D1488320

No End To Yesterday

No End To Yesterday

Shelagh Macdonald

ANDRE DEUTSCH

First published April 1977 by
André Deutsch Limited
105 Great Russell Street London WC1
Second Impression January 1979

Printed in Great Britain by
The Anchor Press Ltd and bound by Wm Brendon & Son Ltd
both of Tiptree, Essex

ISBN 0 233 96865 2

First published in the United States of America in 1979
Library of Congress No. 78–74755

For Marjory's children

And he who gives a child a treat
Makes joy-bells ring in Heaven's street,
And he who gives a child a home
Builds palaces in Kingdom come ...

(John Masefield, 1878–1967)

No End To Yesterday

ONE

Some day in the early 1920s; the outer kitchen of the house in Leander Road, Streatham, London – the house everyone calls Gran's house, though Grandad and various others live here too. Red Victorian brick, a sizeable house in a curving rising row between Brixton Hill and Tulse Hill. From the upper back windows, a view between chimneys of rolling Brockwell Park.

Gran and her youngest, unmarried, daughter Molly (about 24) stand at different stoves, shifting reeking pans. It is Gran's soap-making day. She always has made and always will make her own soap, always has ignored and always will ignore complaints: the rest of the family keep to other parts of the house. Except one, Marjory, a small granddaughter, who (realising the conversation within is about herself) has stopped unseen outside the open back door listening to grandmother and Auntie Molly.

This outer kitchen is the one which Grandad, teasing the women (of which the family has several), nicknamed the Morgue. For it is here, leaning among coppers and boilers, they discuss serious matters and so pick others to pieces.

GRAN: The child should be grateful.
  Naughty? Wicked! We took her from the gutter, gave her a home.
MOLLY: She's hard and that's the truth of it.
GRAN: She won't cry. She's never sorry. Just looks at me. If I could make her *cry*.
MOLLY: A hard child.
GRAN: The way of her mother is the way she'll go.

MOLLY: It's certainly not from Henry she gets it.
GRAN: Poor Henry. *Poor* Henry.

*

Violet had written the date carefully, 8th August 1917.
Henry at once noticed the unusual clarity of the entire page,
dark ink on good paper. That, as well as the fact that Violet
had written only last week, gave him some warning.

Dear Henry, I'm writing to you again so soon because
somebody has got to tell you. The fact is I think you
should try and get home on leave. I was hoping it wouldn't
get this bad but Greta has gone somewhere, just disappeared, nobody knows where. I'm worried because we
don't know where baby Marjory is except she's not with
Greta. Look Henry I know this will hurt but Greta is always off somewhere and God knows where she leaves the
baby some of the time. I'm her sister and I know she means
all right but she never could cope. She gets fed up and I've
looked after the baby before but she stopped asking me
after I told her off. Your family hasn't been much help to
her if I'm honest, everyone follows your mother's lead.
I'm sure Marjory will be found all right but if you can
get home quickly it will be better and maybe find Greta
and sort things out together. I don't mean to stick my nose
in you know that but try not to be too angry with her,
she's been lonely. This is rotten news when you're out
there in the war, I know despatch riders have it hard.
Praying we'll see you soon and you know I'll do all I can.
Your affectionate Vi.

Henry was having it hard. He had ridden his motorbike
through France all week with his bottom covered in boils.
The days were hot, mud ruts were cement. Front-down on his
mattress he read and re-read his letter, folded the paper neatly
back into its envelope, and lay still. When he could force
expression from his face he went to his superiors. He emphasised the anxiety about his missing two-year-old daughter
but travelled back to London conscious only that he had lost
his wife.

*

It was when things began, in Marjory's mind: the day she came to live at Gran's.

'Mind the baby.'

Many legs, lit by fire, paused and passed where she sat.

'Mind the baby.' Gran repeated it to all the legs coming into the big kitchen. Flames baked the skin, lit the walking limbs, all dark beyond. A rug under bare thighs, warm: before had been splintered boards, somewhere. Water poured on to metal, steam clouded across the coals.

'Now look, Henry,' a voice she had heard before in a cold place, the voice with rough-skinned hands, 'you can't go on like this. Just think of your child.'

Faces speaking, legs crowding, eyes and eyes looking, fire jumping in the glistening eyes, hands pulling at clothes.

'Hush hush, no need to cry.'

'She's frightened. Dear heaven, these clothes. All right dear, it's only Auntie.'

'You'll need scissors.'

'There there. Somebody hold her still.'

'Pour some disinfectant in that water. More.'

'These shoes . . . my godfathers, her feet!'

'Into the bath. Deal with that later.'

'The stink. Here, burn that lot.'

'Her hair must be lousy.'

'Soap, soap.'

'Your soap'll take the skin off her.'

'Don't be foolish, Ron.'

'Stop fretting, Henry. She's got a home here.'

'And she'll have her cousin Susie to play with.'

'Count your blessings. She's part of a big family.'

*

Cousins, uncles, aunts, Gran and Grandad, since their youthful marriage in 1874, had added twelve to the population. Fate despatched two swiftly: James was just six when diphtheria took him; Georgie, seldom mentioned, died in a fit at eight months. This left four males, six females, so that, after certain marriages and births, Marjory had eight aunts, seven uncles – not counting family friends who had the titles for courtesy – and a growing number of cousins. On birthdays, cards came with many names: from the same house in

Leander Road, from streets a walk away, from other parts of London. With love from Auntie Molly, Ada, Ellie, Liza, Flora, June, Rachel, Hennie. With love from Uncle Arthur, Joe, Gerry, Ron, Wilfred, Walt, Bertie. And from the cousins' names tacked on, or separate cards from the grown-up ones: Nora, Madge, Susie, Teddy, Harry, Archie, Valerie, Rita, James, Esmie. But every birthday came one odd card out, which said simply: With love from Auntie. The year she was eight Marjory asked Auntie Ellie, for with Ellie one might dare.

'Who *is* this from?'

Auntie Ellie was immediately pink. She darted at things, tidying, though her flat – the top floor of Gran's house – was impeccable always. Like her husband, Uncle Wilf, whose collars never bent, shining smooth beneath his gentle face, and her daughter, Susie, whose boots were never scuffed. 'From a nice lady who knew you when you were tiny, dear,' Ellie gasped.

'Before I came to live at Gran's house?' Before memory.

'I expect so dear, yes.' Ellie groped round cushions for a change of subject.

'What's her name?'

Ellie could not lie, but tried to be vague. 'Oh . . . let me see . . . Violet, would it be?'

'Why doesn't she write Auntie Violet then, not just Auntie?'

Auntie Ellie was pinker, gleaming. '*I* don't know, dear, do I? Maybe she doesn't like – oh, *look* at this mess.' Seizing and crumpling innocent wrapping paper, she looked pleading. 'Perhaps when you're older . . .'

'I am older, today. *Why* doesn't she like to?'

'Oh *Marj*ory, how would *I* know?' A glance at the door.

All her correspondence was opened and read by Gran. (For your own good, child.) Cards and letters were always given with their envelopes removed. But the next year, when she was nine, Marjory had a postcard from the Auntie Violet, a glossy thing with 'Real Photo' inscribed, a picture of a pretty girl with mauve lips, her frizzy hair full of roses. The postcard had a postmark.

'It says Watford,' Marjory pushed the card at Auntie

Ellie, whose hands clutched each other. 'That's where Daddy works, isn't it? Does Daddy know her?'

'I expect so. *I* don't know.' Ellie rushed into her kitchen.

Not that Marjory would ask her more. This Violet, who came from Watford where Marjory had been born, she must have known her mother. And Violet must somehow know that she too must remain as nameless as Marjory's mother, who was rarely spoken of, and never directly or without veils. Except if she cheeked Gran and Gran said: You'll go the way of your mother, young lady. As if it were for the sin of being rude to Gran that her mother had died, struck down.

Marjory wrote in the name Violet on the postcard and sat with it balanced on her fingertips. Watford, where Daddy worked. But she could not ask.

He came only at weekends, but had sent her a doll dressed in lace. The eyes, dark purple, had lashes and closed grace-fully. She would name her Violet. You can play with her today, Gran said, but later she must be put away, you know how you will spoil things. (Why can't you be like Susie?) The doll would join the others in the high cupboard and must be asked for specially: hours of thinking out the request, approaching Gran at an ideal moment. The silver bracelet from Grandad would go there too, and the dainty propelling pencil from Auntie Molly, or they might be lost. Lovely presents, what a lucky girl. But she could wear the green wool dress, edged with ribbon, that Auntie Flora had made, and Teddy had brought her fudge which, with his help, she would eat.

She put the postcard from Auntie Violet in her box. Suppose she met her one day, she might ask her the things they always whispered about, or pecked over in the Morgue, and stopped when she came.

*

'Your dad's waiting.' It was Susie at the bathroom door. She hovered and picked at her skirt.

'I know.' Casually, but nerves shivered. 'Hiding from him? Scared or something?' It might be all they had in common, she and Susie.

Susie quivered. 'I am *not*.' She leaned past Marjory to the mirror, adjusting her satin hair-ribbon.

Marjory saw Susie's reflected face, pale and narrow, the dark brown eyes round. 'Huh, not much. Scared of anyone, you are. Jump like a grasshopper if my dad shouts. Cowardy custard.'

Susie swung and left with an Oh! Marjory saw her buttoned patent shoes run up the stairs towards the flat, then stop. '*You're* the one who ought to be scared, so there.' And she went, leaving the echo of that fact.

In the drawing-room, alone, her father kissed her cheek. 'Hello, Marjory. Have you been a good girl?'

Only a silent half-nod could answer that.

'I hope you haven't been a trouble to anyone, my dear.' He folded his newspaper and placed it symmetrically on a small square table. His collar was stiff, white. He was all neat, polished, pin-striped, looking down through spectacles which enlarged his eyes, soft brown.

'I . . . I don't think so.' But she and Teddy had loop-looped Auntie Molly's silk stockings along the line as they hung in a waving row. Auntie Molly had been savage, and Gran, her mouth small and forward, had added this to the weekly sins to be told to her father. Even Uncle Ron laughing would not make her relent.

'I certainly hope you haven't.' He nodded. 'I'll see you at lunch.' He was out of the room, turning towards the kitchens. The Morgue. Marjory watched her father walk down the hall into the gloom.

Near the back fence was the secret grass. Lying there was to be invisible, on a slope of green beyond 'the heap'. The house had retreated, had sunk into the ground leaving just the roof and chimneys. Here were smells of compost, plants, earth, green things, and in the summer, roses. Buller and Boney, the bulldogs, panted warm alongside. House-sounds had vanished, unless someone called or a door was banged. Hooves and wheels passed muted in the street, sometimes a car engine, sometimes a far clank of trams on Brixton Hill.

Marjory leaned her chin on Boney's back and looked at the bush where the deep red roses would grow, lushly scented. They were stark, pruned. Grandad had cut them last week, standing in the wind, his white hair and beard blown about.

He was tall, the secateurs were small in his hand, he moved aside branches without feeling thorns. Auntie Ada, he said, had asked him to do this for her; she did most of the gardening, but feared scratches. Marjory watched his assault. Why are you cutting them? Got to help them grow properly, he said. See, that's where the new shoots will come, then buds, then flowers. These old bits aren't any use now. She doubted: How do you know? Law of nature, young Marj, remove the worthless and the good will grow. He liked that, said it twice. Roses like a bit of help, you see. A piece chopped here, a little more there. Saves them a lot of trouble. A stake to hold them up. Some water, some food. Food? He kicked the soil. Food's in there. Roses like food, need it to help them to grow up right, just like you, skinny. He laughed, snipping the secateurs under her nose. Mind the thorns on that one, she said, afraid herself to touch the thick bending branch, bristling with hazards. Fine strong rose that, he said, climbs all over. That's why it's got thorns, to be sure, so its enemies will leave it alone and just let it grow. What enemies? she asked. Oh, he laughed, don't ask *me*, but it must have enemies otherwise why would it have thorns?

She saw Teddy's head approaching. His hair, usually in spikes, was sideways and smooth, painted on, as if it were Sunday. The collar was huge in its starched whiteness. The rest of him emerged, dreadfully tidy, a reason for kicking at weedy patches. He screwed a finger into an ear and looked with relish at whatever debris he found there.

'Thought you'd be here.' He flopped down, rolled with the dogs, all grunting. 'Talking to the roses are yuh?' He cackled at this, having caught her once. 'Get ticked off about the stockings, huh? Saw your dad, all stony-faced as usual.'

'Wasn't too bad.' Marjory, he had reproached, can't you try to be a little more thoughtful? I don't want to hear again about you and Teddy getting into mischief. You are a little older than he is and should set an example. Silk stockings are expensive items, your grandmother tells me. 'He just said don't do it again, silk stockings are expensive.'

'Har! Bet Auntie Molly never paid for any of 'em. Bet her fat old Fred gave them to her. Bet he did.'

'Daddy said I should set an example as you are much younger than me.'

'Huh, blooming cheek. Four months isn't *younger*.'

'Oh yes it is then, so there.'

'Gunna be all goody-goody then, like soppy Susie, eh, eh?'

'Oh yeah. Anyway, what're you here for, all dressed up like a sore toe?'

'Going somewhere. Mum says do you want to come? Your dad said you could. He's doing some work or something.'

'Where to?'

'Dunno. S'prise.'

'Why?'

'Oh, you know Mum.'

Auntie Flora would have made a new dress, a new hat, and would be longing to go out in them. Oh Flora, Gran and Molly and Ada always said, you're so extravagant. Look, Flora would cry, drawing silken things from her shopping bag, crêpe-de-chine nightie, only thirty-seven and sixpence from Bond Street. Oh *Flora*, they shook their heads and fingered, what else have you got? Bertie's too good to her, they whispered when she had gone, she goes through more than twenty pounds a week, shocking.

'If you want to come, she says get changed and don't think you're going without wearing a hat and gloves.'

'Ted-dy! Marj!' And they could see Flora's hat beyond the grass: ostrich plumes waved in arcs above blue velvet.

'What?' Teddy yelled.

'Don't say what!' his mother shouted back. 'Come *on*, you two. Do you or don't you want to come?'

'Come on.' Marjory was up, running. 'I'm coming! Where are we going? Auntie Flora, where are we going?'

'Wait and see.' She posed by the rose trellis, a wonderful sight. The dress was dark blue silk, with folds and braid trimming, the skirt with a draped layer shimmering to her calf. The hat was spectacular, she must have spent days on this one. Her pleasure with herself came through her smile. 'Hurry then, Marjory. Get washed and put on your good coat and boots, and I think the soft hat with the cherries. And don't forget to comb your hair, it looks like a floor mop. Oh *Teddy*, your suit. Come and get brushed. Honestly, can't you be left for even a minute?' She seized her son and swept him indoors, plumes undulating.

They leapt and ran to Brixton Hill, impatient for Flora to

hurry. But she walked with care, as if her new clothes had stiffened her neck. She had made a coat to match the dress: Oh, Auntie Ada had cried, you are lucky to be able to make things, Flora, it's just like the coat Queen Mary was wearing the other day in the newspaper. I know, Flora smiled, I know.

Down the road, hopping at the kerb, waiting for her to catch up. Across the tram lines, jigging at the stop. Come on, Mum, come on, Auntie Flora, come on, tram, come on.

'The top, can we go to the top?' Teddy shouted as the tram swayed up to them and waited, throbbing. 'At the front. Can we? Can we?'

'*May* we, not *can* we. Go on then.'

They rushed aboard the shining thing, up the stairs. They had the front all to themselves, like a ship, singing and rolling along the rails.

'Where are we going? Auntie Flora, *where*? Tell us, oh go on.'

'Oh Mum, tell us.'

'Wait and see.'

'I know. The Tower.'

'Nah. Billingsgate, see the fish.'

'What, dressed up? Don't be soppy.'

They changed trams. Once, twice. And then a bus.

'Course! *I* know.'

'What? What Marj?'

'I know. I know, Auntie Flora. I know where we're going!'

'Really?' She was looking in her compact. In public! Gran would be shocked. To wear powder anyway, that was for disapproval; and Auntie Flora had on lipstick too, pursing her full pretty mouth and checking its perfection.

'You're mean, Marj, you're mean, tell me where. Come on, tell. Bah, bet you don't know really.'

'The Zoo, soppy. It's the Zoo, isn't it, Auntie Flora?'

'Is it, Mum? Is it the Zoo? Oh, yippeee.'

'There's a man over there keeps looking at you,' Marjory told Auntie Flora by the lions.

'Oh?' Her plumes did not turn. 'Please don't stare, Marjory.'

'*He* is.'

It was easy as they came to the corner for Flora to glance. 'Why,' she cried, and yet she wasn't surprised, 'it's a friend of mine, Marjory. Goodness me, it's James! James . . .' Flora was flowing towards the man, whose face had flushed, his eyes jumping from her to the children.

'Who's he?'

'I dunno,' Teddy wasn't interested. 'One of her friends. She's always playing Bridge and that with her friends.'

'They're whispering.'

Flora came back to them, bright-eyed. 'James and I have such a lot to talk about . . . you two explore. I'll see you at the Monkey House in an hour.' She gave Teddy money. 'You might want tea or some sweets or something.'

The Monkey House was always saved until last, and there was a system of shallow breathing to take the first shock from the smell.

Flora was late but smiling. She looked as if she could be wearing rouge on her cheeks, but her lipstick had gone.

'Look at this chap, ugh, his bottom.'

'Don't suppose he'd like your bottom either.'

'Children, that's vulgar.'

'Hey, look at him, upside-down. Is he a chimp?'

'This is my favourite. Ah, he's sweet. Teeny.'

'Look at his little hands. Look Mum, look.'

But Flora's eyes were elsewhere, far off.

'Auntie Flora, that fat one's staring at you.'

The black monkey concentrated, scratching. Flora smiled a little beside the cage bars, but did not look.

'Look at him, Teddy, see his face. That black one. What an expression.'

Flora drew out her compact, powdered quickly, straightened her hat. A quick glance, nobody near. Swiftly, the lipstick.

Teddy was nudging: 'Look at him now, Marj, look, look.'

'Teddy! Auntie Fl – ' but Teddy stopped her.

Two seconds' suspense. With wonderful precision the black monkey, his gaze never leaving Flora, his mood unreadable, positioned himself and urinated.

Her shriek was powerful. Men and women ran, asking, exclaiming. The crowd hid Marjory and Teddy so they could laugh, seeing the black monkey laughing also in his corner, rocking and pointing, hugging his belly.

A plume damp, the blue silk darkened, Flora stamped with

them from the Zoo. 'That's the last time you come here with *me*.'

'It wasn't *our* fault, Mum, *we* didn't make him pee on you.'

'You be quiet. Both of you. There's nothing funny.' She loathed them, stalking ahead to the bus stop.

'Auntie Flora, your friend is over there.' Marjory saw the man James dithering near shrubs.

Flora stamped on, not turning.

She refused to sit with them on the bus and the trams. They held their noses behind her back and collapsed giggling into the rear seats.

'Oh, your mum,' Marjory held aching ribs, 'what a scream, oh golly, her face . . .'

And Teddy asked suddenly as they stopped gasping: 'D'you remember *your* Mum?'

'Don't be stupid.'

'I'm not!'

'You are. She's *dead*.' She could dislike Teddy.

He rolled his eyes. 'I mean *before*, soppy.'

'If anybody's soppy it's not *me*. I was only two or something, how could I?'

'So what?' Her ferocity couldn't stop him. '*I* remember being one and a half.'

'Liar.'

'I do! I remember being in my pushchair thing, and I dropped this lollipop, and – '

'Well I *don't*, so *there*, so shut *up*.' She scowled at the window-pane, laughing gone. She hated him, stupid.

'Oh all *right*, peppery-pot.' He began to mutter sulkily. 'Talk about bad-tempered, worse than your dad. Always flying off the handle, blimey.'

'Have a nice time?' Gran and Auntie Ada and Auntie Molly were in the hall as the three entered the front door. Gran saw their faces first.

'Marjory – have you been naughty?'

*

She knew the room. Gaps between floorboards, splinters prickling her legs. Cold, blowing in hard lines. Her fingers were stiff and grey like the floor, her dress too. Her feet hurt, or had no feeling.

Sitting in the corner, hardness pressing into her back, cold blowing up. Out there, outside the door, the bear was on the stairs. Big, huge, a giant, it wore an apron, dirty with flowers. It plodded upwards, heavy, the wood trembled, it stopped. Slowly it opened the door, stood, looked. Vast, dark, it loomed. She pressed to the corner, could not make a noise. Only if . . . if it took another step. Now. Plod, towards her.

'Whatever is she screaming about now?' Gran's voice pierced Marjory's noise.

'It was a dream, just a dream, Marj. Wake up, dear.' Auntie Ellie, fluffy in a bed-jacket.

'Heavens, what a din.' Auntie Molly craned in at the door, Ada was in pale ruffles beyond.

'What frightened you? What was it?' Ellie's hanky, smelling of lilac, wiped her face.

She saw them all standing. 'I don't know.'

'She's all right now,' Gran was brisk. 'Susie, back to bed, you should be asleep. Come along everyone.' She called over the banister: 'No, Henry. Nothing at all.'

Auntie Ellie asked: 'All right now? Good girl.' And when the others had gone, put a match to the gas jet and turned it low. 'Go to sleep then, dear. Soon feel better.'

*

On Monday mornings she was always awake when he came into her room just after six.

He knocked, walked to the chest of drawers. On one corner he placed a small straight pile of coins: silver threepenny pieces he had saved during the week in Watford. He never said anything about them. Her eyes were always closed.

Then: 'Marjory?'

She could turn and sit up. 'Are you going now?'

'Back to work. See you next weekend.'

She nodded.

'What do you say?'

'Yes, Daddy.'

'Be a good girl, won't you?'

'Mm.'

'I beg your pardon?'

'Yes, Daddy.'

He bent, kissed her cheek. 'Goodbye then.' And at the door: 'God bless,' and went.

She got out of bed and took the silver pile. Joeys. Back in bed she counted, turning them, soft-coloured gentle little coins. Later Gran would say: Did your father give you some money? The Joeys would be taken, for safety, changed into a figure in a book. Henry *is* kind.

TWO

*Almost any day in the early 1950s, in Marjory's
home. A discussion (often dogmatic, sometimes
heated) has been going on for some time at the end
of a meal, among her teenage children and their
father about good and evil. At last, impatient at
some sophistry, she must interrupt.*

MARJORY: Oh, I can't be doing with all that
analytical stuff. It was simpler the way we were
taught: there is God, and there is the Devil,
and –

A DAUGHTER: – Nobody believes any of that nowadays, Mum!

MARJORY: Why not, I'd like to know? (*There is
a certain amount of scoffing and she looks
defiant*): Say what you like, it's not so daft in
my experience.

*

Brockwell Park with the dogs, before breakfast: her favourite
duty, one nobody else wanted, or not on days when it was
wet and cold. She didn't mind any of it, even the most glittering frost when grass snapped under foot and paw, making the
dogs bark and dodge.

She was out of bed early, in winter it might be scarcely
light. Into the conservatory; Grandad's parrots moved wrinkled eyelids and croaked Good Morning, Halloo. She snapped
leads on to the scuffling, laughing Buller and Boney. Past
the kitchen door: Gran would be up, scrubbing the table,
blacking the stove. Out of the back gate, along the alley,
across Tulse Hill. Nobody to see, except perhaps a group of
early workers quiet at a bus stop. Big Victorian houses, blinds
down, hiding wrestlers with corsets, waxers of moustaches,
maids lighting fires.

The gate, leashes off, freedom. Sweeping green distances, away, over slopes, into valleys: it was country, London nowhere – or only distant, on the edges, humming. They panted upwards, hurled down, fell and rolled, calling, barking. Sunny mornings the air was all fresh vegetable, the sky endless. Wet days the face drank in rain, the trees hung. Autumn, the sun jumped from behind mad clouds, gusts pushed from behind or beat back, snatching in circles. Only foggy days were the bad ones, with even the back fence invisible behind greygreen; then it was impossible to breathe enough to run, even if anything could be seen, and the dogs must relieve themselves in the alley and wait for the Park to reappear.

The day started perfectly, and might be perfect right through, if it was Spring and sunny like this one, and Grandad was in the conservatory when she went down, fingering plants, answering his parrot, patting the grimacing bulldogs. She could persuade him to the Park for it was Saturday and there was no need to hurry.

No romping and whirling, but she ran and returned to walk with him, to question and talk. Tell me, Grandad, was it true, tell me again, did you really get only half-a-crown a week when you started work? How old were you, not really thirteen? Imagine that, young Marjory, only three years older than you, tiddler, younger than Susie. He scratched his beard, laughed, shook his head. Imagine that. But we went up in the world, step by step, nothing hasty. Hard work, for which people should rightly be rewarded but it doesn't always go like that. And the horses – how long with the horses, Grandad? Oh, thirty years it must have been, managed those stables you know, that big firm in the Tottenham Court Road. Until two things – broke a leg (he slapped his great thigh) and someone invented some engines. Laughing again: silly, eh? But there was always work: did I tell you about looking after the guns they captured in the War? My, what a time. Memories, funny things memories. Wait until you've got as many as I have, Marj, then you'll see. The oldest ones, or is it the ones that counted most, they're as near as yesterday, they never go. But with the horses, Grandad – were you a vet? Lord no. Me? But I knew horses almost like a vet, maybe. Thirty years with horses and you know them. Why are they cruel to horses, Grandad? The man with the coal, he cracks his whip to make his horse jump. Ah Marj, but he doesn't hit him, he only tells him. Why do it, if he doesn't want to hit him, why do it at all? Don't you fret, Marjory, the horse is all right. Horses know, horses know. Grandad – did you always want to work with horses? Since you were little, No, he said after pondering, it just happened so. How can a little child know what he wants to do? She thought: *I* know. She said: But you were glad you did. Oh, I was glad, he agreed. She said: Let's go into the rose-garden near the Hall, the first roses will be out, the little yellow ones, and there are lots of buds.

They came into the kitchen, into the smell of sausages, together. 'Wash your hands and sit down, Marjory,' Gran said, filling plates.

'Hurry up or I'll eat yours,' said Uncle Ron, already attacking toast. Auntie Ada arranged the frills at her wrist and frowned at his manners.

'Morning, Ada. Hello there, Molly.' Grandad kissed his daughters. 'Back late last night, eh, Moll? Good trip?'

Auntie Molly sighed, gave a tired nod. 'Good prices.' She worked in jewellery, something responsible: Gran and Grandad looked proud. Often she brought home uncut gems, casually tipping them on the dining-room table, studying each one before gathering them up to take to some distant dealer.

'Brighton, was it?' Uncle Ron asked through toast.

'And Eastbourne. Fred took me in his car. He's so good, waited around two days so I didn't have to get the train.'

'Such a kind man,' Gran said.

Uncle Fred Barnes, sleek-haired, red-lipped, tight of waistcoat, owner of a Rolls-Royce, was Molly's friend. When he saw Marjory or Susie he pressed florins into their hands and patted them. Fred was the only one of Molly's men friends who lasted. Oh, too *boring,* she dismissed others, though they still called, yearning behind bouquets, for a time. Auntie Molly looked at men in a way that made them sit forward in their chairs like panting dogs.

Uncle Ron prodded Marjory: 'Hurry up there, I'm after your bangers.'

'The child is looking sallow,' Gran said, and was looking towards the Epsom Salts on the dresser.

24

Marjory ate. 'I'm fine, Gran,' she said. 'I'm going to the Market with Grandad, he asked me.'

Gran looked again at the Salts, then at Grandad, who nodded and smiled. 'Very well,' she said.

One friendly day Susie had said to Marjory: It's not his real name you know, Fred Barnes. Marjory would not believe: How do *you* know? Susie, triumphant: He's a Managing Director of some big Insurance Company, he is, honest. Who said? Never mind. What's his name then? Goodness, Susie was shocked, prim: I wouldn't be able to tell you that, even if I knew. You're *soppy*, Marjory punched her, Susie screeched, Auntie Ellie ran to her child and all friendliness ended.

'Did you know,' Uncle Ron tried again to invade Marjory's plate, 'they grow sausages in Holland? I bet you didn't.' He waited for her to look up with the right scepticism. 'In fields. Acres of 'em, row upon row, a bit like hop fields. They harvest them in September, you should see the Dutch sausage-pickers, nipping along the rows with knives and forks. It's quite a skill, don't laugh.'

'Really Ronnie,' Auntie Ada rustled, 'you're quite dotty.'

'You want to watch out though,' Ron peered as Marjory cut, 'for the sausage weevil. Of course they check but sometimes one sneaks through. So you want to cut them up carefully, see. You'll see him if he's there – maybe I should finish yours, just in case – ' her elbows warded him off ' – *I* don't mind the weevil, eaten scores of 'em, little green wiggly things with squashy legs and wobbly eyes – '

Marjory laughed too much to swallow, Auntie Ada shrieked: 'Ron!' her fingers loosening the bow at her throat, her own skin threatening green wobbliness.

'Yes, enough, Ron,' but Gran smiled at her youngest.

Susie said: 'It's all fibs. Our sausages come from Mr Thorpe in Yarmouth, you jolly well know he sends them every month.'

'Susie, Susie – would I tell an untruth to a child?'

'Yes,' everyone agreed.

'You've turned them against me,' Ron moaned at Marjory. 'You've never forgiven me, I know it, for sending you out for a tin of elbow grease, and you asking Mrs Hutton at the shop and everyone laughing.' She still writhed a little, but had to grin. 'And it was a mistake, an innocent mistake.' He spread his hands, widened his eyes, brown like her father's. 'I meant you to get half a pound of greased lightning. As if I would mislead a child!'

'As *if*,' she replied, and he made faces at her like the comedians at Brixton Empire. 'You should've gone on the stage, Uncle Ron.' He was pleased at that.

'The stage!' Gran carried plates from the table. 'Gracious me, I certainly trust none of this family will ever go on the stage.'

'There's a boy in Marj's class says he's going on the stage,' Susie told.

Gran looked as if it were Marjory's doing.

'The whole *family's* been on the stage, *always*,' she disclaimed responsibility. 'They're ever so clever, they can dance and sing and they're funny, you should see − '

'I'm sure,' Gran said, 'but I don't think you should mix with stage people, Marjory, I'm afraid they're not quite nice. You've seen that Music Hall woman along the road, the way she dresses.'

'*Make*-up,' Susie disapproved, 'and necklines showing . . well . . . even in daytime.'

'I think she's pretty,' Marjory said. 'And she's famous, and she's the auntie of another boy in my class, too.'

'I think we've heard enough,' Gran said. 'I'm sure,' she looked at Grandad, 'I don't know what Christ Church school is coming to.'

'Nothing to worry about, my dear.' Grandad smiled at her and passed her favourite marmalade. 'It's a good school, I'm sure nobody doubtful is let in.'

Auntie Molly stretched and excused herself from the table. 'Must unpack, too tired last night.'

'Get a little rest before lunch,' Gran advised.

Molly was searching in her deep handbag. A smooth, solid pile of banknotes emerged. 'Daddy − ' she held the wealth towards Grandad. 'Fred gave me this. Can you look after it for me?'

Grandad, guardian of the family safe, nodded: 'Of course my dear.' And when Molly had gone he said to Gran: 'He must think a lot of young Molly, that Fred.' Gran smiled, they agreed upon his kindness.

Marjory looked at their faces: pleased, innocent. Without

reason she saw the bathroom she shared with Molly; looking in cupboards for more soap, she had found a waterproofed bag of strange things: tubes, an object of rubber like a klaxon-horn bulb, a thin stick reminding one of knitting needles, some round pills in a black and white box, Blanchards Female Pills, it said. Something was sinister, but she took the bag to Auntie Molly's room: I found this, is it yours? Molly nearly struck out, half-wept, raged that she should leave things alone that weren't hers, beastly prying child. And if you tell anyone I'll *kill* you . . . Then she came smiling, ex-plaining. It's not something you'd understand, Marj dear. Medical things. It's just, sometimes I'm not well – I wouldn't want them to know, they'd only worry, that's all. It was true, Marjory sometimes heard her being sick.

'Ready then, Marj? Market?' Grandad stood. 'Get your hat and coat.'

'Don't forget your gloves and *don't* lose them,' Gran's voice followed her.

Auntie Ada gave Marjory a piece of mauve wool. 'Get some more of this for me, will you? Three ounces should do. I got it from the stall nearest the arches. Then I can finish my jumper this weekend.' Ada's knitting was always mauve, or pink. 'Now for heaven's sake be careful, Marjory, it'd be just like you to drop it in the mud.'

'There isn't any mud.' She darted away.

She knew he was a giant beside her, walking along Brixton Hill towards the Market, one huge hand on his stick, the other swamping hers. She could have run for pleasure and leapt paving stones but would not leave that hand. He stop-ped often, talking to friends. Men lifted their hats: Mr Bell, a pleasure to see you. They stood on the pavement talking. She could pull at his hand to hurry him but never did. If the men noticed her they swung their canes in a circle and found peppermints to offer. Ladies smiled at Grandad and straight-ened their hats, asking after his health. And Mrs Bell, how is she? And the daughters at home, Molly and Ada? Such pretty girls. And you've still got a son unmarried – Ron, yes of course. Doing well for himself I hear. And isn't this Henry's little girl? Nine is she? Ten! Well, she's the dainty type, my, how time passes.

You could hear the Market before you saw it, and could see

it spilling on to the road from a distance away. It muddled with the sooty wall, the railway arches, in and out and under and out again on the other side. Stalls sagging and loaded, names painted like circus signs. Ikey's Super Shoes. Bert's Best Shirts in London. Abe and Hilda, Freshest Fruit. Yelling was in the air. A man tossed bargain buttons up and let them fall on his stall, losing none: *Come* on, *you* lot, don't ya know a *bar*gain when yer *seez* it? The lady they called Podge but was Rachel Vice spelt Weiss picked up tomatoes and her voice went from half-way up the Market out into the High Street: Come on darlin' give it a squeeze, see if it's not fresh! That is certainly *not* a lady, Auntie Ada once hustled Marjory past, looking downwards, *that* is a *woman*, and a common vulgar woman furthermore, and there is nothing to laugh at, Marjory. They were all laughing, the men all round, buying the tomatoes and winking at Podge: give us a squeeze, then, go on.

Grandad looked here, there, paused, chatted. This couple had been in Brixton fifty years, this man could remember Grandad as a lad. Cousin Nora had told Marjory she could remember naphtha lamps on the Market stalls when she was little, on winter evenings when she met her father, policeman Uncle Joe, at the Station and they walked home together. The Market was rooted here, growing, hanging, bulging, spreading: impossible to imagine these arches without the people, the noise, the bargain clothes, best value in drapery, a farthing for rice today, crispest apples in the world, Jewish tailors, bolts of cotton and wool, colours, smells. They bought Auntie Ada's mauve wool and resisted some vivid green offered still cheaper; then Grandad aimed himself. Fish for tea today! he said, as if she didn't know. It was always fish-hunger that drove him on a walk to the Market.

He turned over the fish with Mr Stanley at the shining cold stall, discussing each selection. Two connoisseurs, touching scales and pointing at eyes, lifting fins and comparing blotches. They explained across each other's arms to Marjory: See that fellow? Never buy him if his spots are dim, remember, they've got to be bright, see? She nodded but thought of the house later, smelling of fish and herbs and oil as Grandad alone cooked. My sister taught me, he said, and she was taught by my mother and grandmother in Spain. Auntie Ada would flounce upstairs to close her bedroom door, crying warnings to Molly, panting back to the kitchen: Honestly, Daddy, you might have said, my clothes will smell awful. Grandad always laughed, gently turning golden gems, dropping in transparently-thin onion: No better perfume, my girl. Mr Stanley wrapped the fish with cherishing fingers, layers of paper and finally *The Times*. Brain food, he told Marjory. Eat fish and you grow up brainy, that's why your grandpapa's so clever, isn't that so, Mr Bell? Grandad smiled but Mr Stanley could just be disapproving of that. They walked away and she was silent with longing to ask, was it true? He would tease her, tell the others. Suppose she ate a lot of fish and it worked, she might have reports better than anyone's to show Daddy, might do everything she wanted.

Grandad pulled his watch from his waistcoat as they came near the place to cross the road for home. Let's go this way, he said. It was his detour down the short road to the Prison: not a road she would go down alone, or even with Teddy or Susie. Bad people in there, they had told her, suppose they escaped. If you are bad, Auntie Molly said, you'll get locked away. I've a good mind to send you to a home for bad girls and orphans, Gran threatened again last week when Marjory and Teddy had tied up the strings of the blinds, and when she put Susie's best doll's dress on Jimmy the tabby, who never minded. Miss Loyal at school told her when she was six: You are being wicked and perverse writing with your left hand, you are doing it on purpose. She hit her left knuckles with a ruler for such a sin, or sent her to be caned, until Marjory obeyed.

The Prison drew Grandad, an unsolved mystery to be examined again and again. He looked at the high walls and great doors, silent. They stood opposite the entrance, immovably closed with huge locks. Grandad looked again at his watch.

'Bad people go there, don't they?'

'So they say, Marjory, so they say.' And turned his head as the black van arrived. Perhaps he was uncertain whether she also should see; while he still held her hand, he stood slightly in her view so that she must step aside and peer. Silhouettes of heads in the van's darkened windows. A man getting out, speaking through a grille, the doors opening slowly, the van going in, door closing as it moved; gone.

'Well, there goes another lot, Marj.' He sounded puzzled. 'Another lot that didn't grow straight.'

At Sunday School Miss Percival had told them: There is God and there is the Devil, God will show you Good and the Devil will tempt you to Evil. She was tall and gingerish and never swallowed her spit; it gathered at the corners of her mouth so that you had to stare and swallow for her. She said: When you are tempted to be wicked, that is when the Devil is speaking to you. That is when you are supposed to say, Get Thee Behind Me Satan! Miss Percival's face shone with excitement. Marjory asked her: The bad men who go to the Prison, were they tempted? Miss Percival clapped her hands, thrilled. Exactly so, Marjory, exactly so. Those very men turned towards the Devil when he spoke to them.

She told Grandad. 'Miss Percival says they were tempted by the Devil and they listened.'

'That's a way of looking at it, isn't it, Marjory?' He sighed now, but his fish parcel cheered him when she spoke of it.

Miss Percival said every person could be tempted. It was not to be imagined, Grandad being tempted; there was nothing bad in him, and she couldn't be tempted to be bad towards him. Being bad to Gran came without knowing the Devil had spoken: it just came out, answering back, cheek, or something she and Teddy thought of for fun but to Gran was wickedness. Uncle Ron, he couldn't be bad. Susie could, telling tales, hanging round the grown-ups. Auntie Molly could too, Auntie Ada even more, running to Gran if she said something she shouldn't, like Blimey. Auntie Ellie wasn't like that. Soft, Gran said of her second daughter, Ellie's too soft by half. Every human can be tempted, Miss Percival said, every one.

'They don't have prisons for animals, do they, Grandad?'

He stopped in the street and looked at her and laughed. His beard turned up and he took off his hat and put it on again and would not stop, though she was driven to punch his arm furtively and say stop it, Grandad, everyone's looking. Embarrassed, then cross, hitting at him, then the laughter caught and she giggled with him. They tottered along Leander Road still finding breath, Grandad saying Oh my, Marj, you do have some ideas.

*

Under the dining-room table on Sunday, a day too wet for the secret grass, she found Teddy cutting alternate bobbles from the edge of the enormous red plush table-cover. Jimmy the tabby pounced and rolled on the growing heap.

'What are you doing *that* for?'

'Felt like it.' He cackled.

'Gran'll be *furious*.'

'Let her be. Old stinker.'

'She'll think it was me.'

'Nah, course she won't. Hey, Marj – ' he stopped cutting, jabbed the scissors into the carpet ' – we could do *it* today. I had an idea.'

'*Today*? With everyone here?' With Daddy here.

'All the better. Crowds of 'em. Nobody'd know what'd happened. They'd all panic and run about, you bet.' He grinned; she could see his eyes bright in the shadow, his teeth diabolically gleaming.

'How?'

'Poison in the teapot.'

'Honestly, Teddy, you're daft. You'd kill everybody then, even Grandad.'

'In her cup then. I could sit next to her.'

She stroked Jimmy, who smiled and purred. 'What sort of poison?'

'Weed-killer. Saw it in the conservatory, it's Uncle Ron's.'

'Would it work?'

'Why not? She's a weed isn't she? Old stinking bindweed . . .' His guffaws knocked him over to roll on the carpet, almost impaling himself on the scissors. 'She'd just slump forward, boomf, nose on plate. They'd all say goodness, whatever's wrong with Gran?'

They rocked together, the cat stared. Then Marjory said: 'They'd find out, they always do.'

'How d'you mean? Who do?'

'Police. They ask questions and do tests. In the end they always find out, in books.'

'*Books*.' He slashed off a row of bobbles. 'You, you're so *clever*. You jolly well think of something then, smarty.'

Auntie Hennie slapped a hard hand on the table and said: 'My, what a crowd.'

She always said it if she came on Sundays, and louder on a Sunday like this, Uncle Arthur's birthday: Gran had brought out the best damask, silver and glass for her eldest son, it was a fête-day. And everyone looked round at her words and smiled at the numbers, with pride. Gran at one end of the great table, Grandad at the other. Down one side their sons and daughters and their wives and husbands; down the other, the grandchildren.

'Twenty-nine!' shouted Teddy, finishing his count.

'Quiet.' His mother's finger pointed, sharp. Teddy's face was all bright cheek; in his own house he would have grinned until Flora's finger wavered, but here she stayed severe. At Gran's table a child must be spoken to first. Teddy revenged himself on Marjory's leg, pinching. She squeaked and kicked.

'I'm not at all sure those two should sit together,' Gran remarked. Marjory felt her father's face turn.

'Oh leave them.' Flora couldn't think about it, admiring buttons on her cuffs. 'Teddy, behave.'

'I'll keep an eye on them, don't worry.' Nora, on Marjory's other side, nudged slyly.

Nora was something, she didn't care, flicking long lacquered nails, fearless of Gran's disapproval. Marjory promised herself a dress like that one day, in salmon pink or emerald, with feathers instead of fringes, a real Flapper dress. And long beads like Nora's, but also a cigarette holder and red shiny lipstick. And silk camiknickers and a slip the same with coffee lace, as seen in the women's pages of the *London Illustrated News*. Nora had a lipstick, she had shown it: Look, Marj, I wear it for dancing. Does Gran know? Marjory whispered. Gran! Who cares? I'm twenty-one, Marj, Gran thinks she knows but she lives in the last century, it's nineteen twenty-five don't you know, everybody has fun now, it's a lark. But Daddy . . . ? What, Uncle Henry? *He* doesn't mind, he's quite modern really you know. Nora's smile couldn't be read. I've nearly got him doing the Charleston! Her golden head fell back as she laughed but Marjory looked with disbelief. My chaperon uncles, Nora mocked Henry and Ron: they took Nora and her sister Madge to the West End for dancing, Jack Hylton at the Piccadilly Hotel, four shillings. It was Gran's suggestion. It's not right really, Nora admitted, it means they don't meet other girls. And she looked wisely at Gran. Marjory asked: But what about you and Madge and other boys though? Oh, that's different, Nora grinned with her secrets.

'Oh *Nora*, your *nails*,' Auntie Ada was opposite. And to Hennie: 'Your daughters are so *modern*,' with her mouse-laugh.

'Yes, aren't we?' Nora and Madge swung beads, blithe and pretty; their mother laughed.

'Can't stand nail polish.' Auntie Liza, flat-chested, gruff as a man. She came rarely on Sundays now since she and Uncle Walt and their family had moved miles away to Hornsey, but when she came her opinions were as strong as ever, like her arms. Cor, she packs a wallop, Teddy said after receiving Auntie Liza's fist one day at her house. But she was worth visiting for the dirty stories she told other grown-ups that she and Teddy must laugh at silently, and because she let Marjory ice cakes and decorate puddings, and for her children Archie and Val, fifteen and sixteen, friendly and casual. 'Dirty stuff, nail polish,' Liza was fierce with her nieces, 'Not worn by nice people, you know.'

'Oh but Auntie Liza,' Nora said, 'we're awfully nice, awfully jolly.'

'Don't like it,' Liza leaned towards Nora, meaningful. 'Reminds me of certain ... you know ... That Woman.'

The silence made Marjory's breath stop while faces turned towards or away from her. Nora's cheek had flushed. Thump, Marjory's heart. Her father, turning to Gran, might not have heard for there was no flicker.

Auntie Hennie said: 'Rubbish, Liza.'

Grandad's voice rolled up the table. 'I don't know who you mean, Liza, but I imagine the lady isn't present and you know I don't care for speaking about people if they're not here to defend themselves, hm?' It wasn't stern, but Liza was a child again, apologising, earning a smile from her father.

Teddy jabbed a fork at Harry, his brother of three years. Susie hissed: 'You really are a *horrid* little boy.' Teddy stuck out his tongue and Susie cried: 'Oh! Oh!'

Auntie Ellie heard the distress signal. 'What is it, dear?' from the other end.

'Teddy! Oh!'

'Stop it, Teddy,' came Flora's command, though she didn't glance. 'Look after your brother. Ignore him, Susie.'

Teddy looked down at Harry's silvery head with revulsion. Marjory whispered: 'I'll have him next to me if you want.' Harry was harmless, soft and rosy. She had looked after him frequently since his birth, whenever Auntie Flora dumped him and Teddy at Gran's house and rushed away – Must go, friends waiting – often until quite late, when Harry would be bedded down by the kitchen fire in the armchair. Flora would rush in, pick him up, shout for Teddy or agree to leave him sharing Marjory's bed, and run home, five minutes away. She was there always, pretty and smiling, hot meal ready, when Uncle Bertie came home. He owned cinemas, was out at all hours, returning to lavish money and adoration upon Flora, contentedly knowing nothing of half her life.

Teddy heaved Harry between them, thumping him on the bench so that puzzled injury moved Harry's amiable face. 'Sick-making beast,' Teddy told him. Marjory muttered across the fair head: 'What're you so cross about?' but knew it was because of the poison idea.

'I'm not, shut up,' he scowled, looking for evil. And she was back into the day last year when she and Teddy and Harry had gone on one of Auntie Flora's outings. A day by the sea. Auntie Flora crossing the road to a shop, saying: Mind that pushchair, Teddy. Walking down the steep hill. Then Harry's pushchair was hurtling ahead away from them, people screaming, running. Marjory ran, fell, would never catch him, he'd be killed. Teddy stood. Flora shrillest of all, tore down the road on the other side, one hand holding on her new ribboned hat. I couldn't help it, Teddy shouted, it went out of my hands. But Marjory had seen him stare at the top of Harry's head, watched him let go with a shove. Then it was over. The pushchair veered, stuck in railings. Harry was giddily astonished but unharmed. Flora had forgotten within the hour, buying them sticks of rock, fluttering at the waiters at lunch. Teddy spent the day swerving from relief to ill-temper; Marjory said nothing. A few days later Teddy thought of the first plan to murder Gran, the old stinker, on the grounds that he couldn't stand her bad breath and she was always saying Don't, and Marjory became his confidante and willing conspirator.

'Well,' Grandad put down carving knife and fork and looked at them all, 'when everybody's got vegetables we can begin, hm?' He and Gran smiled towards each other and at the crowd they had created. That he loved Gran, found her faultless, was the only thing about Grandad that Marjory found impossible to understand. My beautiful Maggie, what a girl. But she was old and grey with hair in a bun and anger somewhere whenever she looked at Marjory.

She was eighteen, Grandad said, with hair of deep red: beech trees, copper kettles. And her eyes, huge, green-hazel with black lashes. Only the Irish have such beauty. And tiny: pretty and gentle. But don't get the idea she was soft. My, what determination. They were rich, her family, leather and shoes with a famous name: they weren't so sure about marriage to this nobody whose parents had been immigrants. But they would not put her off. And they gave in, she had her way, just like that.

They couldn't have been that doubtful of Grandad. Tall, young, black-eyed, twenty-one. Hard to imagine the face less craggy, no beard, but beauty was there still. Then his hair was black, glimpses of blue, like Marjory's maybe. He was born on a refugee boat from Spain, his parents aiming for freedom in England; they were Jews called Mendoza. A name of romance, why change it? Times were difficult, people had been bad to Jews, they wanted to forget so they chose the name of the first London street they lived in, Bell. He was brought up a Londoner, not a trace of Spanish. My friend Keziah, Marjory told him, is Jewish: she comes to our school but doesn't have to join in prayers, and her name is Hope – is that a Jewish name? He laughed: it might be, anything might be. Why don't you do Jewish things like her family? Sabbath on Friday and candles and special food. Oh, I never learned it, it doesn't matter now. He grinned: I married an Irishwoman. His parents had died when he was four; his sister, grown-up, had looked after him. None of his family was left, though there were photographs in his desk: tall people, proud and bony, Mediterranean. If only Daddy looked like Grandad and not like Gran.

Dishes passed to twenty-nine plates of roast pork; potatoes roast and boiled, spring greens, runner-beans, apple sauce, gravy, rolls and butter, salt and pepper and mustard. Conversation called across, up and down, criss-crossing the arms and dishes. Auntie Hennie saying it was scandalous the way everyone was getting divorced, shooting in and out her awful false teeth to emphasise: after the meal she would belch at the same time. Uncle Gerry telling about his new Rover car, gleaming, beloved, out in the street where he could hardly bear to leave it, a hundred and eighty-five pounds. His wife Auntie June teasing him, nursing their new baby girl; June could look Gran in the eye, which the other intruder, or daughter-in-law, never could. Auntie Rachel, next to her Arthur whose birthday it was, said almost nothing, leaving all to him and her three grown children. She was creamy and beautiful, her hair red: Molly and Ada whispered she dyed it. Uncle Ron played dismayed at Nora and Madge: they had seen the new Noël Coward play – wasn't it awfully frank, weren't you shocked? Auntie Ada trembled: *I* think it's too *dread*ful, the things they say on stage, people don't behave like that. *Course* they do, Nora and Madge cried together, that's the whole point. What nonsense, Molly was sharp. *See*, Teddy mouthed, we could've done it, listen to the row. She said: It really was the best plan so far, Ted. And she had waved a wand to make his good temper return. Here, Marj, Uncle Ron passed a dish, you haven't got any beans with your lovely juicy pork, yum yum. Yum Yum Piggie's Bum, murmured Teddy, so they both spluttered. What's that, eh? Uncle Ron feared to miss a joke, what d'you say, young fellow? Gran looked: What's going on, you two? Henry turned, laughter sank. It was me, said Teddy. Nobody spoke to you, Flora chanted. I've a good mind to separate them, Gran threatened. I'm watching, don't worry, Nora called. Here, she winked at Teddy, have some apple sauce with your piggie. So they could let out the mirth, and Marjory, with a sudden wonderful vision of Gran slumping forward, boomf, nose on plate, almost choked.

'You were going to teach us the Black Bottom, you promised,' Marjory nagged Nora, walking behind her to the kitchen with crockery.

'We can't,' Susie followed. 'Your dad said don't be long. You know what Uncle Henry is.'

If Marjory put back one foot rapidly she could catch Susie's shin. But she persisted with Nora: 'The Charleston then, Nora, let's do it once, we know it, we've got time – '

Nora stacked dishes, turned and swung her beads in one

amazing circle. She was a Flapper, her arms and hands in angles, her eyes and mouth round. 'Right then, begin! Charleston, Charleston, made in Carolina . . .' They flung into the dance, giggling, Susie glancing at the door. But Madge called from the drawing-room: 'Hey! Nora – you coming? We're s'posed to sing something. And bring Marj and Susie.' Beyond Madge the piano plinked, Auntie Flora. 'Coming!' yelled Nora, while still dancing. Then she snatched up her bag, dropped and rescued her compact, apologetically promised: More next time! and bounded ahead.

Susie stared. 'Marj – did you see? That was . . . *powder*. In Nora's bag.'

'I know *that*. She's got a lipstick, too, she showed me. So what?' And added shockingly: 'I liked it.'

'*Marj*. You know what Gran says.'

Marjory was still dancing. 'Only bad girls and girls who go on the stage, bleh bleh bleh. What about Auntie Ada then, *she* gets cream sent from Pond's, and Auntie Molly, she wears powder and even rouge and gets lipstick through the post, so there – ' she jabbed an irritating finger into Susie's shoulder ' – is *she* a bad girl then, huh, is she, *is* she?'

She didn't expect such discomfort on Susie's face. 'Stop it, Marj. You're not supposed . . .' She turned.

The air was still. 'What?'

'You know what.'

'Me? What? What d'you mean?'

'*You* know. Don't be beastly. We're not supposed to know about . . .'

'What? *What?*'

'Oh *you* know. Uncle Fred.' Susie was extremely red.

Marjory gaped. 'I never said anything about Uncle Fred!'

'You did! Oh, you *did*. That's what you meant.'

'You're barmy. What's soppy old Fred Barnes got to do with anything?'

'Oh – shut *up*.' Susie rushed hot-faced towards the drawing-room.

Marjory shouted: 'You're not supposed to say shut up!'

Susie shouted back: 'You're not supposed to shout!'

The drawing-room door opened, Nora looked out. 'Here, you two. Don't you ever stop squabbling?'

'No,' Marjory seethed.

'We are not squabbling.' Dignified, Susie went into the room.
'Why on earth don't you leave her alone?' Nora took
Marjory's arm and drew her in. Everyone was sitting except
Madge and Uncle Ron who were singing Drink To Me Only
with comic effects to Flora's haphazard tune. Marjory's father
was by the window with Grandad, newspapers up. Marjory
whispered: *'Me?'* with an outrage that made Nora ask, 'What
was it then?' while thumping down beside her on the sofa
nearest the door.

'I don't know. Lipstick. She said about Gran saying it was
for bad girls and I said what about Auntie Molly – '

Nora nudged hard. 'Better keep off that.'

'What? Keep off what?'

'How old are you, young Marj?'

'Ten and a quarter. Keep off *what?'*

'And Susie?'

'Nearly fourteen. *What*, Nora?'

'It isn't your business, not at your age.'

Marjory's whisper was a screech. *'I* never said! It was
her – '

'All right. Leave it there.'

They were all clapping, laughing at Uncle Ron's clowning.
Nora joined in, standing as she was called to sing next. Marjory watched her walk along the room, the fringes of her short
dress swinging, her hair like glossy honey. Even Nora. There
was always something they whispered or didn't quite say. But
if anyone ever told her anything, anytime, it might be Nora.
Perhaps she knew about the Auntie Violet. Daddy liked Nora,
even smiled across his newspaper as she started to sing.

'You two next,' Auntie Liza instructed her children, 'after
Nora.' Archie and Val made faces, but would obey. Marjory
grinned at Archie, who had been too far off at table to speak,
and he came and flopped into Nora's place. He was all limbs
at fifteen, good-looking. 'What're you doing these days then,
Marj? How's school?' He always asked, remembering her
saying school was nice. 'When are you coming to see us?'

'Dunno. Maybe in the holidays if Gran says. It's a shame
you don't live round the corner any more.'

Archie fumbled for paper in his jacket. 'Got something to
show you.' But Nora's song ended and he was pulled up towards the piano by his sister. 'Give us We All Go To Work

38

But Father,' Auntie Liza cried, 'There's nothing like a laugh.'

Auntie Molly was at the piano. 'We'll give you a laugh all right in a mo,' she said, 'Got a terrific song for Marj, haven't we, Marj? You know – I Am A Little Beggar Girl.'

Her stomach resisted.

'What song's this?' Gran asked.

Molly giggled. 'One we found the other day in an old book. It's a scream.'

Auntie Ellie looked up, silk thread waiting over embroidery. 'Marjory has a very sweet voice,' she smiled, 'haven't you, dear?' She spoke towards Henry: 'She and Susie are often asked to sing at school.'

'I've got a sore throat,' she croaked.

Archie and Val sang and bowed to applause. Auntie Ellie looked at Marjory then patted her daughter. 'You sing first, Susie. What about the Cradle Song?' Teddy made retching noises behind Uncle Ron's armchair.

'No, Marj first. Come *on*.' Molly's fingers were on the keys.

'Yes, Marjory,' Auntie Ada gaily clapped her hands, 'come along, it's *too* funny.'

'Doesn't look as if Marjory thinks it's funny.' Auntie June spoke across her baby's head and received the glares she was used to from the other women.

'I've got a sore throat.'

'Now, Marj!' Ada simpered. 'Not too sore to have eaten a great big lunch, hm?'

'Come *on*, it's only short.' Auntie Molly flicked the music, looked at Marjory straight-mouthed.

'Maybe she doesn't feel like it,' Auntie June tried again.

'Doesn't *feel* like it!'

'Don't be a spoilsport!'

'Everyone's waiting, Marjory,' Gran said.

Her father's newspaper sank inches. He looked over his spectacles. 'Marjory?'

She looked.

'Be a good girl.' The newspaper rose again.

She went to the piano and looked over their heads at the heavy wallpaper, the gilt-framed photographs, the long tasselled curtains. She watched Molly's fingers play the introduction, there was no escape, heard Ada and Flora giggle.

'I am a little beggar girl
My mother she is dead
My father is a drunkard
And won't give me no bread
I sit beside my window
And hear the organ play
And think of my dear Mother,
Who's dead and far away . . .'

They were falling towards each other with laughing,
Auntie Molly leading Ada and Flora with a chorus of:

'Home, home sweet sweet home –
There's no place like home,
There's no place like home . . .'

She went through the shrieks to the sofa near the door.
'Don't look so tragic,' Nora murmured, 'they don't mean any
harm.' Auntie June wasn't laughing, but tugged jerkily at her
baby's dress. Grandad and Uncle Ron and Daddy were still
reading, hardly aware. Grandad looked up, smiling at the
noise, asking: What's funny? Susie was at the piano singing willingly, high and clear:

'Little feet, tired with play,
As the sun fades away,
Bring my baby home to rest
On a mother's loving breast . . .'

She slid to the door and out, to run upstairs. Susie's song
finished, she heard the clapping, lovely darling, lovely. I am a
little beggar girl my mother she is dead.

Someone was coming up the second stairs. It might be Daddy;
she rubbed at her face.
'You all right?' Archie came round the door. 'You've been
gone ages.'
'I'm not crying.' Staring out of the window.
'Who said you were?' The bed bounced as he sat down.
'We've got to go in a minute. Look, I didn't show you this.'
She looked, but kept her face down. 'What is it?'
He had a drawing, pencil and crayon. 'It's a dolls' house
I'm going to build.'

'It's lovely.'

'Soppy. For you, I mean. For Christmas maybe.'

'Oh!' She looked up then. 'Honest, Archie? Will you really? Honest?'

'Course. Shall I?'

It was a beautiful drawing. Five rooms, tiny furniture, a kitchen with a stove. 'You'd have to ask them, Gran and Daddy.'

'I did.'

'Oh. What did they say?'

'They said all right, if I really wanted to.' Archie grinned because she stared.

'Can you really make it, just like that? Even the furniture?'

'Yeah, easy. And paint it too.'

'What colour?'

'What d'you want? I thought, white and brown furniture, and the outside of the house – what? – green?'

'Blue would be nice.' Nobody had blue.

'Right-ho, blue then.' He stood and swung the door. 'I'll have to run.' He folded his drawing, looked at her. 'Auntie June was in a temper when you went, she and Auntie Molly had an argument. It was fine!' He laughed, then shuffled his feet. 'I stuck up for you a bit too,' he had to tell her. They grinned. He almost went, then came back to say: 'Oh, Teddy's been packed off home, his Mum whacked him. He cut the bobbles off the table-cover. Gran thought it was you and he owned up and bash! Auntie Flora gave him one.' Archie's enjoyment was huge. '*He* didn't care, you know old Ted.' He was away. 'Bye then, Marj, see you soon.'

She heard him thud on the stairs. 'Bye Archie.' Then she ran to the door and called: 'Archie – thanks. Thanks ever so much.'

*

It was nearly dark, the bear was coming. Splintery wood quivered under her. Rustle, plod. The bear stamped, was hurrying. Scrabbling at the door, snuffling, whispering, breathing. The door opened, opened. Her scream was stuck, she pressed backwards, hard, cold. They came towards her, big people, not the bear, hands coming towards her gleaming in the dusk. Somebody tall, a shining police hat. Another hanging back. A

41

lady's voice but deep; I'll have her, I'll have her, let me take her. Hands on her legs, rough as sandpaper. Poor little mite she's frozen, there there don't cry. They were going to give her to the bear, it waited on the stairs. Hush there don't cry, god what a smell. Out, out, the bear, the bear. No bear. Nothing. There, see, nothing to be afraid of, all safe now, rough hands on her forehead. Cold air, cold. Here, wrap this round her: the man that hung back brought warm wool. Some shouting, noise, engine, pushing. She was sitting on the pavement, cold, legs around her, jerking, kicking. Long silk legs, someone is crying. Long silk legs by wheels, trousers moving past, grunting. The engine; loud, crack, by her ear, silk legs lifting, going, leaving. The deep voice with rough hands: Think of your child. The motorbike is going down the street, silk legs, gone away, Daddy is crying. Marjory woke on the edge of sobbing, her throat big and aching. She lay without noise, inexplicably sad.

*

When her father said goodbye he paused, coughed a little. Then he said, looking towards the window: 'Next weekend I might bring home a friend to meet you, Marjory. For lunch on Sunday.'

'Oh,' she said. And she knew, it was a lady.

'I hope you won't be a disappointment to me.' If it had been less austere it might have been a plea. 'I hope you will be a good girl.'

'Yes, Daddy. I will.' What is her name?

'That's good.' His lower lip jutted, moved; he might be smiling slightly. 'Right. Goodbye.' The pause. 'God bless.'

She counted the Joeys. Let her be nice. Let her be able to look Gran in the eye like Auntie June. Let Daddy marry her and they could live somewhere else, with her, far away, and hardly ever see Gran.

THREE

A rare visit: Susie to Marjory. Both are in their fifties. Their childhood and family are almost all their conversation.

SUSIE: Gran and your feet. You always go on about your feet.

MARJORY: No wonder. Always cramming them into shoes too small.

SUSIE: Oh come on! We had all our shoes made to measure, hand-made, Covent Garden.

MARJORY: *You* know damn well I could hardly ever wear mine new, or I'd scuff them. God, I had to have an operation on my feet ten years ago.

SUSIE: That wasn't because of Gran.

MARJORY: Those tan and patent shoes she made me wear, I'll never forget. Even when I got that huge blister – what a fuss about nothing, Marjory! It was Auntie Ellie, your mum, took them off me in the street and I screamed. It went poisonous, into my leg – don't you remember? They said only sea-water would cure it. I was five, I was so scared of the sea I had to sit on the sand with my foot in a bucket.

SUSIE: Honestly, Marj, your feet were awful when they found you. Your shoes'd been on so long your toes were all bent over, like that. Mother told me.

MARJORY: Hmph. Well Gran certainly carried on the good work.

SUSIE: Oh, Marj, you always did exaggerate.

MARJORY: Good God, you sound just like Auntie Ada.

SUSIE: Gran was strict, but she was kind. You've got a lot to thank her for, Marj.

MARJORY: Yes, Susie. (*She laughs*)

*

Christ Church School stood back a little, as if respectfully, from its large church. Solid railings not too high, a swaying fence alongside. The bricks were round-edged, comfortable, the colours of soft rust. The doors, dark shining green, opened to warm dusty wood aromas, and chalk, desks and paper, paint, gabardine, carbolic soap, gym-shoes, books, pencils, ink.

Mr Beach, tall and chalk-blurred, always ginger-jacketed, famous for the single long hair that grew straight out of his right ear, loomed between desks, exercise books in hand.

'Interesting, Marjory.' A book dropped before her. 'Even if your opinions are a little unorthodox.' She thought he grinned but when she looked up he was gone, letting books fall with his comments on other desks.

'Eight out of ten? Stone the crows.' Keziah craned across the aisle. 'Can I read it?'

Marjory's English composition, 'People in My Family', ended:

'I like animals better than people mostly, except for Grandad who is very old and white-haired and Uncle Ron who is funny, and also some cousins, Teddy who is about my age and Nora who is grown up with her hair done in ear-phones, and Archie who makes things, and also my friend Keziah Hope who lives in the next street to me. Other people are usually not so nice, they can be strict or silly. Animals never are, and are never wicked. Jimmy our tabby is always in a good temper and even lets me put clothes on him, and Billy the white rat who is really Uncle Ron's will sit on my shoulder, and Buller and Boney are best of all, they are bulldogs. Grandad also has some parrots which talk and are nice too, and Uncle Ron has some pigeons. I must say that everyone in our family likes animals even the ones who are not as nice as the animals.'

Walking home, a distance behind Susie who confided with other big girls, Keziah said: 'Hey, you put me in it, honestly, Marj, fancy doing that.' She jumped on and off the gutter, not looking at Marjory. 'Is it true? Liking animals better?'

Marjory said: 'I should've put in Auntie June really. She's nice. She took us to the boat race and made this ginger cake all covered in lumps of ginger and almonds sticking out of it like teeth. You know what?'

44

'What?'

'I'm going to be a vet.'

Keziah stopped jumping. 'A vet? Honestly? Like Mr Stopps? Blimey.' She considered. 'That's very good, Marj, it really is.'

'Don't tell anyone.' A glance at Susie's back.

'Won't your dad let you?'

'Dunno.'

'You'll have to ask.'

'You don't *say*.'

'When it's scholarship time you'll have to, when they decide what you do next. You might as well ask now.' As if it were simple, asking your father. Then Keziah remembered the composition. 'You could ask your grandad.'

'I could I suppose.'

'Why don't you then?'

'*Oh*.' Marjory made the kerb her enemy, kicking it. '*He* won't be the one who says.'

After a while she asked Keziah: 'What was yours about? Excellent, he said.'

'About when my grandmother died.'

Marjory's head came up. 'Honestly? How did she die? Did somebody kill her?'

'Don't be *stupid*, Marj. She just died. She was *old*.'

'Oh.' She skipped along looking sideways until Keziah's scowl went and then asked as if with sympathy: 'How old was she?'

Keziah forgave. 'Nearly eighty. She was nice.'

Gran was only sixty-seven.

*

'I want you in the kitchen, Marjory.' Gran in the hall on Saturday morning as Marjory ran downstairs with the words in her mind: Daddy will bring the lady tomorrow.

'Oh, but – '

'Yes?'

'I was going to do my painting.' Holding up a box of Reeves and a poster. 'For the prize, you know, at school. Susie's doing it too. Everyone is. There's this poster you see – given out by Triplex Stoves and they're giving prizes for the best paintings of the different foods and the stove and – '

'Thank you, Marjory, we heard all about it yesterday. You can do it later. But I want you in the kitchen *now*.' She turned.

'I don't need it, Gran, honest. I've been. I went this morning, cross my heart I did. Really, Gran, there's nothing left to *do*.'

Gran stopped, her face dismayed. 'Marjory! Try not to be so coarse, if you please. *I* shall decide what you need or do not need. Now put down those things and come along.'

'The child's looking sallow,' Gran said to Grandad, who shelled peas at one end of the kitchen table while talking to Uncle Ron. 'A good dose of salts will put that right.' She said it every Saturday unless Marjory had ready some escape.

'Honestly, Gran, I don't need –'

'Please stop arguing, Marjory.'

She would not cry, but watched the fresh hard peas jumping from pods, tried to listen to Grandad and Uncle Ron, who – after an apology to Gran, for Grandad did not approve of politics before ladies – talked of miners and bosses and strikes, meaningless. Louder sounds were the tumbler, the tin, the spoon, the kettle beginning to boil. One and a half tablespoons, scrape of tin, clump of lid pressed back, steaming water pouring, stirring.

'Sit down.' Plunk, the tumbler on the table and hot steam under her nose. For the rest of her life, for ever, her whole inside would heave at the smell of boiling water. 'Drink it up.'

Gran stood.

'Come along, Marjory.'

'It's too hot.'

'I added some cold. Come along.'

Ron noticed. 'Go on, Marj, it's lovely.' To his mother: 'What is it anyway?'

Grandad chewed peas. 'Hold your breath, that's the best way.' As if she didn't know. 'Do as your grandmother says, my dear. She knows what's best, doesn't she?'

Fast, through shudders, it was gone.

'That's better.' Gran took the tumbler, lost interest. 'You can go now if you want to.'

Marjory sat a few seconds, not moving. Then she ran, reaching the downstairs lavatory in time to fall on her knees and feel her entire body try to turn itself inside out. Retching, swearing, oh damn and blast, stop crying, stupid fool. Her throat ached too much to swallow. She couldn't go and settle to painting, experience told her that. In a while there would be sharp pains and another rush to the lavatory where she would sit in griping misery until nothing else could happen. If her father were coming – but that was tomorrow, with the lady – he would say: You're looking a little pale, Marjory, are you getting enough fresh air? In the evening Gran would remark: You are looking much better now, Marjory, more colour.

Marjory kept her head down over her painting after lunch, sitting outside with Buller on the conservatory steps in the sun. She heard Gran's quick feet, round the corner from the back door. 'Ah. There you are. What are you doing?'

She loaded her brush with yellow ochre. 'Painting.'

'I want you to go to the mill for flour, with Teddy. He's just arrived with Auntie Flora and they're going out shopping afterwards, so hurry.'

'Oh Gran – can't we go later? Can't Teddy go on his own?'

'Really, Marjory, I've seldom heard such selfish talk. You know perfectly well that Teddy cannot carry twenty-eight pounds of flour alone. Your painting will wait.'

'We've got to hand it in at the end of the week.'

'Stop arguing, Marjory, and come.' Gran walked away.

Marjory plunged her brush, fat and yellow, into the jar of water. Do this, do that. Lump a great bag of flour, hurry up, don't argue, nag nag. Quick with irritation Marjory jumped up from the step, to say *damn* aloud as her paint jar lurched and fell. She snatched away the poster as a yellow pool spread across Gran's scrubbed step. Oh, too bad, silly old stinker.

She and Teddy grumbled together down Leander Road and round the corner to Brixton Hill. Honestly, what did Gran want all that flour for anyway? She's still got four bags left, Teddy had seen them. That store cupboard, you'd think she was expecting a war or a famine. Sacks of rice, great jars of treacle, and flour flour flour. Probably Auntie Ada used it for powder, that's what her face looked like, flour. *Plain* flour, Teddy decided, so they sniggered across the tram lines and into the gravelly road where the mill stood. Teddy put money into a floury hand, a thin dusty man put the sack between them and teased them about their strength. Teddy scowled and grumbled again going home. Couldn't Gran get it delivered like anyone else? Ah, she can't stand it if anyone's doing nothing, or what she thinks is nothing, makes you spit, when'll I get my painting done? All right for you, I've got to go shopping with my Mum, new coat, ugh, why don't you come? Can't, I'm s'posed to clean the silver and anyway there's the painting. Yah, lousy rotten sport, go on then.

Jimmy the tabby was wide-eyed and anxious on the back sill as Marjory went into the garden. She stroked him but he was oddly preoccupied, sinking from her hand. Gran was arranging sheets in the sunlight, anger in her movements.

Then Marjory saw Buller. 'What's the matter with Buller? Buller – here boy. What is it?' The dog shivered, shrank and whined by the wall. Boney stood near fretfully.

'Don't speak to him. He's been a very *bad dog*.'

Buller quivered through his skin. Marjory looked from him to Gran's pursed mouth. 'Buller? What's he done? Here, Buller – '

'*Leave* him.'

'Buller wouldn't be bad! What's he done?'

'Just look at that then. Wouldn't be bad! Filthy!' Gran was pointing at the conservatory steps. At the yellow puddle. 'Disgusting. He knows better. I whipped him. *Bad dog, bad.*' Buller whimpered and pleaded.

'But Gran – but Gran – ' words stuck, at last came. '*I* did that – *I* did it!'

Gran's face, astounded then furious. '*You* did it? *You?* Don't be foolish, Marjory, and don't tell – '

'*I* did it, it's my paint water, I spilled – *he* didn't – he wouldn't – ! It's not *that* – not *pee*-water – '

'*Marjory*! Watch your language and stop telling me lies. You are a wicked girl.'

'I'm not, I'm *not*.' She might choke. 'It's paint water, *paint*, you can *see*, you – you – Oh, Buller wouldn't – *oh*!' She turned her back between Gran and the trembling dog. Rigid, she would not cry with her there, cruel, horrid. She felt sick. Buller. She heard Gran breathe in and out noisily, heard her flap a sheet, gather pegs, start to walk back to the house. She knew the next words.

'Your father, Marjory, shall hear about this.'

48

Buller oh Buller I'm sorry it's my fault. Her hands shook at his neck, she led him down to the secret grass.

'You been crying?' Teddy, back from shopping.

'What do you want?'

'They said to find you. You're supposed to do something or other, the silver. What've you been crying for? Blimey, Marj, you're all swollen up.'

'Nothing.'

'Not much. *I* know. Gran told Mum you'd been telling fibs again. Out of sheer wickedness, she said.'

'Oh Teddy.' She rested her head on the calm warm of Buller's back. 'I hate her. I just hate her, that's all.'

*

From Auntie Molly's room Marjory could see the road, the corner of Elm Park where her father would appear, if they walked from the tram stop. Now perhaps he was getting off the tram, putting his hand under the lady's elbow. Now they were waiting to cross Beechdale, now Endymion, now coming to Elm Park Road, turning. Count to twenty and they will appear. He would bring her that way, not through the short cut where it was harder to walk in smart shoes and there might be litter. Now they would turn the corner, now. But her eyes had glazed on the milkman's pony by the time her father appeared, and she saw him like a stranger.

He was slim and neat, this man, walking with a bounce, swinging an umbrella. His head turned, quickly amused, she saw him laugh at the lady. She had laughed, she had fair hair quite short and modern showing below the close blue hat. Her coat was blue, bluebell blue, the gloves darker: a hand swiftly touching the man's arm as the laugh ended. The couple stopped a few yards from the door. She spoke, he answered. He shook his head. She took a step, stopped. They spoke again. He led her to the door.

It was Daddy. They were here. Marjory ran back to her room and stared at her face and combed her hair again.

'Clara, this is my daughter, Marjory. Marjory, I would like you to meet Miss Clara Finch, a friend of mine.'

She wasn't tall, only to Daddy's shoulder. 'Hello, Marjory.' Her hand was thin, smooth.

'How do you do.'

'I hope you'll be a friend of mine too.' She had an oval face, eyes were never that blue. Marjory smiled back: 'Yes.'

'Yes, Miss Finch,' Gran told her.

But Clara smiled at Marjory. 'It's all right.'

'Manners must be remembered.'

Her father kept his hand on Marjory's shoulder after kissing her. 'Been a good girl?' He was almost jovial.

'Ho ho, better not go into *that*,' Molly said from the window chair; she and Ada snickered.

As never before, he seemed not to hear them, but asked: 'How's school?'

'You like school?' Clara asked.

'Yes, I do. I like it.'

'Thank you, Miss Finch,' said Gran.

'Thank you, Miss Finch.'

Her father was settling his lady, who had glanced quickly at and away from Gran with a blush, in the velvet chair. 'What do you like best?' she asked.

'Oh, writing and reading and drawing and sports, but I like it all really.' She heard Gran breathe, and added: 'Miss Finch.'

'She gets good marks on the whole.' With disbelief she heard her father. 'She likes books; don't you?'

Susie shifted in the corner, sliding a magazine down her front. 'Marj brought a school book home on Friday, I saw it.'

Marjory was hot. Silence. Then Gran spoke: 'What book is this, Marjory?'

'A book Mr Beach gave me.'

'*Gave* you?'

'Mr *Beach*?' Susie half-laughed and turned slippery pages. 'That old meanie?'

Her father's mouth looked uncomfortable but he hung on to good humour. 'What's it all about then, hm?'

'It's a book called *Lorna Doone*,' the words dragged, 'and he gave it me.' She looked hate at Susie.

'Gave it *to* me,' said Gran.

Clara's slim hand had taken hers. 'How nice, I used to love that book. I wish I'd been given it by my schoolteacher. Was it a prize?'

50

She loved her. 'Yes, Miss Finch.'

'A prize!' Gran, Molly, Ada. Susie's mouth, open, said nothing.

'Goodness me, dear,' said Ellie.

'A prize?' said her father. 'Well well. What was this for?'

'Is it true?' Auntie Ada whispered to Susie, who was behind her magazine again, shrugging.

'Reading, it was for,' Marjory said.

'I thought prizes were only at the end of term,' Auntie Molly still didn't believe.

'Mr Beach never *used* to give any,' Susie said.

'Why didn't she tell us? She never *says*.' Ada was peevish, there was no scandal.

'This is a new idea then, is it?' Clara's hand still held hers.

'Yes, Miss Finch. Just prizes for three things in our class. It was Mr Beach's own idea, to do it every month. One for reading, one for writing, one for sums. My friend Keziah got the sums one and she nearly got the writing too. I came third for it.'

'Well well, we must enquire at the school about this,' Gran nodded at Susie.

'Congratulations,' Clara smiled, and her father said: 'Yes, well done, Marjory.'

On the way to lunch she trod on Susie's foot and kept treading even after she yelled.

Inevitably Clara asked them at table: 'What do you want to do when you grow up?'

Susie said: 'I'd like to work in a nice office. A secretary.'

'Very pleasant too, dear,' Auntie Ellie said.

'Auntie Ada works in an office,' Susie told Clara. 'Don't you, Auntie Ada?'

'Yes, dear.' Ada's fingertips touched her lace collar, patted the neat corrugations of her hair. 'And it can be very pleasant, as your mother says, as long as you choose the right place and the right kind of people.' But she sounded vague as if she preferred another subject, immediately asking Flora something about a Bridge party. Ada had worked in, and tearfully and suddenly left, several offices: Oh mother, she would weep to Gran, the people weren't really gen*teel*.

'And you, Marjory?' Clara turned the blue gaze.

Marjory said: 'I don't really know yet.'

Grandad smiled, gesturing to Teddy to pass Clara vegetables. 'Something to do with animals I should think,' he said, and she jumped, 'she's good with animals.'

She cut up her cabbage, head down, glad it was a smaller gathering this Sunday.

'Really?' Clara was looking, waiting.

'I'm sure,' Gran said, 'we'll do our best to find her something respectable.'

'I have a cousin,' Clara Finch told Marjory, 'who is a farmer. He says you have to be strong to work with animals – strong willed as well as strong physically I mean. I don't think I could do it, though I love animals.'

'I see what you mean,' Gran smiled. 'You're the frail type, delicate.'

'Oh – ' Clara's laugh was startled, 'I'm not weak or unhealthy or anything. I meant – '

'The wrists. You can often tell by the wrists,' Auntie Molly said.

Marjory saw her father look at Clara's wrists.

'I know the men will want to talk,' Gran said as napkins were folded. 'And so do the ladies.' As they stood she put an inescapable arm through Clara's. 'We'll have a lot to chat about, won't we? Ellie, where did I put my knitting? Molly, Ada – you bring coffee, won't you? Marjory, Susie, when you've helped clear the table run and play. Some fresh air would do you good. Teddy, go and wash, I know your mother's ready to be off.' She smiled at the men: Grandad, her sons, Ellie's husband, Wilf. 'Don't you interrupt us too soon now, only don't quarrel over politics, Henry and Wilf.' Uncle Wilf, tall and mild, was left-wing, Marjory had heard her father say. It sounded undesirable, but he was kind and thoughtful. It was a mystery, he and Ellie producing Susie as a daughter. Clara smiled a plea towards Henry but he was looking at his mother. She was led away, fair and bright on Gran's dark arm.

Teddy went: he and his mother were off to meet Uncle Bertie from the cinema and then on a train for tea with friends. Marjory looked at Susie. 'I certainly don't want to play with you,' she said, 'I'm taking the dogs for a walk.'

Susie smoothed her dress. 'You are very rude, Marjory. Anyway, Gran said Buller's still in disgrace, so you can't.'

52

'Gran can say what she damn well likes.' Marjory's tongue came out as she pranced away.

'Oh! That's swearing. I've a good mind to tell her. And I'll tell Uncle Henry too and see what his soppy Miss Clara Finch thinks of you then.'

She came with menace towards her cousin and yelled as Susie fled: 'I'll get Teddy on to you!' It was a threat with real meaning. The last time Teddy had acted as her agent he had pushed Susie's head into the garden drain.

The Park had more people on a Sunday afternoon but still space enough not to see them. She ran with Buller and Boney away from paths, dodged madly round trees, pouncing on the dogs so they yapped and veered away wild-eyed. Miss Clara Finch, Mrs Henry Bell. She'd be nice, she'd never hit you, Buller, for something you didn't do. Maybe she'll let you and Boney come and live with us, and she'd let me be a vet and we'd never see Gran again.

She dreamed back through the longer grass, the dogs snuffling near. It was cloudy now, a day when the breeze made face and hands chilly though it wasn't cold. The trees on the rise there were silhouettes. A couple stood by the big oak trunk like part of the tree; a man, a girl, heads bent to touch, then together like one person. Then two again, joined at the hands, walking down the slope towards her. She had been staring, very rude; she ran and whistled the dogs so the couple wouldn't know. So she stopped with shock when Uncle Ron's voice came: 'Hello, Marj.'

'Oh.'

He didn't let go the girl's hand. Both faces were smiling: Ron at Marjory, the girl at Ron. The girl's short dark hair was shiny but untidy; she glanced once at Marjory, kindly, but kept looking at Ron, standing close.

'I said hello.'

'Hello, Uncle Ron.'

He laughed at her, the girl laughed. Then he looked again at Marjory, his handsome comic face bright, and put a finger to his lips while his eyes pointed to Leander Road. She nodded and grinned too, and waved as they walked past her though they didn't look back, the girl with new bobbed hair and soft loose coat showing long calves, Uncle Ron saying something in her ear. He had brought girls home before: not this one, at whom he looked seriously though laughing. There was May with the chestnut hair and dark eyes: I do believe there's something false about those lashes, Molly murmured. And fair Elsie: But her *accent*, Ron dear, said Gran sadly. Doris, neither fair nor dark: mousy, they said, and I didn't think nice girls wore dresses like that. One visit, then gone. Uncle Ron, where's your nice friend? Oh, he'd wink and make it a game, I expect she found a man more handsome or richer; but there were lines at his mouth. And Gran with her arm round his shoulders, kissing him, you deserve much better my dear; satisfied.

Marjory ran. Buller, Boney, come *on*.

'I'm glad you're back,' her father said. 'Miss Finch has to leave soon, her train goes at five-thirty.' Clara held a tea-cup which might be trembling.

'It's lovely, Marjory,' she said when she was shown the prize book, but her glance flicked from it to Gran and Henry.

There was time to show her the roses in the garden. 'They're my favourites,' Marjory said, 'I have sort of conversations with them.' She waited, for she had told nobody that, but Clara did not tease, bending to smell the early blooms.

Then she asked: 'Does it help?'

Marjory nodded, and reached to pick just one, pale pink and thornless like Clara; neither open nor closed, its face waited. 'You have it.' Clara took it silently. 'You will come back, won't you?'

'If – yes, probably, I hope so.' She did not look towards Henry, who stood by the conservatory with Molly and Gran, but her head moved minutely.

Won't you marry Daddy?

'I've got a lot of things to tell you.'

'To tell me?' Clara looked surprised across the rose.

'Yes.'

'What sort of things?'

'Things I want to do, I want to be.' She looked towards the house, saw her father listening to Gran. 'It's a secret, I haven't told them.'

'Not even Daddy?'

She shook her head; they looked at each other.

*

When Miss Clara Finch left she bent to kiss Marjory. 'I hope,' she said privately, 'you are strong enough to do it all.'

Small and blue, down the steps. Daddy with his hand under her elbow. They walked down the street, not laughing. Their heads moved quickly as they talked. Once hers lifted with a jerk. Then round the corner, gone.

Gran closed the door, slow and certain. She looked at her daughters: Molly, Ada, Ellie. Together they walked down the hall to the kitchens.

At supper she heard them speaking sweetly to her father, softly tearing, viciously protecting. He did not speak to her much again except to say goodnight, hardly glancing at the *Lorna Doone*. He did not mention Buller and the paint water: perhaps Gran had said nothing.

'See you next weekend,' he said in Monday's dawn.

'Yes, Daddy.' Bring her back, please bring her.

'Be a good girl.'

'Yes, Daddy.'

'Goodbye then.'

In the pause she nearly shouted it: 'I liked her, Daddy.'

'I beg your pardon?' By the door his eyes looked big.

'I – your friend, Daddy. Miss Finch. I liked her, she's nice.'

'Oh. Yes, I see. Yes – good.' He coughed.

'Goodbye, Daddy.'

'Goodbye. God bless.'

*

'We need,' said Mrs MacTavish, who taught Physical Training, 'volunteers for junior hockey practice.' She stood gym-slipped and vastly-bosomed before the class in the playground. 'To prepare for next year's team, on Saturday mornings – '

Marjory's shoulder came near to dislocation as her arm hurled upwards.

'You're a bit on the small side,' Mrs MacTavish sprang from foot to foot; her huge breasts swung and the nickname Floppy went sniggering down the class line. 'Don't want you getting injured, do we?' She was an enthusiast.

'I can run fast.'

'She got two goals last games, don't you remember, Fl – Mrs

MacTavish?' Keziah succeeded in making the class noisy.

'Thank you, Keziah, I remember very well. Quiet, everybody.' Mrs MacTavish folded her arms and stood still. 'And are you merely advising, or volunteering too?'

'No, miss. I can't Saturdays.'

'Then please be silent. Now, Marjory. You were centre-half weren't you? Hm. All right.' She wrote on her pad. 'We'll give it a try.'

*

'Marj says,' Susie put particular weight on the second word but otherwise spoke as expected, 'she's been picked for junior hockey.'

Marjory filled her mouth with cake to stop the grin.

Auntie Ada said: 'I expect she was making it up.'

Gran said: 'Hockey? What is this, Marjory?'

Deliberately she chewed and swallowed, looking at Gran whose mouth shrank, waiting.

'It's practice for next term, for picking the junior team.'

'Oh, you're not actually *in* the team then,' said Ada.

'Not yet.'

'I hate hockey,' Susie said. 'It's dirty.'

'Well are you picked or not?' Gran asked.

'Mrs MacTavish is going to decide after a month or something. We have to practise every week and then she chooses.'

'No wonder,' Molly observed, 'your shoes get in a mess.'

'I wear my boots for hockey, hockey-boots.' Saying nothing about kicking a ball around with Teddy and his friends, or racing the boys down the playground and vaulting over their horse.

'It's not a very *lady*like game,' Susie said to her mother. Ellie smiled and stroked her arm.

'When is all this to be?' Gran asked.

Marjory looked at her, very straight. 'Mrs MacTavish said, be there at nine-thirty sharp Saturday mornings. We play until about eleven so I'll be home ages before lunch to do any jobs.'

'I see.' Gran poured tea. 'And in time, I trust, to have a bath before your father arrives.'

'Oh *yes*,' she said with such gaiety that Gran looked up quickly.

56

'Good girl,' Grandad said, taking his cup. 'And the fresh air will do you good, no doubt.'

Marjory looked at the dresser. Goodbye for ever, Epsom Salts, after three horrible years. She caught a glance from her grandmother's closed face and returned a bland one. In some way the score for Buller was even.

*

My Dear Marjory, wrote her father neatly on coffee-coloured paper, It happens that I won't be able to see you next weekend after all as I shall be working rather difficult hours which make a visit impossible. So I decided to drop you a line or two instead. Not that there's a lot of news in Watford, just a lot of work. I will look forward to hearing about all your activities when I come the following weekend, and perhaps we can go out somewhere together. Maybe you'd like to think of somewhere you want to go. Please ask Grandad to let me have a line to know how Gran is, I know from Auntie Molly that she was getting a cold and I know how they can go to her chest, or maybe you will write to me yourself if it doesn't take you away from your school work. I hope you will do everything you can to help at home. Please give my fondest love to everybody and be a good girl and don't give any trouble. Your affectionate Daddy.

Please God, Marjory prayed, if it is your Will perhaps you could let Gran's cold go to her chest and she wouldn't be able to breathe and it wouldn't hurt her if she died like that would it? And please let Daddy bring home Miss Finch again.

Dear Daddy, she wrote, Gran said I could write to you. It will be nice to go out somewhere when you come like we did before on the tram ride when you showed me places in London. Please may Teddy come too? At school we are keeping silkworms and Miss Robinson said we could keep some at home if we are allowed. I am playing hockey on Saturday mornings now and if I'm good enough I might be in the team. Gran is all right, so is everybody except that Billy the rat was sick yesterday but he's better now after Uncle Ron gave him some brandy. Lots of love from Marjory.

She sat with her pen for some time before slowly writing: P.S. I hope you will bring your friend again one day.

'I don't think, Marjory,' Gran said, 'that your father's friends are any of your business, do you?'

The letter was sent without the P.S., and Miss Clara Finch was never mentioned again.

FOUR

A Sunday in 1931. Auntie June has cornered Henry after lunch and they have been talking for some minutes; Henry looks increasingly bemused.

HENRY: Goodness, June, I hardly know what to say. I always understood from Mother and the others that Marjory was a difficult child, rather a handful. Of course I took their word for it – what do you expect? They were here, I wasn't, most of the time.

JUNE: Honestly, Henry, you cant be *that* dim. Fact is you're downright Victorian – it never occurred to you a child might be right and the adults wrong. Did it?

HENRY: I suppose not. But –

JUNE: And you've always thought your mother's word was gospel – the lot of you. Even Gerry, though thank heavens I've changed that a bit. Yes, I know they call me a trouble-maker. Well, it's been worth it. Good thing if you let a sensible woman put *you* in order, though it's a bit late for Marj, the damage is done.

HENRY: Damage? What on earth do you mean?

JUNE: Oh, nothing terrible. I just mean . . . well. if she can ever trust, really *trust* anyone in her life, I'll be surprised. God, no wonder she prefers animals! But perhaps one day someone'll come along with some love for her, and bang! that'll be it, nobody'll stop her. And a good thing too.

HENRY: Really, June, you say some extraordinary things.

*

She ran and bounded along the alley to the back gate. Mrs MacTavish had said: Good, Marjory. Daddy wasn't coming,

59

no sins to be reported. There was tea at Teddy's, Auntie Flora was taking them to one of Uncle Bertie's cinemas, free: it was Buster Keaton. Do everything right this morning: clean boots and hockey-stick in the scullery, have a bath; Gran, are there any jobs you would like me to do? All holy, the way Susie could be.

The dogs galloped to her at the gate, laughing round her legs, darting round the windy shrubs. She gave them fresh water from the garden tap, stopped to smell the roses. The deep red standard had bloomed quickly and now bowed at the neck, its perfumed head too heavy to hold up.

'Shut the door, please,' Gran said as she stepped into the kitchen, 'with *less* noise, Marjory.'

The kitchen was filled with suspense. Its centre was Auntie Molly, who was eating a late breakfast: she had been out to a party last night with her Fred; Marjory had heard her come in, bedroom floorboards creaking, not long before the birds started to sing.

Gran and Grandad, Auntie Ada, Auntie Ellie, Susie: all looked at Molly. Susie looked round at Marjory with widening eyes, turning down her mouth quickly: something important had been said.

Molly continued to spoon her breakfast cereal into an offended mouth. She always ate cereal or puddings with a teaspoon, to preserve the shapely bud of her lips. Teddy had told Marjory that Auntie Molly had heard that women with big mouths were big somewhere else unmentionable, and ever since then she had eaten with a teaspoon. She swallowed, turned large dark eyes on her audience, and spoke again. 'All I know is, there were ten sixpences in that pocket and they are not there now.'

Gran said: 'Now, Molly, let's be sensible. Where did you leave your coat?'

'On the back of my door, I told you, Mother. I put it there when I came in from work, and the change was in the pocket.'

'And you didn't wear it last night?'

'To a party? I wore my green, I said. Then I was sorting out my handbag this morning, went to the pocket for the sixpences – nothing there. Empty. Five shillings, I ask you. Well, *some*body must've taken it, it didn't *walk*.'

Grandad said, anxious and frowning: 'Come, Molly, there could be a mistake. Another pocket, or a hole in it.'

'Daddy . . .' Molly was patient. 'I've looked everywhere, and there's no hole in my pocket.'

'But who could have taken it?' he asked. 'Who *could*?'

'*I* don't know.' Molly laid down her teaspoon. 'But *some-* body did.' Her glance flicked quicker than a lizard at Marjory.

'*I* didn't!' she cried, seeing the thought: their bedrooms, side by side.

'Didn't say you did,' Molly smirked.

'I don't want any bad feeling,' Grandad rubbed his palm along the whitened edge of the table. 'This is most upsetting.'

Susie said: 'Maybe you put it in your purse last night, Auntie Molly, and then forgot.'

Auntie Ellie looked hopeful but Molly said: 'Don't be silly, Susie.'

Auntie Ada looked from Molly to Marjory across her coffee cup and sighed, clicking her tongue.

Gran said: 'There'd better be a search, that's the only thing for it.'

Uncle Ron came in. 'Search for what?' He was brisk and clear-faced, peering into the coffee-pot.

'Molly's lost some sixpences, that's all,' Grandad said.

'Lost! I didn't *lose* them.'

'Spent them I s'pose, eh Moll?' Uncle Ron nudged her, 'Wild living, *I* know, lavishing your sixpences around town.'

Molly didn't smile, nobody did. Uncle Ron made faces to himself.

'Come along,' Gran said. 'I'm sure we'll find them.'

Auntie Molly said, pushing Marjory's bedroom door, 'We might as well start here, it's nearest.'

Marjory stood, hating. 'I didn't take anything.'

'If you didn't, we'll soon know, won't we?'

Auntie Ellie's hands were squeezed together, she hung back on the landing. 'Oh Molly. Shouldn't we look in your room first? It's only fair.'

'For heaven's sake, Ellie. I've looked there, I turned it up-side down.'

Molly and Ada opened drawers, lifted clothes, opened the

wardrobe, felt in pockets. Gran shifted things on the window-sill, searched Marjory's school satchel.

Auntie Ada lifted the pillow from the bed, looked in the nightie-case, flopped them back and looked round the room. 'What about in there?' She was pointing at Marjory's box.

'It's private,' Marjory said, not hopefully.

It stood on the chest of drawers, the box that her father had made for her last Christmas. It was her only privacy, that treasure box: the lid locked, although in fact Gran had the key. Even so, it clicked smoothly shut and looked unassail-able. It was polished mahogany with some fine strips and designs of a lighter wood inlaid. Glass-fronted doors into which the lid fitted, and through the glass gleamed the brass handles of drawers. One for letters, one for jewellery, and a top layer for sewing things. Lift the heavy lid and it was satin-lined in jade green, with a mirror. It was the best present ever, and Grandad said: Your father is a craftsman.

Molly seized the lid, fingerprinting its polish, and pushed it up; she flicked open the doors.

'It's private,' Marjory tried again.

'Don't talk nonsense, Marjory,' instructed Gran.

Molly pulled out the bottom drawer, closed it. Then the middle one. She stood without moving, the room was silent. 'There they are,' she said.

The sixpences, an incriminating pile, sat next to Marjory's turquoise pendant. Marjory heard Gran and Ada say together: '*There*,' and Ellie: 'Oh no!'

'Oh Marj,' Susie whispered.

It didn't matter what she said, shouted, screamed. Their faces stayed stiff, appalled, moving away. Molly picked up the money and slapped the box lid down. Gran turned Susie, moved everyone from the room, closed the door.

'Be quiet, Marjory.'

'I didn't – I didn't – '

'Stop that dreadful noise. Behave.' Gran's face was small, hateful. 'You cannot argue with the facts, Marjory, not even you. You have been wicked, wicked. Ungrateful. You will stay here until you are ready to apologise. And you will certainly not be going out to tea or anywhere else. You should be ashamed, after everything that's been done for you. As for what your father will say to *this* . . .'

She was gone. Marjory heard them all move along the landing, voices low. 'There, you *see?*' 'Whatever will Henry say?' And Auntie Ellie: 'Maybe there's some mistake, Molly – couldn't there be?' Molly's exasperation, fading down the stairs.

'I wish,' she sat on the bed, 'I wish Teddy would put poison in the teapot and kill them all.'

Auntie Ellie, hardly speaking and miserable, brought lunch on a tray. No pudding, and it was syrup sponge.

Marjory asked: 'Did they tell Grandad and Uncle Ron?'

Auntie Ellie nodded, her hands clasped, she was almost in tears. At the door she said: 'Marjory, won't you say sorry to Auntie Molly?'

Marjory stirred her spoon in the soup. 'No.'

'Oh dear.'

'I didn't take them.'

'Oh *dear*.' Auntie Ellie went.

She heard Auntie Flora and Teddy arrive, watched at the window until Teddy came to signal and caper in the garden. She pushed up the sash and leaned out: forbidden, but disgrace could be no greater.

'Hey, Marj – did you pinch them?' he yelled.

'No I didn't!' she shouted into the wind.

Almost instantly Auntie Flora was there, smacking his head, dragging him indoors. Marjory was out of sight, window closed, in the same second. She kicked the skirting board until the paint chipped.

Susie came with tea, eyes down. Bread and butter only, no jam or cake. She put down the tray and walked to the door, where she hovered. 'I'm not supposed to talk to you.'

'Shut up then.'

'Ooh you are *rude*, Marj. I was being nice.'

'Har har.'

'They're all in the kitchen, they won't let me listen but I heard some. I don't know *what* they're going to do to you. Gran's furious, Grandad's all sad. Uncle Ron said he didn't believe it, Molly got cross. Why d'you do it, Marj?'

63

'I *didn't*, you stupid – fat-headed – *pig*!' The bread and butter was on the floor as she rushed at Susie.

Susie was quick; the door closed between them. She spoke through it. 'You're horrible and rude and I'll tell Gran, so there.'

She heard Susie run downstairs. She picked up the bread, fluff on the butter. Then she lay on her bed and cried, because of Grandad, all sad.

With the bedtime cocoa came Gran.

'It is very simple,' she told her. 'All you have to do is say sorry to Auntie Molly.'

Marjory did not reply but looked at her grandmother, making herself cold, without feeling.

'You should be ashamed. Auntie Molly, who has always been so kind to you.'

Marjory looked.

'Very well.' Gran's mouth was the smallest ever. 'You will get up in the morning and walk the dogs as usual. You will then return to your room and have breakfast here. And you'll stay here. Nobody wants your company for meals until you have shown how truly sorry you are. It is very fortunate for you that your father isn't here this weekend, and only Auntie Flora to lunch tomorrow so the whole family need not be upset.'

Marjory had discovered when she was five or six that if she made herself think of something else she could look at Gran as if she wasn't there: then her own feelings became distant, painless, non-existent, while fury built up behind Gran's voice.

'And you will go to bed the *minute* you have finished that cocoa.' The door closed behind her quite loudly.

She hoped Grandad wasn't up. She went quietly to the conservatory; even Gran in the kitchen shouldn't hear. And stopped: Uncle Ron was there, munching a hunk of bread, fingering some plant cuttings.

'Hello, Marj.'

She took down the dogs' leads. 'Hello.'

'Hey.' His hand held the back of her neck. 'What've you done that's so wicked?'

64

'Nothing.'

'Nothing, huh? What'll they do to you when you really do *something*?'

She said: 'I didn't, honest. They think I did.'

He chewed, frowned. 'Hm, difficult that.' Picking up a plate from the bench: 'Did you get any tea or supper?'

'Some bread and butter for tea but I dropped it.'

'Hungry?' He was holding out the plate. A chunky piece of crusty bread, thick butter, dark marmalade.

'No.'

'You can have it, I don't want it. You know me, eyes bigger than me belly.' He laughed.

'Don't you really want it?'

'You don't think I'd give it away if I did?'

'Thanks, Uncle Ron.' She took it and ate. The dogs slavered and begged.

Uncle Ron leaned, looking out of the conservatory and down the garden. Sometimes he looked old, lines down his face, but he was young, in his twenties.

'So,' he said. 'What do you do, eh, Marj? They all think one thing and you think another.' He was smiling a little but there was a thought beyond herself and the stolen sixpences. 'Give in, eh? Is that it?'

'No.'

'Never?'

'I didn't do it.'

'Ah.' He was looking into distances again. 'Well, at least that's *clear*.'

The dogs were jumping, knocking against flowers.

'I'd better take them,' she said.

'Yes, go on.' And as she was going he called: 'Anything I can do, Marj?'

She stopped and shrugged, then shook her head.

'Oh well,' he said.

She ran with the dogs to the Park.

Auntie Ellie brought her meals, sometimes silent sometimes pleading. Auntie Ada ruffled past to her room; she could feel the look at her own door, light brown and contemptuous, as Ada sniffed. Auntie Molly held loud conversations with Ada across the landing about the ingratitude of children today. Susie did not return.

Marjory did her homework, read, drew. She had one short, shouted conversation from the window with Teddy, who also smuggled Jimmy the tabby to the stairs so she could call him up for company. Gran came in the evening again with cocoa.

'How long do you intend to keep this up?'

Marjory shrugged, looking through her.

Gran breathed. 'When you come home from school at lunchtime and teatime you will come straight to your room. Do you understand? At *once*. Unless you are prepared to apologise.'

Coming down the main stairs to go to school she saw Auntie Ada below, her tallness bent over the small table, peering at and sorting the post. Then she held one envelope, square and mauve, to her bosom. It would be from Mr Waverley, the young gentleman who had called for her three times carrying posies of flowers. He had flat black hair, a black cane, patent shoes. His notes came on mauve paper always. Marjory had watched Mr Waverley, through the door-crack, waiting for Auntie Ada in the drawing-room; Ada, in a new blouse of many frothing borders, had flapped him angrily away. The other evening Auntie Molly had kept him company as he waited; she was expecting her friend Fred Barnes at any moment to take her to the theatre, she said, did Mr Waverley like the theatre? Mr Waverley was blushing as Molly leaned from her chair, and jumped up and dropped his flowers when Ada hurried in all perfumed. He was shy, fancy a man that shy. Marjory saw Auntie Molly snuffle a laugh to herself as she left the room.

*

Keziah asked: 'Well, who did take them?'

'How would I know? Susie, I suppose.'

Keziah thought. 'She wouldn't, would she? I mean, she's a bit soppy, but – '

'Well *I* didn't, that's all *I* know. So who else was it?'

'Maybe you did it in your sleep.'

'Don't talk such absolute stupid lousy *rubbish*.' Marjory walked away across the playground and didn't look at her for the rest of the morning.

'Hey – Marj – ' Keziah caught her up at lunchtime. 'I didn't mean – well, *I* don't think you did it.'

Marjory kicked at a fence. 'All right.'

'Maybe Susie did, if she wanted to get you into trouble.' Susie walked aloof with her friends, whispered and glanced. 'How can you find out?'

'Dunno, can't think. Gran says I've got to say sorry but I damn well won't. I don't care if I stay in my room for ever.'

Every day Gran said: You are being very foolish, very wicked, ungrateful, silly, thoughtless, selfish. I cannot think what your father is going to say. Saturday, Daddy, came nearer. Every day Marjory said: I didn't take them. Gran quivered. I cannot imagine what Henry has done to deserve a daughter such as yourself.

On Thursday she said to Keziah: 'I might run away.'

'Where to?'

'Could I come to your place?'

'Yes, but they'd look there first.'

'I could go to Auntie June and Uncle Gerry in Putney. She's nice, she wouldn't tell. She sticks up for me.'

'She might have to tell, if they nagged her.'

'I could go to the docks and hide on a ship and go to America or somewhere.'

'What all on your own?'

'Teddy might come. And he could bring some money.'

Running away before Saturday: the idea expanded. She wanted to tell Teddy but rarely saw him on week-days, he left earlier for his school. He might want to come; Auntie Flora always gave him money.

Marjory was so deeply inside her thoughts as she came in the front door, she almost didn't see Auntie Molly in the dim hall. And somebody else: Ada's Mr Waverley who must have just arrived. Auntie Molly said Oh! at the sight of the evil-doer and turned away, beckoning the visitor to the drawing-room. As she went upstairs Marjory heard Molly whispering: telling him, of course.

She pulled angrily at her school coat in her room: a button shot off, careering under the chest of drawers. She shouted

Damn and Blast and hoped they all heard. She'd have to sew it on, Gran would only moan. She found the button, went to her box for needle and thread. And as she opened the lid she stopped breathing.

Lying on top, on the jade-green satin and next to her silver thimble, a ring. It was large, of gold and garnets. It was Auntie Molly's.

She stood holding the box-lid up. She could hide it – under the rug, behind the wardrobe. Or throw it out of the window.

Auntie Molly was coming upstairs. Humming, cheerful. Marjory was hot, cold, her heart jolted. She shut the lid, opened it. The ring lay shining, awful. She breathed in, picked it up, and pulled open her door fast as Molly reached the landing.

'Marjory!' Auntie Molly jumped. She was carrying one of Mr Waverley's mauve envelopes, it must be for Ada. 'What do you think you are doing?'

Marjory stretched out her hand, the ring lay enormous. 'This is yours, isn't it, Auntie Molly? I just found it in my box and I didn't put it there. Here you are.'

Molly's mouth opened, closed, opened. She snatched the ring. 'What a dreadful story!' she cried. 'What a very wicked trick, what a terrible thing to do!' And she was running downstairs again, calling her mother.

Marjory shut her door, sat on the bed. Stupid: why hadn't she thrown it away? Or even put it back in Auntie Molly's room. But then, Molly might have missed it immediately and come looking, before she'd had a chance. Susie: she'd do something horrible to Susie, she'd tell Teddy to think of some beastly trick.

She waited for Gran, who came quite soon and stood just inside the door, small and tidy, lace-sleeved. Hardly moving, only looking at Marjory. She had a cameo brooch at her neck which rose and fell, or quivered, very slightly.

'I am *most* distressed.' Her voice came sharp and straight. 'So, I know, will your father be. Molly has told me about your foolish deception. What have you to say?'

Marjory bent her mind away from the face before her, so hard in dislike and anger; away from the thought of Grandad; away from Saturday and Daddy. She looked beyond Gran and thought of herself as a stick, a leafless hard prickling twig, and made her voice as unyielding: 'I found it in my box and I didn't put it there.'

Gran breathed; in, out. She decided against speech, and went.

In the Park in the morning she thought: Today I'll have to go. If she left extra early for school she might catch Teddy at his house. She could tell him to come in the evening with some money and they'd go. She would take Buller, maybe even Billy rat too. To wait for tomorrow was impossible: her father, shocked, ashamed, not believing her, believing Gran. And if he told his friend about it, Miss Clara Finch, what could she think? I must go, I will go, Marjory muttered as she ran back with the dogs. And she would leave a note in her room: it would say she was innocent, had done nothing, and would come back only when they were all sorry.

But she was held back by Gran telling her to polish her boots: *Not* while you are wearing them, Marjory. Unbuttoning, polishing, buttoning up again. She was too late for Teddy: by ten minutes, said Auntie Flora's cold face.

'Maybe your dad'll believe you, Marj,' said Keziah, but said no more when she saw Marjory's face.

Auntie Ellie brought her supper tray guiltily, as she brought all meals, as if she were breaking some rules and really she should be bringing bread and water only for the criminal, like in the Prison. She whispered, afraid of being heard speaking to her.

'Marjory, dear, couldn't you just say sorry? I mean, for your own sake. Your daddy will be here tomorrow and you know how – well, if you said sorry they might not tell him, might they? If I put in a word for you?' Ellie gasped a little.

She was tempted, she felt it. That Daddy shouldn't know. But she could see too clearly Gran's face and Molly's and Ada's as she made the apology. She said: 'I *can't*.'

She would stay here for ever, for years, a prisoner in a dungeon or a tower. She would get ill here, and die. She would write a long letter to be opened only after death. It would shame them, a letter about how she had died a wronged person, a victim, innocent. Her father would never forgive himself. And with luck she would come back and haunt Gran and make her die of fright.

Saturday morning. Gran came. 'Drink it,' she said, holding a tray with a steaming tumbler of Salts. Hockey had been forbidden, a note written to Mrs MacTavish. Marjory felt sick, her stomach turned and turned when she thought of her father.

'I don't want to,' she said. 'Thank you.'

'What you want, young lady, and what is good for you are two very different things,' Gran said. 'Come along. Take it.'

Marjory took the tumbler.

'Drink.'

She looked into the hot, disgusting glass. Gran waited, arms folded.

And then: 'Mother! Mother – are you there?'

Auntie Ellie was calling from the top of the house, over the banisters. Gran went on to the landing to answer. Ellie wanted some advice about a dress she was altering for Susie: could she come up for a while when she was free?

Gran was out of Marjory's room for less than a minute. Enough for her to pour the Salts into one of her wellington boots which stood in the wardrobe.

Impossible to read or do her homework. Fear went through her body, from her stomach outwards. All of her waited, listened. Every sound was gigantic. Auntie Molly was going out for lunch. She came upstairs to change: drawers and doors opened and shut, water ran in the bathroom. Marjory could smell her perfume as she hurried past. Auntie Ada saying: You look smart, Moll, who is it you're lunching with? And Molly laughing, acting as if it were secret when it was sure to be only fatty Fred Barnes. Uncle Wilf came thumping down from the flat, Susie running behind asking about going to the shop where they had the cream meringues, knowing she could hear her, the rotten pig; not that she could eat a meringue, or anything. Auntie Flora arrived: she heard the front door bang open, only Flora arrived like that, calling her mother, shouting at Teddy and Harry to stay tidy for heaven's sake. Then silence for a time: Flora had gone through to the Morgue, they'd be talking about how to tell Henry, all of them wanting to help, Gran and Flora and Ada and Molly.

Molly was changing early for lunch so she could be there, giving Henry a sad kiss. Grandad had gone out: it was ladies' business, all this upset.

After the quiet she jumped to hear Teddy's voice. He was singing – yelling – the Felix Cat song, doing their game, top volume to reach her room. Although she was shivering she laughed, picturing him. Bent, walking with hands clasped behind, in circles, then up the stairs going thump, thump on the loudest words . . .

> *'Felix kept on walking*
> *Kept on walking still*
> *With his hands behind him*
> *YOU would always find him*
> *BLOW HIM UP with DYNamite*
> *But HIM you couldn't kill . . .'*

. . . and now, a flying leap from the stair just reached, down to the hall with a crash . . .

> *'. . . MILES INTO THE AIR he flew*
> *He just murmured TOODLE-OO*
> *Landed down – '* (another crash)
> *'in TIMBUCTOO –*
> *And kept on WALKING STILL!'*

Last holidays they had invented the game, when it rained and they had to be indoors, and the song was always on the wireless.

Silence again. Teddy had gone maybe, might appear in the garden. Then with a shout he began again and she could hear him laugh behind the raucous singing:

> *'MARJ'RY kept on walking*
> *Kept on walking still . . .'*

He had got as far as *'BLOW HER UP with DYNamite but HER you couldn't kill!'* at screaming pitch, when Auntie Flora's shriek came even louder and he was pulled away. She heard the stubborn words: *'SHE just murmured TOODLE-OO. . . .'* and then a smack brought silence. Ted, good old Teddy.

Her mouth tasted terrible and her face was cold. She heard the front door close behind her father. It must be him, everyone else had hurried to the hall. She held open her door but couldn't hear Gran's words. They all murmured along to the kitchens.

Shocked, regretful, they were whispering to him in the Morgue. They wouldn't call her yet. Auntie Ada would touch his arm, Ellie would be crying, Auntie Molly and Auntie Flora would be full of right, indignant for him, condemning her. Gran would do the telling, her thin-edged voice going straight to the point, no emotion except a touch of triumph that something had been proved. I'm sure she doesn't get it from you, Henry. No Grandad to add softness. No Uncle Ron: he had gone out earlier, she'd heard him call goodbye, to meet his dark-haired girl maybe. Daddy would be listening in horror and shame, then he would be angry. He would apologise to Molly and to his mother for her wickedness.

She decided. Whatever he said, or they said, she would say nothing. He would question her, but she would not open her mouth. That might be easier. Otherwise she would have to protest, she knew she would cry because of his disbelief and then Gran would be pleased. Silence. He would punish her, and then it would be over.

There was a rustling along the hall as she came downstairs to the drawing-room. They would be waiting, Gran and her daughters. Perhaps they would creep along to listen at the door.

Her father stood by the fireplace. She closed the door behind her and stayed, hands still on the knob. They looked at each other: he had one thumb tucked into his waistcoat pocket, his other hand on the mantelpiece. His eyes were large and unavoidable, his mouth tight.

'Come here, Marjory.'

Five, six steps forward.

'My mother has told me what you have done.'

Silence.

'It was very, very wicked, Marjory, as I hope you know. I am *extremely* disappointed in you, deeply ashamed.'

Say nothing. She looked at his toecaps, very polished, glassy brown. She was aware of space all round her, nothing to hold. The thing was not to cry, to try to keep her heart quiet, to think of something else.

His words were quicker, sharper. 'This is disgraceful ingratitude, to your aunt and to your grandmother. They have shown you generosity, given you a good home, and you repay them by . . . by *stealing*. I'm shocked, appalled. You have enough money, beautiful possessions, excellent clothes. There can be no reason for it except wickedness.'

Her mouth clamped, it was all dry between her lips and teeth.

'Have you anything to say, Marjory?'

Shake of the head.

He breathed deeply and spoke very clearly. 'I want you, Marjory, to apologise to your Aunt Molly, and to your grandmother, and to everyone else for causing so much trouble and distress in this house. I was doubly ashamed to learn that you had refused to do so. Indeed, I could hardly believe my ears.' He paused but she did not look up. 'I am going to call everybody into the room now and you will make your apology in front of me.'

This horror was more than anything expected. 'I didn't do anything – I didn't, Daddy!' Her voice was strange, high and croaky.

His cheekbones reddened and his voice shook. 'Marjory! Please do *not* tell lies. If there is anything worse than a thief, it is a thief *and* a liar.' He walked past her to the door. 'And now you *will* apologise.'

She could run out, down the road, away –

'Mother. Molly. Marjory is ready now.'

They walked in, she felt them coming round behind her. Gran, her mouth pea-sized; Auntie Molly dressed up to go out, something victorious in her walk; Auntie Flora in a new cloche hat, checking it in the mirror; Auntie Ellie sighing, sitting in a corner; Auntie Ada drifting to the window, turning to view all the room. Gran and Daddy stood together at the fireplace, Molly nearby. Everyone looked.

'Well, Marjory?' Her father's feet were apart, his legs very straight.

She looked at the Persian carpet, the pattern fawn and blue and brown, very intricate, rather boring. She said, very low: 'I haven't done anything, it wasn't me.'

Gran gasped. Molly, quivering anew, cried: 'Well!'

'I am so sorry about this, Henry,' Gran said. 'I really did believe that at least, when you were here . . .' Maybe now she actually would send her to a home for bad girls and orphans.

73

'But I regret to say, Henry, she has shown no remorse at all, not a tear.'

Molly stamped. 'It's quite obvious she isn't at all sorry, not at all, and she'll probably do it again.'

'You have my word, Molly,' he was like an iron rod, 'that she will do no such thing. Furthermore she will apologise. Marjory.'

Marjory looked at the carpet and swallowed. Her father's feet shifted. Molly's dress made shiny noises as she folded her arms. Gran sighed through her nose.

'Marjory. Look up at me.'

She looked but his face was unbearable. 'I didn't do anything, I won't say sorry, I didn't take them, I didn't!' Her mouth was collapsing, she dropped her head at once.

'Go upstairs.' He didn't shout. 'Go this minute and do not come down until you are ready to apologise. You will stay there for as long as it takes. And if you have not thought better of your actions before I leave on Monday I shall have to decide what steps to take. I am ashamed of you, Marjory. Think yourself lucky you are not being thoroughly spanked. Now go.'

In the hall she passed Susie. Stupid cat, listening. Stupid all of them, horrible, she hated them. She slammed her door so hard it bounced open again : she kicked it shut. She fell on her bed, screaming in her throat with a rage too painful to be understood, and discovered Jimmy, breaking rules, under the eiderdown. He purred as she hugged him.

Now Auntie Ellie did not speak at all when she brought the tray, and the house was quiet. Teddy had gone, the day went on, on. She had read enough, she didn't feel like drawing and besides her pencils needed sharpening. She looked out : it was sunny sometimes, the roses swayed in the rough breeze. Everyone would be here tomorrow for Sunday lunch, they'd all be told. Nora would believe them and think her wicked. They might tell Archie to stop making the dolls' house. It was horrible, all of them whispering and thinking.

She hated, and hated. Oh, so many things to hate Gran for. Making her wear shoes even on the blister because they matched the coat. The Salts. Wait until your father hears. Bad girls, orphans. Buller. If I could make her cry. And Susie

74

she hated, making them think she'd pinched the *Lorna Doone*. And Auntie Molly: I Am A Little Beggar Girl, and if it wasn't that it was Swannee with my mammy waiting for me praying for me and all of them laughing. Auntie Ada looking sideways and whispering about That Woman: the hairdresser who used to come sometimes to the house to do their hair for special occasions – I say, Ada murmured, doesn't she remind you of G . . ., mouthing a name and glancing at Marjory so that she felt inexplicable shame. You'll go the way of your mother. And all of them she hated, for listening when Susie told: Marj had to do some lines, Marj got the cane. Or if she let slip something good that had happened at school, they said: Is that true, Susie? Is Marjory making it up? And for that birthday when her name had been on the wireless, Uncle Mac's voice unbelievably saying her own name and address: Go and look in the far pocket of the billiard table for a special surprise. And she ran, and there was a piece of screwed-up paper and a bit of ribbon. They laughed, Molly and Ada and Flora and Gran. Spoil-sport, Marj, where's your sense of humour, it's only for a lark. Fancy, we had our name on the wireless!

Gran appeared very early on Sunday and stood at the foot of Marjory's bed, hands on the brass rail. 'You will not be walking the dogs.' Marjory lay looking just past her shoulder. 'But don't imagine you can laze about all day. You will get up as usual.' At the door she said: 'And make your own bed and I shall come later to see that it has been done properly, and your room tidied and dusted.'

Gran herself always made all the beds. It was her own ritual, unexplained. She wore a particular bed-making apron, first going round the house pulling back clothes for a thorough airing. Then after breakfast round again to make each bed with precise smoothness: sheets tight, pillows exact. And in the late afternoon came the last rounds, this time to turn back each counterpane and a measured triangle of sheet. The whole business of the beds was sacred; her linen cupboard was a holy lavender place. That Marjory should make her own bed suggested that it might now be contaminated by her sinfulness.

Gran was looking at a hairy dent on the eiderdown. 'Has that cat been up here?'

Jimmy had left in the early hours. 'No,' Marjory lied, unfaltering.

Gran continued instructions. 'For the rest of the day, you will do your mending. Auntie Ellie will bring you your stockings, and there are some other things which need darning or buttons.' She left, unaware of Marjory's stuck out tongue and crossed eyes.

She could hear them all in the hall as they arrived for lunch. Uncle Ron teasing Nora and Madge about their short dresses, nearly showing their knees! Teddy's cackle, Auntie Hennie's deep voice, Auntie Flora and Uncle Bertie, Auntie June calling to Gerry to bring the baby's shawl from the car, the baby crying, Uncle Joe's mild greetings and soft laugh. All acting as if she wasn't in the house. She sat with Jimmy on her lap and darned another heel and was glad when the noises faded towards the kitchens or drawing-room. Except that now they would be telling.

The beef on her plate was red, seeping, the sort she couldn't swallow. Usually Uncle Ron sneaked such slices off her plate to help, giving her any crispy outside he had. Or it would be served up again for supper: that wasn't so bad, it was usually reheated and less red. She ate the edges, Jimmy had some, she left the rest. There was no trifle, only two Rich Tea biscuits. Auntie Ellie crept in and out with the tray.

She could give in, it would be easiest. She only had to say sorry and not look at the faces. Maybe then if she could find out who had really taken the sixpences and the ring, it would turn out better, for they would have to apologise for making her tell lies, forcing her to say sorry for something she hadn't done. They'd always have to believe her after that.

The piano was plunking, they were singing. Buller and Boney chased the wind in the garden; did they wonder where she was? Probably Uncle Ron had taken them out this morning, or even Daddy or Grandad.

She could get a suitcase from Auntie Ellie's flat and creep out in the night.

Somebody was coming upstairs: creak, softly. Daddy? She had a cold feeling, the hint of a nightmare coming true. Creak. Then the door swung: it was Teddy, and Billy rat on his shoulder, a bag of Sharps toffee in his hand and some stolen cake. His hair hung in spikes on his forehead and he grinned his demon grin.

'I said I was going in the garden. Here, have some cake, it's all sticky.' He tipped Billy rat on to the bed and sat there himself. She could hug him but he would recoil and blush. He gave her the bag of toffee, craggy lumps broken with a hammer. 'You can have it all.' Then, feeling that such generosity should be explained: 'I've got the rest of the tin at home, Dad bust it up for me.'

Teeth stuck with Sharps Creamy, she told him what had happened.

'What d'you think then? Susie did it?'

'Well I didn't. Somebody did.'

'Trust Susie. Huh. *She* won't own up. You'll be here for ever, Marj, until you're a little old lady with white hair.'

'I'm going to run away. One night.'

'Crikey. Where?'

'Don't know yet. I thought of going to Auntie June's, she'd believe me. I could find my way I think on the trams. Only Keziah said they'd make her tell.'

'Uncle Gerry would. He's soft.'

'He's nice.'

'Yeah, but they all do what Gran says.'

She drummed her feet against the bed. 'Well, the other thing was a boat, hiding on one and going to America or somewhere.'

'You wouldn't! Would you? Would you? Hey, Marj – can I come too?'

'Oh yes – I was going to ask you, Ted. We'd have to have money and some food, and you can get money easier.'

'Yeah – easy. Tell you what, I'll see what I – '

'Teddy!' His mother's voice, downstairs.

Hands over mouths, eyes staring. 'Shh,' Marjory said needlessly.

'Teddy – where on earth are you?' Flora's voice was further away.

'I'd better go,' he hissed, 'she'll find out I'm not in the garden. Listen, I'll try and sneak back, or I'll give old Keziah a note or something and she – '

'I *thought* as much!' Susie, her grown-up face on, pushing the door open with one finger.

'Oh clever clever,' chanted Teddy, hiding the toffee.

'*And* Jimmy, *and* Billy rat. Well!'

'*Well!*' Teddy imitated. 'You just tell and –'

But Susie was already at the banister rail.

'Auntie Flora! Here he is – up here.' A pause. 'With *Marjory.*'

'You mean cat!' Teddy yelled. And he sprang, fists like hammers.

Susie screamed at the first blow and slapped him on the ear, loud. She tried again but he shouted with fury and rushed into her. Pummelling, punching, kicking, biting, they were against the landing wall, Teddy fighting as dirtily as he could to make up for being smaller. He made no more sounds louder than a grunt but Susie's shrieks were terrible. Marjory sat on her bed watching them through the open door, waiting for everyone to rush upstairs, an odd feeling of distance while she said Go on Teddy at each grunt or scream.

'Susie – Susie darling, whatever – ' Auntie Ellie running first.

Auntie Flora followed. 'What the devil's going on?'

Susie screamed louder, Teddy's attack grew wilder in the last seconds before they were seized. Then everyone was there, pulling him off, Flora shaking and cuffing him. Teddy's Sunday collar was sideways, blood on it from one or both of them. Auntie Ada: Beastly little boy! Auntie Ellie and Auntie Molly: There, Susie, don't you cry. Fancy hitting a girl! Uncle Ron halfway up the stairs: Here, what's happening? sounding amused. Everyone shouting, chaos, Susie sobbing. Nobody looked at Marjory: Ada stepped forward and pulled her door closed. She opened it again, quietly, as the noise moved down the stairs: Flora lecturing, Teddy protesting, everyone shouting him down. Auntie Ellie and Susie were just leaving the landing. Oh Mummy, Susie wept, he nearly bit the nipple off my left one. Somehow the words reached Teddy. He yelled back: Next time I'll bite 'em both off! Flora's hand landed painfully, Uncle Ron gave a snort.

Marjory rolled laughing on her bed, laughing again at Billy rat jumping aside to watch, whiskers quivering. Hooray for Teddy, hooray that she hadn't said sorry, hooray that they would run away and never come back.

She watched out of the window at dusk as the street lamps came alive one by one across the back gardens of Medora Road. The church bells started to ring. It could be quite creepy, going away in the night, all dark and cold. She thought: If I pray to God while the bells are ringing, to make Gran die, and she dies before the bells stop, then that would mean God agrees with me and it wouldn't be wicked. She knelt by the window, pressing her forehead to the sound of bells.

But Gran lived. Minutes after Marjory had straightened stiff knees she came to light the gas jet. She did not speak, but breathed with meaning.

Just after six her father came to say goodbye. Morning light and a smell of shaving soap, his collar very stiff and clean. He stood between the chest of drawers and the door. This Monday there were no Joeys, he did not kiss her.

'Have you anything to say to me, Marjory?'

Sitting up, she looked at her bent knees and her hands clasped around them, and shook her head.

'I beg your pardon?'

'No, Daddy.'

Silence for some time. Then he said: 'I want you to think very hard, Marjory, about how very wicked you have been. And when I come next Saturday I want to learn that you have made your apologies as you should. If you haven't – well – I cannot say what we shall have to do about you.'

She kept her eyes down.

'I am going now. Goodbye.'

'Goodbye, Daddy.' She looked up: she would never see him again, goodbye, Daddy.

There was no God bless.

'I have to go before Saturday,' she told Keziah, 'or they'll send me to a bad girls' home.'

'They wouldn't!'

'Or an orphanage. I'm half an orphan.'

Through Keziah they arranged it, with notes. Teddy would come to the back gate at eleven on Friday night. Marjory must leave it unbolted: she would come in that way from school. He would whistle the first notes of the Felix Cat song, she would creep down, take Buller from the conservatory, they

79

would go; Teddy knew how to get to the docks. He was thrilled: We'll go to Hollywood, Marj.

Marjory spent hours working out the note she would leave, reproaching them; she would sign it Marjory Greta Bell, with the Greta underlined, aged nearly ten and a half.

'Couldn't you leave it until next week?' Keziah asked. 'They might change their minds.'

'I can't. They'll send me away, I know they will.' Keziah's eyes were down, the lashes dark, her fine skin pale. 'I'll write to you though, cross my heart.'

'I was going to ask you home for Friday. You know, the Sabbath. You always asked about it and Mummy said you could come.'

'Oh.' The candles, the special food. 'Oh *Kez.*'

'Never mind.'

'They wouldn't have let me anyway.' She saw Keziah's nose changing colour. 'Why don't you come with us?'

'*I* don't want to run away!' Keziah was ferocious.

Thursday after school: one more day to go. She pushed open the big door of Christ Church, carefully, slowly. Empty. She slid into the good smells, the soft light. Polish and incense and matting-dust and candle-wax. Creeping into a back pew, she hoped Father Cheshire wouldn't come. He was nice, big like Grandad, a large but quiet voice. But he would say: Hello, Marjory, and how are you? Anything I can do, young lady? She sat for a while, waiting, hearing her own breath whistling in her nose. Nobody came.

Please God let it be all right. Let me and Teddy go to a good place and don't let them find us until they know I didn't do it. Please let them find out what I said is true and make them sorry. Amen.

Friday morning: Marjory emptied her school sportsbag into the bottom of the wardrobe, ready to pack in the evening. She went to the bathroom to get her sponge-bag and face flannel; she would get the rest tonight. Auntie Molly came from her bedroom as Marjory reappeared on the landing. She sniffed, closing her door with deliberate care. Marjory slammed into her own room. Stupid cat, wish she'd fall downstairs.

She was pulling up her school stockings when she heard

Molly rustling, back in her room. But then – that was Molly's voice down below, saying she must just get her scarf, that was her tread on the stairs, the click in her ankle. Marjory's hands, straightening the stocking, were still.

A door-handle rattled. A gasp, a flurry. 'Ada!'

Auntie Ada, whimpering, protesting: Don't be silly, Moll, I was only looking at it, how could you think . . . Molly's voice, very high: Ada! It was *you* – Ada. Marjory's door was shut, impossible to hear all the words; she could not move to open it. *Ada* – my godfathers whatever will Mother say – I didn't, Molly, I didn't, how could you believe – Ada crying, whining, running after Molly down the stairs.

Marjory unfroze: she opened her door. She heard them meet Gran on the lower stairs. Ada: It isn't true, Mother, don't listen to her, Molly's being beastly . . . Molly: I *caught* her, Mother, it was *Ada*, look, my necklace . . . And Gran: You'd better both come downstairs with me. The whimpers, the accusations, faded. They had gone. Marjory pulled on her school coat, picked up her satchel, went slowly down to the front door and down the road.

It was Susie, catching her up, looking so prim, that made her realise the amazement and she rattled out the news: 'It was Auntie Ada all the time who pinched the things, so there, so *there*.'

'Auntie Ada! Are you mad, Marj? Anyway, you don't say pinched, it's vulgar.'

'Auntie Molly just caught her, you should've heard the row. She had a necklace. Don't believe me if you don't want. You'll see.'

'Auntie Ada!'

'There you are, *see*. You thought it was me.'

Susie did not look at her: 'Well *you* thought it was *me*, so there.'

They said no more. When Keziah appeared from her street Marjory ran ahead.

'Golly,' Keziah said, 'what a scream. Now they'll have to say sorry to you. But, Marj – aren't you furious with them all? I'd be *livid*.'

'Don't know what I am.' But some outrage began to filter through the numbness. 'I am, I suppose – but a fat lot of good *that*'ll do me.'

'Teddy'll be cross. He wanted to meet Rudolf Valentino.'

'Ah.' Gran was in the hall when Marjory and Susie entered the house for lunch.

Marjory headed for the stairs.

'Marjory.'

She stopped, too embarrassed to look round.

'Come into the kitchen with Susie. We are having soup and macaroni cheese.' Gran was walking along the hall.

Marjory glanced at Susie, whose eyebrows were high, and stuck out her tongue.

Grandad sat at one end of the long table reading a paper. He folded it as they came in. 'Well well. Hello, young ladies. Come and sit down.' He winked at her, but he was not really so jolly.

'Wash your hands.' Gran ladled soup.

Auntie Ellie was placing napkins and cutlery. 'Hello, my dears,' she said, smiling and anxious. She touched Marjory's shoulder as she passed; Marjory did not look at her.

They washed hands and sat. Marjory felt her face set, serious; she said nothing to anyone. Auntie Ada was missing. She was usually at lunch when she didn't have a job. With the daring of curiosity Susie asked: 'Where's Auntie Ada?' all innocence.

'Hm?' Gran seemed absent-minded, everyone else looked at their spoons and forks. 'Who? Oh – upstairs somewhere. Busy. Now, pass the bread, Susie.'

There was little talk. Marjory thought: They'll wait until tonight, when Auntie Molly's here. Then they'll say it was a mistake and Auntie Molly and Auntie Ada will have to say sorry, ha ha serves them right, horrible things.

But she was nervous after school, going upstairs to take off coat and boots. What did you say when somebody said Sorry? They would all look at her. That's quite all right! Airy, very polite. Or: I told you it wasn't me and you didn't believe me. All righteous. Or nothing, awkwardly.

Halfway up the second stairs she heard a sound from the morning: Auntie Ada weeping. But now it was shakier after long hours, Auntie Ada was speaking in a drawn-out tremble. Then came Auntie Molly's voice, bland and cool.

Marjory arrived quietly on the landing. Auntie Molly's door

stood open: Molly sat in her buttoned chair, ankles languidly crossed, looking at Ada just inside the doorway. Ada's back was to Marjory, her chestnut hair oddly frizzed and uncombed; one hand held a hanky to her face, the other crumpled something mauve: notepaper. Molly smiled a little.

Neither looked at Marjory. She walked past to her room and went in, but left the door slightly open and stood near.

'*I* knew it, *I* saw, don't think I didn't . . . I'm not stupid . . .' Ada sobbed.

'For heaven's sake, Ada. One boring lunch.' There was a yawn.

'You . . . *you* stole . . .'

'Ha, don't make me laugh. I wouldn't steal *him* if he was wrapped in gold leaf.'

'*Oh* – you're hateful, Molly. He was going to take me to . . . now he says . . . oh how *could* you, Molly? It was the same with Percy – you did it then, didn't you? *I* know. *Didn't* you?'

'Go away for pity's sake.' Molly's shoes squeaked together as she stretched. '*I* can't help it if your boy friends are so damn pathetic.'

'You're horrible, horrible!' Ada was crying too much for more words. She ran along the landing.

Molly's acid voice followed: 'And keep out of my room unless you're invited.' Marjory wanted to shout: *And* mine!

The walls shook as Ada's door shut.

Marjory heard Molly's small snuffled laugh, like one of the dogs when they'd snatched the other's bone.

Nothing was said. At tea and at supper Auntie Ellie and Grandad spoke with particular kindness. Uncle Ron made jokes and Marjory laughed deliberately loudly: nobody protested. Gran was the same as before, as if nothing had happened, as if nothing unjust had ever been said, hateful cat. It was half an hour before Auntie Molly even looked at Marjory; when she did she spoke with irritated politeness. Marjory gazed scornfully. Auntie Ada was still upstairs.

Keys had appeared. Molly's door was locked. The key was back in Marjory's box, another in the wardrobe. She locked both with relish and hid the keys behind her books.

At bedtime Gran said: 'When you take out the dogs tomorrow, Marjory, remember to put on your wellingtons. It's very muddy underfoot.' Marjory thought: The Salts! I haven't tipped out the Salts. She snorted, and Gran looked up quickly, so Marjory blew her nose.

When he came next day her father said: 'Well, Marjory, well. I'm pleased that everything is all right in the end. Good. Now – how are things at school?'

In the afternoon Teddy careered into the house, his mother behind him. Flora went straight through to the Morgue.

'Hey, Marj – hey, Marj – ' Teddy capered around her like a lunatic terrier, his sulks about America over. 'Mum's got a great surprise – if your Dad says yes – if, if – you just wait, you just wait!'

'What is it, Teddy? Come on – tell. What's going on?' She chased him round the garden but he escaped always.

Auntie Flora came to find them. 'Marjory, I've asked Henry if he will let you and he says yes, as long as you are a good girl.'

Teddy pranced. Marjory said: 'What?'

'We're going for a week to Yarmouth during the holidays. If you like, you can come too.'

FIVE

*One spring day in the 1970s, two women stop at a
London store window: MARJORY and a DAUGH-
TER. 'Oh look – ' Marjory points ' – those Easter
baskets.' It is a bright display, yellow chicks and
coloured eggs. 'They used to make them just like
that when I was a kid.' Daughter: 'Aren't they
smashing?' They walk on; Marjory continues: 'Mind
you, I never got mine on the proper day – I'd
usually been Wicked: No Easter Eggs for you my
girl. Ha!' Marjory laughs: 'Teddy used to share his
with me once we got outside, and Susie if I
smarmed round her.' Daughter: 'You must've had
yours on the right day SOMEtimes Mum.' Marjory:
'I suppose so, but that's how it seems, looking back.'
Perhaps she sees some sadness or sympathy on her
daughter's face, for she speaks briskly: 'Oh, things
like that used to make me howl once, but I can't let
them bother me. Anyway, kids accept a lot, God
help them.' Daughter: 'D'you think so?' Marjory:
'Don't get the wrong idea. I reckon they thought
they were doing their best for me, and it was only
Gran I really hated – I felt she hated me. But we
had an awful lot of good times too, you know.
Don't forget that.'*

*

Teddy began the holidays with the neatest idea yet for mur-
dering Gran.

'The thing about a good murder,' he said as they lay with
the dogs and cat on the secret grass, the scents of plump roses
all round, 'is that it has got to look ordinary.' He spoke as if
lecturing.

'What do you mean?'

'I mean, it's got to happen in such an ordinary way, nobody
thinks it is murder.'

'Not like poison in the teapot, then.'

'D'you want me to tell you or not?'

'Get *on* with it then.'

'An accident, that's the thing.'

'Push her out of a window? Under a tram?'

'I'm serious, Marj, stop it.'

'Well *what* then?'

'Listen. What does Gran do every single day at the same time, always?'

'Go to the lav.'

'No.'

'Black the stove.'

'Nah.'

'Nag at me.'

'Oh come on, Marj.'

'*I* don't know. *Tell* me.'

'I thought you got the class prize. You're not very bright, are you? The beds, the beds!'

'Oh.' Gran's ritual, wearing the special apron: airing, making, turning down. 'So what?'

'Think, dimwit.'

'Hold a pillow over her face? Tie her up in a sheet and dump her in the laundry basket? Hide under a bed and – '

'Oh shut up. I'm not going to tell you now, so there.' Teddy was up and would have walked away but Marjory had his ankle.

'Ah, come on, Ted. I was only kidding. You're being so slow, telling. Come on. We'll go and get some sherbets after – Grandad gave me two bob.'

'What for?'

'Getting the prize. Come *on*.'

'Promise?'

'Promise.'

He sat, and looked intent. 'Look, it's all got to happen when she goes round the last time, in the afternoon, when she turns back the covers and everything.'

His seriousness reached her at last. 'At about five or half-past, that is.'

'Right. Now, when she goes up to Auntie Ellie's flat, last of all, she takes ages – she stays and has a cup of tea.'

'Wonder why Auntie Ellie doesn't turn down their own beds?'

'Dunno – who cares? Habit, I suppose. Anyway – it's then that we do it.'

He was waiting, so she said 'Do what?'

'You know those top stairs where they're dark, and they do that sort of turn, quite steep? Well, what we do is loosen the rod there, just take out a screw or two. Then when she comes downstairs again, she wouldn't notice, the carpet'd slip and she'd fall down to the bottom and break her neck, snap.'

She looked at Teddy; he looked back, his face bright, and dug his heels into the grass. *'Well?* What d'you think? It'd work, wouldn't it? Nobody would know. They'd just say the rod was loose, it was an accident.'

'You know what, Ted – I think that's very, *very* good. I think we could do that.'

'Hey! Honest, Marj?'

'Honest.' She thought a while, pulling grasses and sucking the ends. 'There's only one thing.'

'Oh blimey, trust you.'

'What if Auntie Ellie comes downstairs first?'

'Don't be daft, she never does, you know she doesn't. She stays until Uncle Wilf comes home and then they come down before supper.'

'Suppose – just that once – '

'She won't, she just *won't*, so stop going on and on thinking of things. You don't want to do it, that's what.'

'I do, I do – God's honour I do, Ted. It's a really brilliant idea, we'll do it.'

'That's all right then.'

'When?'

'Can't come tomorrow or Thursday. Friday.'

'I'm going to Keziah's on Friday if they let me.'

'Saturday we go to Yarmouth. It'll have to be after we get back.'

'All right.'

'Agreed, then?'

'Yes. Agreed.' Then she said: 'Teddy – d'you reckon we're being tempted by the Devil?'

He sat up straight. *'Course* not! Don't be soppy. We'll be doing everybody a favour.' He thought a while, then added:

'But just to make sure, we could pray for forgiveness after we've done it, then it would be all right, wouldn't it?'

'I suppose so.'

He was up. 'C'mon. Sherbets.'

*

'Grandad.'

He was alone in the drawing-room in the brown leather chair by the window, his hair and beard very white against the blinds. He was reading a magazine, there were rust-coloured pictures of horses. He looked over the steel-rimmed spectacles he had bought in Woolworth's: only pair he'd ever been able to see through he claimed. 'Hello, tiddler. How's big-eyes?'

She leaned near his shoulder. 'Can I – may I – ask you something?'

'Hm. Why not?' He studied a saddler's advertisement.

'You know my friend Keziah, I told you about her. You know, Keziah Hope, the one who is Jewish.'

He looked up properly. 'Ah, *that* Keziah.'

'Her mother said can I go to their Sabbath on Friday and stay the night. Can I, Grandad? Can – may I?'

He took his glasses off, scratched his beard with them. 'Well well.' He smiled at her.

'I can be back early on Saturday and walk the dogs and everything, and get ready to go with Auntie Flora.'

'I don't really see why not,' Grandad said, 'if Keziah's mother has invited you.'

'I can then? I can?'

'Better ask your Gran just to be sure.' So it was not to be avoided. 'She's the one who runs this household.' He smiled at this comfortable fact and returned to his sepia horses.

It took hours to ask but then Gran said: 'I suppose it's all right, it's only up the road. I just hope you'll be good, Marjory, and not be any trouble to Mr and Mrs Hope, and remember to say thank you for having me and do as you're told.'

Only the mother lights the candles, Keziah told Marjory as the dusk in the warm room glowed, Mrs Hope's long full-lipped face was gold above the two tall flames; her hands made giant shadows on the red walls as she spoke the soft blessing of these lights, strange Hebrew like a melody. She looked towards her husband, smiled, looked at Marjory while the smile stayed.

They stood waiting by their chairs. Keziah's hair shone blackly; she was like her father, pale skin a shock beside the hair, the same short curving nose. Benjamin, eight, was slender like his mother, a remoteness in his calm face.

Mr Hope wore a skull-cap, his fine-fingered hands took over the shadows on the walls as he blessed the wine. His voice was deep, beginning to sing the *kiddusch*; its tremor echoed in the candle flames, moving through the silver, the glasses, shining things on the sideboard against the rosy wall, the shadows; thanking God, Keziah had explained, for the gift of the fruit which made the gift of this wine. Everything in the room was taken up in the Hebrew words, merging in warmth: around her, through her, within, at a long distance. A feeling not to be grasped, something won, something gone, known always but barely glimpsed, serene and sorrowful, included and left out. Now the family sang together, words meaningful and meaningless, rising, spreading, filling the room, rich as the velvet at the window, father's and mother's voices winding together at the depths, Keziah's and Benjamin's curving above, separating, linking.

Keziah's mother touched her hand: her eyes were black and soft; there was bread, slowly uncovered by Mr Hope. Two loaves, for the two dispensations of manna falling from heaven to save the Jews in the wilderness: plaited loaves, a symbol of marriage. Now he cut the bread, now he shared it, now each must take a life-supporting pinch of salt, and now a strange sip of wine.

Only the mother serves the food. A smell of herbs and comfort as Mrs Hope put spoonfuls of hot spicy meat on the plates; then she passed vegetables, offered steaming within silver. The mother, who put a quiet hand on Benjamin's curling hair, laughed at Keziah's jokes, grinned unsurprised at her husband when their daughter announced she was going to be a barrister. We always knew she could argue, didn't we, Reuben?

My grandfather is Jewish, Marjory told them after the meal, after the last singing, the thanks for food received, had risen and filled the room and faded. The taste of sugar and cinnamon was still on her lips.

So we've heard, said Mr Hope, and wasn't he from Spain? But my grandmother isn't, she apologised. Mr Hope smiled: It must be through the mother's line, though the Lord knows why. He nudged his wife: It can't have been the men who decided, I'm sure. Marjory spoke quite loudly: I haven't got a mother. Mrs Hope said: No, we know. Marjory said: I don't think she was Jewish either. Well, Mr Hope was reasonable, everybody can't be, can they? You're still a bit Jewish, Marj, Keziah told her, about a quarter; even if it is men's blood it's still Jewish blood. She'll prove anything, that one, her father laughed.

And he laughed louder still when Mrs Hope asked her about Christ Church, and she told them about Miss Percival and God and the Devil: And Susie was Confirmed, and I'll have to be, and if you're not very good then the Devil can get you. You sound scared stiff, Keziah said, fat lot of good being a Christian is if you're scared stiff. Mrs Hope said: Christ was a good man, whoever he was, one can't deny that. Mr Hope laughed: He was Jewish. Marjory said: *Was* he? Nobody ever said that before; she was startled. They all laughed now, the candle-light all round them; she got the giggles at Keziah imitating her surprise.

You can come whenever you like, you are very welcome, Marjory, Mrs Hope said in the bedroom, and bent to kiss her forehead.

I wish, she told Grandad, I wish I was Jewish. Well, big-eyes, aren't you? A little bit Jewish? He put his large hand on top of her head, where it felt heavy and safe. Gran said: Don't imagine Marjory that you can go off to Keziah's house every week, no matter how enjoyable it is and how exceptionally kind they are. Next term you will have a lot of work to do, scholarship year. You have to think about what else you want to be in life apart from Jewish. My goodness, she said in general, sometimes I wonder what goes through that child's head. Upstairs, Marjory, and get changed and collect your things together. Auntie Flora will be here in a couple of hours and you've done nothing. And I, Grandad said, must be off to Market; he swept up in one hand the copious square American-cloth bag which was the sign he aimed to buy quantities of fish. Have to go without you this time, Marj, won't be long. She watched him from the middle landing as he left the house, black hat over white hair, stick swinging happy arcs. If Grandad had married a Jewish lady, Daddy would be Jewish and might also have married someone Jewish, and the world would be different.

Marjory buttoned coat and gloves as she ran from the dining-room into the hall. Auntie Flora was there pushing Teddy before her, pulling Harry behind. Gran was calling Marjory! up the stairs, then: Oh *there* you are. Come on come on! cried Flora, we'll never catch that train, where've you been? Had to say goodbye to Buller and Boney and feed the silkworms – is Grandad back? Must say goodbye to Grandad. Good Lord, child, you're only going for a *week*. Auntie Flora twirled between Marjory and the hall mirror. He's in the kitchen – now *hurry*.

Marjory ran through to the scullery calling him, opening the door to end on a screech. She was in a nightmare, or a mad joke. The floor writhed. And over at the shallow sink Grandad, half turned from her, wrestled with a nest of snakes. But he was laughing, snatching at the slithering wriggling forms as they spilled and escaped over the top of the sink, across the stone floor, an undulating threshing panic. Oh damn these eels, keep still drat you. He might have had eight arms, the long sharp knife in all of them, flailing and seizing, then turning to the chopping board with a captive; but the pieces he chopped still leapt and jerked, refusing to surrender. Then he dived back to the sink, fighting the living fleeing writhing mass, shouting laughter and curses. Jimmy the tabby stared pop-eyed from the back door, between predatoriness and amazement at several giant eels lashing and whipping round Grandad's ankles.

Grandad! What have you done? She hardly understood her own question. He hooted and turned, knife gleaming: Bought too many, that's what. He was red with mirth and bending and chasing his dinner. Greedy, that's what. Mr Stanley told me, best ever, fresh from Billingsgate, grab them while you can. Grab them, that's a good one. Filled up my bag, he did. My mistake was tipping 'em all in the sink at once. He snatched at the whips round his feet. Give us a hand, Marj, come on. Can't – oh I can't, Grandad. I've got to go, Auntie Flora's waiting – oh *Grand*ad, you're not going to *eat* them are you? Look at those bits, they're still jumping about. Certainly *am*, my girl, he cried jubilantly, downright delicious they are, come here, you fiend. He pursued a serpent towards the back-stepping cat and carried it convulsing to its death. It's just the nerves that jump, Marj, don't worry, they're dead all right. She shouted goodbye and slammed the door on it all. Come on quick, Auntie Flora, Teddy, come on, I'm ready. Flora said: There's no *panic*, my dear, it's not *that* late, and your hat's crooked. Ugh – it was Grandad – he's got eels everywhere – I ran out . . . Eels! Auntie Flora paused while Marjory shuddered. Eels for dinner? Flora might almost reverse her entire plans. Oh rotten luck, we'll miss them. Marjory had the front door open: I'm *glad*, I am. I don't *ever* want to eat eels.

The hissing and smoking of Liverpool Street. Boys running, ladies pursued by porters, steam slipping or rushing from towering engines. Loading cases: a wicker hamper, five hat boxes, three suitcases, a brown parcel. Auntie Flora smiling at the porter, forgetting to tip him, smacking Harry for dribbling boiled sweet on his new smock, straightening her hat in a speckled mirror. The soot and plush smell of the compartment; Auntie Flora made them spread everything on the seats: We don't want anyone else, do we? Sit down, sit down.

Stiff new clothes underlined the excitement: buttons straining on shoes, straw hat clamped to the ears, unwrinkled gloves. Don't touch those ledges, they're filthy. Yarmouth, Yarmouth, we're going to Yarmouth. Waiting for the train to move, hearing it belch and sigh: Sounds like Auntie Hennie, Teddy said. Smell of dirt and sulphur, jolts of doors slamming, near shouts, distant answers, shrill whistles; the train slid past a man with a flag. That was his job, standing here every day with a flag, unbelievable. We're moving, look, we're moving.

Sandwiches in the hamper, apples and chocolate and liquor-ice sticks too. Cor I'm hungry, said Teddy: there's cake with dates. No, Auntie Flora said, definitely no. We're on this train positively hours, we will have lunch not a minute before half past twelve. Flora with three newspapers, DIVORCE SCANDAL a headline she hid, four magazines, smoking a wanton cigarette. Gran would have a fit: Teddy blackmailed her for just one puff.

Grimed houses, jumbled and broken back yards: They keep their coal in the bath, don't they, Mum? Rows of streets and chimneys, a market flashing colour, skinny kids waving at a level crossing. Then bigger gaps between buildings as the city was diluted with green patches, then trees, richer houses, parks, fields, lines of hedges, lanes. Let's have the window open a bit, such a lovely day. Look, horses! Look, Harry, gee-gees. It's all country now, all of it – when will we see the sea? See the sea, see the sea. That huge house, like a castle, rich people live there, rich as the King, rich as the Prince of Wales. Fields followed fields: Marjory kept waiting for them to end, cut by roads and streets and buildings, enclosed and limited like Brockwell Park. But they had no end, rolling on, dipping to streams, rising to spinneys and on again; after a while she relaxed with the interminable greenness.

Can we have lunch now, Mum, can we? *May* we, how many times do I have to say. It was half past twelve on that church clock, Auntie Flora, I saw it. Come on then. Watch your manners, Teddy. Blimey, Mum, my bit of cake's much smaller than Marj's. Don't say blimey, I don't know where you hear such disgusting language, stop fidgeting, leave Harry alone, you'll go back on the next train. And don't gobble, both of you, you'll be sick and that'll be a fine start to the holiday. Ooh, it's all black: a tunnel, isn't it dark, I can't see you, Ted, where are you? Pooh what a pong, we should've shut the window. Ah you lousy stinker, you pinched my cake. Marjory! Where *do* you pick up such dreadful expressions?

Look, look – there's the sea. Over there – it is, it is. We must be nearly there, it can't be far. It was a grey-blue horizon, misted and infinite. How far, Auntie Flora? Five minutes. Come on, get yourselves tidied up.

Horse-drawn carriages waited in the station yard as well as motor taxis. Horses – please let's go with a horse, Auntie Flora, Marjory jumped among the luggage. Do keep still, child: we'll have to have a carriage anyway, with this lot. Flora stood beside bags and boxes, one silk leg slightly before the other, her lace-edged lawn dress showing half a knee-cap, waiting for the gentlemen she knew would help.

The horses clopped, the carriage swayed from the yard.

Can't you smell the horse-pee? Teddy asked. The sea, there it all was, huge and startling: the air rushed at their faces, salt and seaweed. Cockle stalls, the beach. See those big sticks of rock? They've got writing right through. Is it true? How can they? Marjory felt herself surrounded by impossibilities. No you may not get out now children, we shall stroll later. Look, Marj, Punch and Judy — it's super, he bashes everyone on the head.

A tall red-brick house, stained glass lilies in the door, *Sea Haven* in gold, net curtains very white. Here we are, let me comb your hair, Teddy. This is where Mr and Mrs Thorpe live and they are very respectable so please be on your best behaviour all of you. Put your hat straight, Marjory, it looks most unladylike, hands out of pockets, Teddy, leave your nose alone and don't grizzle, Harry. How much is that? Keep the change *do*, too kind, thank you *so* much.

The Thorpes, the same who sent sausages monthly to Gran, were a drawing from a book. She was spherical, creased at neck and wrists, dark blue eyes sunk in a peach face, grey hair pulled into a high bun. He towered, limbs thin as drainpipes, sunken face long above a white beard, cut square across his chest. When they spoke to each other she looked at his watch-chain, he the top of her head.

Mr Thorpe ignored the children, bowed to Auntie Flora, carried the luggage and disappeared. Mrs Thorpe smiled at them all, learned their names, showed them round. Here is the bathroom, be sure to turn off the light when you leave; yes, it's electricity but small boys mustn't turn it on and off or they'll go up in a blue flash, won't they? An enormous bath, you could drown in it, Teddy declared. A high cistern above the lavatory: Avalanche No. 2 lettered across like a warning or threat. Now, Mrs Thorpe said, in the daytime the children won't want to be running in and out, will they, they can use the lavatory outside. There, in the garden, see the green door? There's no chain to pull, so you have to take water from the rain-barrel there — you can see the pan hanging up, can't you — and just pour it down the toilet when you've finished. Don't forget now, will you? There's good children. I'll leave you to unpack, then come down to tea. Who would like some meaty Yarmouth sausages and home-made jam?

Teddy and Marjory shared a room; Harry was with Auntie Flora next door. Until maybe Auntie Ellie comes with Susie at the weekend, and Susie will be in with you. Crikey, Mum, you never told us that, ugh. Teddy if you don't behave you'll feel something to grumble about, and let me tell you I won't hesitate to send you straight home, alone, with a luggage label tied on. Who cares, Ted? Marjory leaned from their window; there's days and days yet, we can see the sea, look at all those people going in the big hotel, cor, isn't it *hot*.

Gloves and stiff shoes might be discarded: But you must wear a hat, Marjory, don't you know how strong the sun is? Only the other day a little girl nearly died of sun-stroke. Goodness what a summer, everyone said, it hasn't rained for weeks, pity the poor farmers.

Treats piled on treats, too many to believe or contain, with a tremor of fear lying somewhere underneath that it would end or spoil or never come again. Ice-cream nearly every day, fizzy red pop from the corner shop where the man put the fizz in through a tangle of tubes, one halfpenny. Cockles and mussels, sandwiches, cream puffs, toffee apples, rock, potted shrimps, brown crusty bread, peaches and cream, gingerbread men: all flavoured by salt air and sun, like foods of a magic land that might float away while your eyes were shut. Auntie Flora in wide hats, sometimes a parasol if they were stopping somewhere posh for tea. Punch and Judy, tap-dancing and singing on the beach concert platform, a real Pierrot, a con-juror with rabbits from nowhere. Speak Your Weight, Win Your Fortune, Gypsy Lorelie Reads Your Palm for Twopence, What The Butler Saw. Sand: warm on top, damp and cold deeper down; to lie on, to throw, to run through and kick. Water for ever, going on and over the world's edge, warm and soft at the fringes, then cold, bitterly salt; splash, flop, look for creatures. Along at the quay, herring boats gliding, men call-ing, girls with Scottish voices sorting and gutting slithering heaps of fish, hundreds, thousands. Why do they do that for a job? she asked Mrs Thorpe. I dare say it's the one thing they're good at, and I dare say it pays. Fancy doing that, all year, fish and fish and fish. Better than starving, my girl, though they say they can never wash the smell away. To go through life smelling of fish. But then they would marry fishermen and wouldn't notice, and the children would smell of fish as well, and it might be a comfortable thing, belonging, all fishy together.

I could live here for always, Teddy, it's like being in Heaven, feel how hot the sand is just here. You won't go to Heaven, Marj, you're much too wicked, you and me will go to Hell. You'll be roasted alive then, Ted, roasted. Nah, don't you believe it, Marj, we'd have some fun, everybody'd be wicked, wouldn't they? In Heaven they'd make you be good all the time, blimey. They'll probably send you to Heaven, Teddy, it'd be a real punishment having to be so good.

The only thing I don't like is that outside lav, Ted, it's beastly. There's not much rainwater in the barrel, I can't reach properly, then I can't pour in much water and then it stinks, pah. Look, Teddy showed her, stand on these bricks and then you can reach – go on, try. Oh do it for me, Teddy, I'm busting to go I can't wait. Yes you can, think of something else. You are mean, Ted. On to the bricks, leaning down into the rain-butt, pan in hand. Reaching, a dark reflection reaching up. Bricks collapse, feet flail, a terrible dive. Ow! Teddy! Come back, help, I'm in the barrel, eeugh, Teddy! Crikey, Marj, Teddy cackling, banging the barrel with his hands, helpless: you dope, Marj, what d'you do? Shut up, Teddy, help me get out. Only the top of her head showing. I can't, Marj, I'll tip it over, pull yourself up. There's nothing to put my feet against, it goes outwards, how can I? Mum! Mum – Mrs Thorpe – Marjory's fallen in the barrel! Dark, and wet: there'd be little things swimming in the water. Teddy! Auntie Flora! Oh, you silly little girl, however did you do that? Come, give me your hands. Now, Teddy, and Mummy, hold the barrel still. Here she comes: my, she *is* wet. Never mind, accidents will happen, come in and get dried. Oh *Marj*ory, Auntie Flora was less cross than she might be because of Mrs Thorpe, the things you *do*, lucky that's an old dress. Hey, Teddy, Marjory confided later, I pee'd in there. Ugh, *Marj*! Well *I* couldn't help it, I was busting, think yourself lucky that's all I did.

Where does your mum go, anyway, every evening? They watched her walk below their window, flowered hat perfect, gloved hands with a neat handbag. *I* dunno, playing Bridge, dancing and all that. She just likes lots of people around, that's what it is. Why can't *we* go out, it's still daytime, other kids are still playing on the beach even, look. It's not fair. You know what, Teddy, your mum's getting a bit fat. A bit *fat*, Marj? Don't you know *anything*? A bit fat, eh, Marj? He had a particular smirk. What d'you mean, Teddy? Stop looking like that, what d'you mean? She's not fat, soppy, she's got a baby in there, it's a baby. A *baby*? You're a fibber, you are. I'm not, you daft thing, Marj, don't you know babies grow inside? He jabbed her nightdress. In there, in your stomach. How can it? How does it get in there? How will it get out? My dad put a seed in her of course, what d'you think? It'll get out through her Thing, there's a hole that gets bigger. A *seed*? Bees Catalogue, she'd seen it in the conservatory. How could he put a seed in there, you're pulling my leg, Ted. It's easy, he puts it in her with *his* Thing, and stop laughing like that, Marj, it's true. Uncle Bertie planting a seed in Auntie Flora with his Thing, it was hilarious, ludicrous, how could they, but it was strange too, did everyone? Stop fiddling with yourself, Teddy, she stopped laughing, you know Auntie Flora says it's bad for you. Look at mine, Marj, I bet you never saw one look like that before. Teddy! What've you done to it? It's gone all – oh, your Mum will be cross! Teddy was cackling, rolling on the rug: You are soppy, Marj, you don't know anything, not anything. She would not speak to him again until he explained, and then was silent again with surprise.

A day of clouds came, a breeze, sun here and there. Not a day for the beach, let's go to the countryside and have a picnic. Auntie Flora put on a simple straw hat. Suppose it rains, Mr Thorpe warned across the marmalade, it hasn't rained for weeks, you'll be caught. No no, it won't rain, Flora decided, and the smell of the fields will do them good. Fields. Like the fields the train had passed by, endless pastures.

They caught an open-topped bus: a big fuss folding Harry's push-chair, the conductor holding up a noisy crowd for the sake of helping Flora and touching her hand. They blew out of town, the sea sinking away, and it was country quickly. In ten minutes Flora said: We're here, come along. It was a curving road with little lanes to left and right, vanishing into long greenness. The conductor waved and winked, the bus went and left them in the silence.

Just a wind in the hedges and trees, some insects and birds: no other sounds. Hedges leaned, flowers and grasses over-filled the ditches, wild roses turned their clear flat faces to the sun, rambling wherever they chose. You can pick some if you want, Auntie Flora said. *Oh no*. Marjory threw out her arms as if she would protect the blooms. Leave them, they belong here, they're free. Flora rolled her eyes up. Let's go down this lane, kids, it's like a tunnel. Look, a gate, a lovely meadow. We'll walk across, have our picnic by those trees, see? Open the gate, Teddy, help him with the hamper, Marjory.

The ground was level enough to shove or pull Harry's push-chair; anyway, he placidly accepted lurch and bump. Isn't it lovely, children? Smell the grass. How pastoral it all is! Halfway to the trees, Flora saw the cows; or Teddy showed them to her. Look, Mum, those cows are coming this way. Cows! Where? Oh my godfathers – bulls! She let go of the push-chair, dropped her bag and ran back towards the gate, tripping, making shrieks. Teddy looked at her, at the cows, at Marjory, at his abandoned brother, again at his mother. *Is it cows, Marj?* She picked up Auntie Flora's bag, plonked it on top of Harry. Here, she said, you carry the hamper on your own. Hey, Marj – shouldn't we run? They're getting near. His mother was almost at the gate. Maybe they *are* bulls. They're only heifers, stupid, she told him, hauling Harry back; they're wondering who we are, that's all. How do *you* know? I just *know*, she sighed, that's all. Flora now jigged in the lane, giving sharp cries: Why didn't you run? Why didn't you *run*? Quick, quick. Marjory manoeuvred Harry through the narrow opening allowed by Flora, and said nothing. Don't you look at me like that, Marjory, insolent girl. They ate their picnic in the green lane, the heifers looking pool-eyed over the gate bars. Marjory gave them salt, they licked it from her palm. Ugh, how *can* you, Flora turned away. It's nice, they're only curious, they wouldn't hurt us. Look, Ted, they've got tongues like sandpaper. Flora said: I like animals but you are pe*cul*iar about them. Marjory looked at the big sad pretty faces and did not speak. But on the way home they passed a pub called *The Red Cow* and Flora laughed and went inside to buy them crisps. Going into a pub on her own, I'd like to see Gran's face. Oh pooh, Marj, Teddy sighed, his gaze down the road, Mum doesn't care.

Gangs of young men and girls, marching from the sea-front at the dusk of long evenings, arm in arm, singing. Students

from some University, I believe, Mrs Thorpe's round nostrils
narrowed at breakfast, such a noise. Mr Thorpe said from his
oblong beard: I imagine they are taking a rest from their
arduous education.

Teddy and Marjory leaned on the windowsill. I like them,
they're like Nora, having fun. Think of Gran's face: no gloves
or hats, bare legs even, the men with arms round the girls'
waists. (Like Uncle Ron and his girl; did Daddy put his arm
round Miss Clara Finch?) Listen, Marj, listen – what they're
singing, hear that? The tune was Coming Round the Mountain,
the words something else, belted out by the line of men, the
girls giggling: Ooh stop it, everyone'll hear, ooh aren't they
rude, aren't they *bad*? They sang the song most evenings and
another equally intriguing to Oh! Susanna. In three evenings
Teddy and Marjory had pencilled out nearly all the words:
they sang them just out of Flora's hearing but could not help
laughing. *What* are you singing, you kids? Coming Round the
Mountain – what did you think? I don't like the look in your
eye, my lad.

Sam lived next door, a year or so older. He was thin and
ginger, said he lived on shrimps and ice-cream winter and
summer and went swimming even if it snowed. Yah what a
fibber, Teddy said, but forgave easily for Sam owned Slither,
a grass-snake a yard long, green and lithe and marvellous.
Marjory slid it between her fingers; it was smooth, beautiful,
graceful, not slimy and rebellious like Grandad's eels. It looked
at her intently, little sharp eyes unblinking, mouth curiously
stern. What if he was ill, Sam? Would you take him to a vet?
Course I would, but he's never ill. Let's frighten Susie with
him when she comes, Teddy said – can we, Sam? If you want,
Sam said, Slither won't mind. Marjory asked: How do you
know he's a he? Honestly, Marj, Sam was lofty, you ask
some very silly questions. But he didn't know: she saw him
secretly inspecting Slither later.

Susie arrived on Friday afternoon with Auntie Ellie, and
might have been suspicious of their welcome; but she came
innocent and eager to the garden to meet their friend Sam.
Slither made his appearance. Susie screamed, stepped backwards, tripped on the grass and showed her knickers, getting
green on her new white skirt. Oh, oh take it away, a snake,
help, stop him, Marjory, oh you horrible thing I hate you,

Teddy, Mummy, Mummy! Ellie panted round the house: I do hope you're not being naughty and unkind already, we're all supposed to be having a lovely time together, she pleaded. We were only showing her Slither, Auntie, he won't hurt, he's not a proper snake, anybody knows that. Wouldn't harm a soul, would you, Slith? Well, dears, I don't know that it can be very hygienic, can it?

Susie's revenge followed soon. She found the scribbled songs and ran to Flora and Ellie. Ellie pushed the paper into Flora's hands: You'd better deal with this, dear, really I wouldn't know what to say, wherever could they hear such things? Flora came and stood, folding and unfolding the songs. Teddy answered her: I don't know what you mean, Mum, what's wrong with them? The students sing them, we only wrote them down, we didn't know they were bad, did we, Marj? Flora looked unsure, a rare thing. Just don't do it again, that's all, such songs are not nice, they're vulgar, do you understand? As she left the room Teddy called: Mum – what does fanny mean, anyway?

Truce with Susie: the week was not to be spoiled. Anyway, Marjory said, she's all right *really*. Teddy chased them both along the quay with a dead herring but Susie herself laughed at that. They showed her Punch and Judy: he's beastly, she said, but came back to watch again even though she said it was for kids. I'm fourteen, almost grown-up. You've got bosoms, Teddy said when she turned her back to pull on her nightdress, why? Don't be silly, Teddy, all girls get them. You haven't got any yet, Marj. I'm not old enough, soppy, who wants bosoms anyway? *I* don't, Teddy said, and they all screeched at the idea until Auntie Ellie came and told them to be quiet, settle down, and started them off again by asking what was so funny.

Shopping for little presents to take home: a brooch, a hanky, tobacco, a Yarmouth egg-cup. A Kiss-Me-Quick hat for Uncle Ron, a tie-pin for Daddy. Sam asked her: What are you going to get for your mum then? It shook her, somebody not knowing. I haven't got a mum, was all she could say, and Sam was so dumbstruck she felt sorry for him. After they got back to the house he offered: If you haven't got a mum, would you like Slither instead?

I don't want to go home, Ted, do you? We'll come another

time, Marj, Mum said so. Did she really, honest? One more concert, the singing and conjuring. One more laugh at Punch fighting the crocodile, beating his wife. Last splash in the sea, last look at the herring-boats, the frowning girls cleaning wave on wave of fish. Goodbye, Sam, see you next year maybe, see you again, Slither. Thank you for having us, Mr and Mrs Thorpe. It was lovely, my dears, come again. Don't forget your sausages, have a nice journey, be good now, take care of your mother, be a big boy. Mr Thorpe pushed a parcel of sausages into Flora's hands; Mrs Thorpe smiled and whispered about eating for two. Teddy nudged Marjory, Flora slapped his shoulder, they were rocking down the road and past the beach and mysterious far horizon, past the men calling over the shell-fish, past the toffee-apples, to the station. Don't look so gloomy you kids, enough to turn the milk sour.

And now the green fields swooped behind them, soon to be cut by roads then vanishing with suburbs and city. Back to it all. Still, here was the Park: for all its limits, the murmured reminder of traffic at the edges, when you were in it with the dogs it was endless.

Did you have a nice time? Wipe your feet, children. My, don't you look brown. Did you wear your hat, Marjory? Just like foreigners, said Uncle Ron, look at Marj – touch of the tar-brush there I'd say. Got my bangers?

And what, Grandad asked at tea, did you like best? Susie said: The beach, all the sand, it was hot and yellow, and ladies' dresses and fish and chips. Teddy said: The sea and splashing around, the fishing boats, Punch and Judy and Amusements and sticks of rock. Marjory couldn't put them in order, so many things: The water, all blue, and the concerts – this conjuror who made white rabbits appear, and in the country there were flowers growing everywhere, red and yellow and pink, and Sam next door had a grass-snake this long, bright green, and one day there was a huge rainbow and a sunset and – Oh, hark at her, Auntie Ada tittered, she's making it all up as usual. Gran said: A *snake*, Marjory? Are you sure? Did you really see all those things? I did! Of course I did. And Susie said: It's true, what Marj says is true. Marjory stared at her. Gran said, Oh well, if Susie says so.

Marjory lay awake in the light evening and laughed under the sheets at the thought of having Slither as a mother, and because of Teddy's fiendish expression when he'd said: Don't forget the plan, what about the day after tomorrow?

Teddy turned a screwdriver over in his fingers: 'I pinched it from Dad's shed, isn't it wizard?'

'D'you know how to do it?'

'Course. Easy.'

The secret grass was rough and hot. Billy rat found shade between them, the dogs gasped. She thought: I'll write to Daddy afterwards. Dear Daddy, I'm afraid Gran is dead, she fell downstairs this afternoon and accidentally broke her neck. Don't worry about anything here as I am helping as much as I can.

She told Teddy. He said: 'Honestly, Marj, you are a twerp at times. They send telegrams to everyone when somebody is dead. You know: Gran dead stop come at once stop neck broken stop accident stop.'

'Oh. Do they? Oh. What for though? Why come at once? It'd be too late, she'd be dead.'

'They always do, that's all. Isn't it tea-time yet?'

And Auntie Ada called. 'Marjory! Teddy! Come and wash your hands, tea's ready, we don't want to wait all day.'

'I'm not hungry, I've got butterflies.'

'Yah.' Teddy shoved the screwdriver into a pocket. 'Don't be cissy. I don't care.'

'Neither of you has a clean plate,' Gran said as the meal ended. 'I trust you aren't sickening for something.'

'Too much sun I dare say,' Auntie Ada said. 'Or lying about on damp grass.'

'It isn't damp,' Marjory said. 'It hasn't rained.'

'Dampness, my dear child,' Ada leaned towards her with protruding eyes, 'does not always come from the rain but from the earth itself.'

'Only if it's rained,' Marjory insisted. Auntie Ada was so irritating, stupid great face, eyes all round and bulgy and fluttery. People said: a handsome girl, elegant, fine features, pretty. Marjory couldn't see it; Ada was soppy.

'Please don't argue, Marjory,' Gran said.

'No, Gran.' That could be the last time you say don't argue.

'I hope you're not being insolent.'

'No, Gran!' Marjory smiled, Gran stared.

'There could be a heavy dew,' Auntie Ada said, 'couldn't there?'

'Yes, Auntie Ada,' Marjory and Teddy said together, and laughed.

'That's enough,' said Gran. 'Go along outside and find something useful to do.'

They waited for half past five. 'It'll be lovely afterwards,' Marjory said. 'I'll never be moaned at again, or only a bit by Auntie Molly and Auntie Ada. Uncle Ron'll let me do what I want, so will Auntie Ellie. And Daddy might marry Miss Finch and we'll go and live in Watford, and Grandad and you can come and see us, and Uncle Ron will be able to – ' she choked, invented a cough.

'What?'

'Nothing.'

'Uncle Ron will be able to do what?'

'I dunno. What he likes, I suppose.'

'You were going to say something.'

'No I wasn't. It must be nearly five o'clock, mustn't it?'

'We should've gone to the Park to make the time go faster. But then we might've come back too late. It'll strike five in a minute and then we won't have long. We'll see her go past the landing window. You see.'

'I feel a bit sick.'

'Think about something else.'

'I can't.'

Auntie Ada's curls appeared beyond the grass. 'Marjory? Are you there? I just want you to pop down to the shop. Marjory!'

They flattened. 'Oh stripe me pink,' said Teddy, holding down the dogs.

Auntie Ada's voice came nearer. 'Where *are* you – Teddy? Marjory?'

They heard her, to herself: 'Dratted children.' Dratted! From Auntie Ada. Marjory almost went Ooh, I heard that! the way Susie would.

The back door closed.

'There she goes, there she goes!' Teddy was squeaky.

'She's gone, soppy.'

'No, you dope, Gran – look – crikey we nearly missed her.'

Gran's small figure in copious bedmaking apron vanished from the tall landing window on the way up to Auntie Ellie's flat. 'She's early.'

Teddy's face was pink. Marjory's heart was beating against the ground. 'We'll count twenty slowly and then we'll go,' he whispered.

'Shall I wait and keep guard?'

'Ssh, I'm counting.' Then he said : 'No, cowardy custard, you've got to keep guard at the stairs. Come on.'

They went in through the conservatory, fearful of every noise, fearful of Ada or Grandad appearing. Then through the dining-room, carefully into the hall. Wait. Fast, up the main stairs. Listen. Silence. Up the next. They were out of breath, as if there had been ten flights.

'Wait here.' Teddy pushed her near her bedroom door. 'You can see up and down. If anybody comes, cough.'

She leaned on the doorpost trying to breathe more quietly. 'Go on then, go on.'

Screwdriver shining, Teddy crept up the stairs towards Ellie's flat. It was very simple and soundless. He was down beside her, saying 'Come on, quick,' in seconds.

'You done it? Already?'

'Yes – come *on*.' His hands might be shaking as he thrust the screwdriver away.

They were back with the dogs, not remembering the hurtling run from the house. They rolled gasping on the grass, Teddy laughing as if he were in pain.

'Now we just wait,' Marjory said, 'until bump bump bump and a scream.'

'It'll be ages.' He was turning over the screwdriver again, jabbing it into the ground.

'You ought to hide that, it's the murder weapon.'

'Maybe we ought to go out somewhere.'

'I'm dying to go to the lav now,' she wriggled.

'You daft thing, you should've gone when we were indoors, you know you can never hold it.' Then he said : 'Blimey, so am I though.'

After a while she said : 'What if she doesn't fall?'

'Bound to. It'll slip on that corner, bound to.'

They lay saying nothing and when Marjory looked at Teddy

he was glazed, distant. 'Ted – Ted I've got to go, I've just got to, I'll burst, I'll wet myself.'

He sat up. 'We could be quick and still be back here in time. Come on. You go to the downstairs one, I'll go up, I'll be quieter than you.' It was hardly true but downstairs was nearer and she was uncertain of getting that far without disaster. They ran.

Back on the grass, warm and empty and comfortable. Teddy was still in the house. Maybe somebody saw him, Auntie Ada wanting her errand done. Come on, Teddy, come on. She didn't want to be on her own with the bumps and the scream.

He came running. 'Slowcoach,' she hissed. 'Where've you been?'

'Had to hide from Auntie Ada,' he flopped down, 'and I saw Grandad.'

'What's the matter?'

'Nothing.'

'Yes there is. Look at you, all funny.' His face was in the grass, not watching the windows.

'No I'm *not*, Marj.'

'She ought to come soon. Any minute now it'll happen, it'll be over.' Her heart began to bang again.

Teddy's face was almost white.

'Do you feel sick?' she asked.

'No. Shut up.'

'I do. I think I'm going to be sick. Ted, is your heart bumping? Mine is. Oh, I can't stand it. Oh come on, Gran, get it over with.' But when Gran fell and died, would she jerk about like the chopped-up eels?

Teddy had turned on his side, looking at Marjory in an odd, rigid stare. He spoke through his teeth. 'The thing *is*, Marj, the thing is – ' He stopped, swallowing.

'What?'

'The thing *is* – nothing *is* going to happen.'

Some of the stiffness went from his face but he still stared. 'Why not?' she said at last, but was looking at the screwdriver in his hands.

'I did them up again.'

'What – just now?'

'Yeah.'

She looked at the house, and there was Gran. Walking

downstairs past the high landing window, disappearing, show-ing again just head and shoulders at another window. Down, down, alive, bedmaking apron on, neck unbroken.

'Why, Ted?' She realised her heart was quiet, Teddy's hands weren't shaking, his face was the right colour.

He dug at the ground with the murder weapon. 'Oh, I dunno.' After a pause he said : 'I saw Grandad.'

They stayed there until they were called for supper. Neither of them said, but they both knew : they'd never do it now.

SIX

*MARJORY (speaking to two of her children –
grown up and with children of their own – who
are discussing modern parenthood):
I don't see the point in going into all that psycho-
logical stuff, analysing everything. What good does
it do to know that? If you've got it in you, you
have, and that's that. You have to get on with
things no matter what, work out your life for yourself.*

*

It is a time for work and you may as well be aware of it,
Mr Beach told them as he climbed into his high desk and
adjusted ginger sleeves. Scholarship in the New Year. Ceaseless
hard work. The only way you'll achieve anything worth-
while in your lives, remember that. If you have an aim, work
for it. Work.

Yes, Marjory, Mrs MacTavish bounced, you are in the
hockey team, well done. And if you work hard you should do
very well. I think we can say that you make up in grit and
speed for what you lack in stature. So keep at it, eh?

Uncle Wilf sat at the long kitchen table, his face sunken,
his collar undone. A man wants to work, he said, but it takes
more than just wanting. Susie whispered: Daddy's lost his job.
Pale Auntie Ellie's hand was over Uncle Wilf's gentle wrist.
Uncle Ron slapped the table and stirred his tea: You'll find
another, good Lord, man. Uncle Wilf, his eyes reddish, said:
There'll be more, not just me, we're heading for a bad time,
Ron, and you may as well face facts, there'll be trouble; there's
injustice, just listen to the miners, you wait, chaos there'll be.
Uncle Ron knew better, he laughed: Come off it, Wilf, nothing's that bad, I'm a boss, I should know. In other words,
Uncle Wilf said with a sour look very unfamiliar, you *don't*
know. Uncle Ron clattered his spoon and would have spoken
angrily but Grandad stopped them: Not now, boys; glancing

at Gran and Susie and Marjory who all stared behind teacups.
Uncle Wilf got up and left, Auntie Ellie running after him,
Susie was suddenly crying, Grandad gave her chocolate cake,
saying: Go easy, eh Ron? It's a shock for a man when he
wants to work and do the decent thing by his family, and
sometimes the ones who should help don't always seem to,
although – he sighed – I'm sure they mean no harm either.

*

'. . . and the Second Prize for the Triplex Stoves Painting
Competition,' said the Reverend Smiley, Headmaster, at
morning Assembly, 'has been awarded to Marjory Bell.'

Faces turned, Keziah prodded. She had to walk all the way
to the platform behind the big girl who had won First. The
books were beautiful, a set of leather-bound in warm red:
The wild flowers and herbs of Britain, their medicinal and
culinary uses. Fancy that, Keziah said, when you're a vet you
can feed herb medicines to the cows.

The lamplighter went ahead, unhurried but businesslike, as
Marjory turned into Leander Road. The long pole reached
like a wand as the man glided beneath on his dark bicycle;
a glow from nowhere. Windows were lighting too, lace
shaking, heavy curtains moving together. Red brick blackened
into solid shapes, dusk became dark around each street-lamp.
The air was cold; smell of horse-droppings from the road,
soot from a chimney, soup from a doorway.

'Is that Marjory?' Gran came into the hall. 'At last, child.
Hat and coat off here, wash your hands in the kitchen, everyone's waiting, nobody wants cold food.'

Only when the steak and kidney pie was steaming on all
plates did Gran ask. 'And why were you so late? And where
did those books come from?' The red leather pile was on the
sideboard.

'Mr Beach wanted to see me.'

'Not lines again I hope.'

'About singing at Christmas.'

'Why didn't you tell Susie if you were to be delayed? I
can't think how many times you've been told – '

'I looked for her, she'd gone.'

'*I* was looking for *you*,' Susie said.

'And what's this about singing?'

'This Christmas Show at school, that's all. We always sing in it, Susie and me.'

'Susie and *I*.'

'Mr Beach wants me to do the Page in King Wenceslas in one of the intervals.'

'A solo?' Auntie Ada said. 'You?'

Uncle Ron said: 'Good for you, Marj. Hither page and stand by me and all that? Shall I come and be the King?'

'A boy called Joe Bale's going to be King.'

'Whatever will you wear for it?' Gran said. 'Will something have to be made?'

'There's a costume, a kind of green tunic thing. They think it'll fit but it might need altering.'

'I suppose Flora could look at it.'

'And when is the play?' Grandad asked. 'We'll all have to go and see it, won't we, and hear Marjory's solo?'

'Is it true?' Ada murmured to Susie, '*Is* she doing a solo?'

Susie said: 'I really don't know,' putting down her knife and fork and folding her hands. 'The only thing *I've* been told about the Christmas Show is – '

Marjory got there first, making it a mockery of a grand announcement: 'Susie's going to be the *Virgin Mary*!'

Outcry. Auntie Ellie, all delight: Really, darling? Auntie Ada: How wonderful – now that really is a solo! Auntie Molly: Fancy you not saying, Susie. Gran: Well that *is* an honour I'm sure. Uncle Wilf, some of the gloom moving from his mouth: That's nice, Susie, well done. Uncle Ron: I suppose I can't be Joseph, can I? And Buller and Boney the ox and ass? Grandad: My, my – congratulations both of you, what clever girls. Auntie Ada had some blue material, perfect for Susie's robe. Gran could find gold foil for the halo, swaddling bands for the infant Jesus, the smallest doll.

They were eating the baked custard when Gran remembered the books again and asked. Marjory looked at Susie: 'Didn't you tell them?'

'Goodness no. I was sure you would want to.'

'Come, Marjory – what are they?'

'Triplex Stoves.'

'I beg your pardon?'

'The painting competition. You know, the poster – we had

to paint the stove and all the different foods.' She looked at Gran : both saw a yellowish puddle.

'I remember,' said Grandad. 'It was a big thing, wasn't it, that competition? Lots of schools? You mean you got first prize, Marj?'

'No, only second,' Susie said.

'Only second,' Marjory spoke at the same time.

'Good heavens,' Auntie Molly said softly while teaspooning pudding, 'whatever could the others have been like?' She giggled. Ada, anxious always now for her sister's approval, trilled an echo.

'*I* think second prize is jolly good,' Uncle Ron said, leaning back his chair to reach the books. 'So what did they give you?'

Grandad held out a hand. 'May I see?' Ron gave him two of the four volumes.

'I say,' Uncle Ron touched the leather reverently, 'these are posh, Marj. Beautiful illustrations, look at this.'

'How lovely,' Auntie Ellie said. 'How lovely, Marjory.'

'Well well, hark at this.' Grandad was grinning into the first volume, at the prize notice stuck there. 'It says : "The eggs and bacon looked delicious and the beef beautifully roasted".' He laughed. 'What nice people.'

'I should think so,' Gran said. 'You look after those books, Marjory, they look very expensive to me.'

'The First Prize,' Susie said, 'was even better. A sort of encyclopaedia, great big books.'

'Fancy Marj winning a painting prize,' Auntie Ada said. 'When you think how she colours those fashion drawings in the magazines, all those dreadfully bright colours. I'm always saying, why not a nice grey dress with a white collar? Much more ladylike.'

*

'You know that boy Joe Bale who's barmy about football?' Keziah said on the way to school.

'He's going to be King Wenceslas.'

'Look. He gave me this for you.' Keziah was holding out an envelope. 'He did, honest.'

'What for?'

'Don't ask me. You've gone red, Marj.'

Joe Bale was tall, with brown hair gold at the edges and

eyes the same colour. He was in the next class up from Marjory; only when she joined the boys at sprinting or football had they ever exchanged words, usually breathless and practical.

Dear Marjory, This is to say that I am glad you will be in the Christmas Show and be the Page, I just heard. I like you. I live only in Holmewood Gardens, can I walk home with you? I'll wait by the gate so if you walk by I'll know it's no. Love from Joe Bale.

'Marj's got a sweetheart!' Keziah danced round her.

'Shut up, you,' Marjory shoved her. 'If Susie hears, I'm for it.'

'What are you going to do, Marj? Walk home with him? "Good afternoon, Marjory, may I carry your books?" What a lark.'

'I can't just walk past him, can I, with my nose in the air? I mean, he's King Wenceslas and everything.'

'*And* he's nice.'

'You'll come with me, won't you, Kez? Then if Susie says anything I can say he was with you.'

'Hello, Marjory,' said Joe Bale, and actually lifted his cap. Keziah snorted.

'Hello,' she said.

They walked for some way, and at last he spoke.

'You do your Scholarship soon, don't you?'

'Worse luck. Did you do it?'

'Yeah. Failed English and Geography. Pooh, I don't care, didn't want to go to High anyway. I'm going to Tech.'

'When?'

'When I'm fourteen. I'm going to be a builder and build super houses. What d'you want to do?'

She looked at the pavement. 'Don't know yet.' Keziah coughed hideously. 'Well,' Marjory said, 'I only *half* know.'

'That's all right, you don't have to tell me.' He had stopped, looking lofty. 'I live here. Or shall I come to Leander Road with you?'

'Oh no!' A glance at Susie, some yards ahead.

'That's her cousin,' Keziah told him. 'She'll tell tales to her Gran, and her Gran's ever so strict.'

'Oh,' he said. 'Bye then, Marjory. Bye Keziah.'

'Bye,' she said, unable to add his name.

'I *say*,' Keziah laughed, 'he's quite besotted.'

'You're daft.'

'I think you hurt his feelings.'

'It was your fault. Going "kreeuh kreeuh" in that stupid way. He wouldn't have known otherwise.'

'Oh honestly, Marj – why shouldn't you tell him? What's so secret about being a vet? I think you're a bit silly about it, so there.'

'I'm not, I'm not!' Marjory stood and shouted, and knew that Susie looked. 'I'm just *not*, so shut *up*.'

'*I* heard you quarrelling with Keziah,' Susie said at supper.

'I wasn't.'

'You were shouting. In the *street*.'

'Goodness, Marjory,' said Gran, 'I do hope you would not be so common.'

'And there was a boy with you before, I saw him. I bet you were squabbling about him.'

'What boy is this?'

'Joe Bale, the one who's going to be King Wenceslas.' She put boredom into her voice and lied. 'He's a friend of Keziah's, and we weren't quarrelling, so there.'

'There is no need to use that tone, Marjory.' Gran put down a plate hard. 'It seems to me there's far too much on your mind this term besides work.'

*

It was freezing, the trees stiffened, air cut between. Grass in daggers, patches of black across the paths, ice to slide on. Gran had looked out from the kitchen as Marjory gathered the dogs: I hope you've got on your woollen vest as well as your bodice, it's exceptionally cold for December. They ran all the way, Marjory feeling nothing but dead cold on her face, her fingers hurt as she undid the leads in the Park. Come on, Buller, Boney, quick, run, run. They warmed soon but the wind stung. We'll go back on the shrubbery path, not over the grass, it's sheltered there – come on, fetch, fetch. She threw sticks to make them race ahead. It would be warm in the kitchen, porridge on the stove, hot milk, brown sugar. Down the slope of path, now the shrubbery. Rhododendrons spiky without flowers, crowding privet, dark shrubs thick and low, huddling, secret, tall and frozen, making no sound. Then Boney swerved, Buller made gruff sounds and stopped. There was a man, facing her, stepping out. His trousers were undone, how awful, she'd interrupted him going to the lav behind the bushes. He said quietly as if she should explain: Well? She stood: Oh – excuse me! And jumped backwards. Buller screamed and growled, she felt his paw under her foot and his teeth in her leg, then she leapt and ran. The man shouted after her angrily: How would you like me to look at you like that, eh, eh? Icy air in her throat, down the path, along the fence, the gate. Only then could she look: Boney was with her. Buller was far behind, limping.

'Wher*ever* have you been?' Auntie Molly came into the conservatory with Gran. 'You'll be late for school.'

'At last,' Gran said. 'Uncle Ron was just coming to look. What on earth have you done to your stocking?'

Molly saw the bandage on Buller's foot. 'Look at Buller! Look! What've you done, Marjory?'

'It was an accident.' Marjory gave the dogs water.

'It would be,' Molly said.

'I sort of stepped back suddenly and trod right on his foot and it hurt so much I don't think he knew it was me and he bit me.'

'I hope you're not inventing this,' Gran said.

'Look at the hole in my leg.'

'The hole in your stocking's a lot bigger,' said Molly.

'He *bit* you?' Gran peered at the wound and said: 'Gracious. This must be cleaned. The dog must be punished.'

'No, Gran – he didn't mean it. He was hurt. His pad was all split and bleeding, I took him to Mr Stopps and he had to put in stitches, that's why I was late.'

'You took him to the vet? On your own?'

'I had to, it was pouring blood. He was ever so good, weren't you, Buller? I held him and Mr Stopps did it. He said keep the bandage on, bring him back at the end of the week. We can pay then, one and six.'

'Come with me, Marjory. That legs needs iodine. Then you'd better change your stockings and mend that one tonight.'

Iodine didn't sting that much if you turned your feelings

away. Mr Stopps had told her: You're doing excellently there, Marjory, only wish some of the grown-ups could handle an animal as well. She asked him: Mr Stopps, would I be able to be a vet? He looked across the bandages: Is that what you want to be? Yes, she said, is it easy? He laughed: No, it's hard work for a lot of years, but if you want to you can, yes, why not? You can do anything if you really want to, don't you think? She said: Yes. She thought: I will then, I will.

*

'Stone the blooming crows,' Keziah muttered over her drawing of Welsh mining areas, 'my hands are blue. Why can't we sit nearer the stove? I'll get chilblains, I know I will.'

'I already have.' Marjory rubbed desperately at her heel, swollen inside a tight boot.

'No talking. Work quietly.' Mr Beach spoke without looking up.

Keziah held out wrinkled paper, pale toffee in lumps within. 'Have a bit of this,' she mouthed. Whispered demands rose around her: Mr Beach looked and shouted. Heads ducked, chewing.

'In two minutes,' now he was looking at his watch, 'we shall discuss the Christmas Show rehearsals. Be ready to finish what you are doing and put away your Geography books.'

Two minutes. The toffee was huge.

Books slapped shut, papers shuffled, desks banged. Mr Beach read names from his list, rehearsal times for different groups. Shepherds, angels, people at the Inn. Marjory fought the lump of toffee; impossible to finish, he would get to her soon. Children stood as their names were called, said: Yes, Sir, to their instructions, important.

'Spit it out,' Keziah saw Marjory's panic. Marjory shook her head, pointed at her jaw: her teeth were sunk in the toffee, immovable.

'Now,' Mr Beach announced her doom. 'The solos.'

Marjory released some teeth but they were instantly embedded again, Mr Beach was looking across her head.

'The three Kings, and the Angel Gabriel.' Three boys stood, then another. They took their orders, sat. Marjory's face twisted frantically the moment Mr Beach looked down, but

114

her teeth were fixed. 'Now,' he said, 'it's been decided that as well as the solos between scenes there will be a few before the Show begins, in front of the curtains. We need someone who will sing the Brahms Lullaby – Marjory Bell, I think you will do very well, and you will have plenty of time to change for the King Wenceslas Page. Right?'

She stood, hopeless. And nodded.

Mr Beach looked. 'Right, Marjory?'

She mumbled ludicrously. Keziah choked. Mr Beach lowered his papers and waited. She tried to open her jaw without betraying the toffee, and felt her eyes roll.

'Marjory Bell. Have you lost your tongue? May I expect the courtesy of a reply? You have been selected to sing the Brahms Lullaby. I would expect you to be honoured but not, I assume, struck dumb.' The class sniggered.

Her face was hot, the toffee cement.

Mr Beach lifted one hand and pointed at the floor beside his desk. Marjory walked slowly down the aisle towards him, face down, struggling without hope.

'Marjory.' She had to look up, could not disguise her bulging face. As always when he was angry, the single long hair stood straight out from his ear: it had less fascination today. 'I see,' he said, and looked at her a long time without speaking. Then: 'When you are ready, I would be glad to hear an apology.'

A moment of fear when she thought her teeth would be pulled out, stuck for ever in the toffee, then a dreadful sucking noise, her jaw opened: 'Sorry, sir,' she said through stickiness. The class collapsed, Mr Beach shouted, Marjory spilled the toffee quickly into her hanky.

It was inevitable: Mr Beach opened his desk, Out came the Punishment Book and cane. 'Go to Mrs Popham, tell her six.' He put the instruments into her empty hand.

In the corridor near the cloakroom she finished the toffee and screwed up her sticky handkerchief. Then upstairs, across the landing: Mrs Popham, Senior Mistress. She knocked. Mrs Popham sat among open files, books, papers. She looked up as Marjory closed the door and sighed: 'Oh *Marjory*. What is it *this* time?' As if she were there every day, but it was weeks since she'd had the cane: not doing all her homework because she'd been at Auntie Hennie's that weekend and couldn't be bothered. Well if you really haven't got any homework, Auntie Hennie had said, you can decorate the trifle. Mrs Popham sighed again, wiping her pen: 'How many?' She took the Punishment Book.

'Six.'

Mrs Popham wrote: Marjory Bell, six strokes. A column was headed: Reason. Another: Comments. 'And what did you do?'

'Got my teeth stuck in some toffee so I couldn't speak.'

'Eating in class.' She left the Comments for Mr Beach. 'All right. Hold out your hand.'

Mrs Popham's hair, all over the front half of her head, was a moving sea of tiny sausage curls. When she shook her head, or exerted herself with the cane, the curls slithered shinily brown from side to side, rolling down towards one ear, then to the other, never quite reaching the tops but looking always as if they would spill right off. It was something to watch while the strokes were delivered, three on each hand.

In the cloakroom the cold water was icy; a few seconds took the sting from her palms. She went back to the classroom and stood by Mr Beach until he looked at her and took the book and cane. He said: 'Consider yourself extremely fortunate, Marjory, that you are not losing the Wenceslas solo, but since the costume has been altered to fit you we can do little about it. You will not, however, be needed for the Brahms.'

'No, sir,' she said. She didn't mind the caning really, he could have given her more than six: Mrs Loyal had given her eight for writing left-handed. He could have taken her right out of the show, he was really nice. When she had won the cup for a hundred yards at sports he'd said it was all right if she didn't want to take it home. She hadn't explained that Gran would be horrified, saying running was unladylike, especially with *boys*. But he had looked at her and said very well, Marjory, if you would rather; and put the cup on the classroom shelf. She thought of saying: Sorry about the toffee, or even Thank You. Either would be embarrassing.

'Are you waiting for something, Marjory?'

'No, sir.'

'Then go back to your desk. We haven't got all day.'

'I did think,' Keziah slid along some ice, 'of owning up and saying I'd given you the toffee, but I didn't see the point in two of us getting the cane.'

'*I* think you should've,' said Joe Bale.

'Oh, hark at holy Joe. I bet *you* would've, ha ha, if you'd got chilblains on your fingers too.'

'Yes,' he said. 'I would, even if.'

'Oh pooh,' Marjory said, 'it doesn't matter. Didn't hurt anyway, and I finished the toffee.'

'Did you cry?' Joe asked.

'Who? Me? No I did *not*.'

They parted at Holmewood Gardens, sliding their different ways home. The lamps were lit. Leander Road was all ice, sheets glimmering across. The coalman's horse was down the slope, waiting outside their house: he was late. Grandad had perhaps been out to give the horse sugar, she might be in time to get more. Poor horse, cold, steam from his nostrils, pulling the heavy cart all day. Under the lamp she saw the coalman saluting someone from next door, then pulling the horse's rein. Gee up there, damn you, she heard him say on the bitter air. From the top of the slope she could hear the hooves slipping, pulling, slipping. He couldn't move the cart, ice under his feet. The man shouted, cold and enraged, hauling at the horse's mouth: decrepit old nag, knacker's yard, dog food, kill you, stupid beast. The hooves: clang, slide, clomp. She was running down, slipping, lurching into gates. The man was dancing, a demon in the lamplight, jumping at the horse's head. Punching its face, yelling, pulling, punching again. Marjory fell over, was up, running. Don't you do that! she was yelling as loudly as he. Don't you do that, you horrible man! And she was upon him, tearing at his leather jerkin, hanging on his arms, kicking his boots: Stop it stop it. The horse's white eye, its head jerking from the man's hand, the savage fist; the man red and spittly at the mouth, yelling, mad, shaking Marjory off. Stop hitting him or I'll get my Grandad and he'll kill you, he will. Get off, you damn kid, little bastard, don't you bite me. Yanking at the horse, hooves desperate to obey, muscles pulling. She ran at the front door, banging, shouting: Grandad, Grandad! Falling in as it opened: light, and Gran saying All this noise, whatever – But Grandad

just behind. Grandad, stop him, stop him hitting the horse . . .
He walked down the steps, calm and large in his heavy coat,
came to the man and put a hand on his shoulder. He spoke,
something quiet, the man stepped back and Grandad had the
reins. Something he said, or something in his touch, it could
have been a spell: the horse stepped forward slowly and
pulled. The hoof was firm, the cart moved. Carefully Grandad
led the horse to the top of the slope, Marjory walked beside
him wiping coal-dust from her gloves on to her coat, not looking round at the man following. At the top Grandad gave him
back the reins: There, just be calm, a horse will understand
that, he said with kindness, almost apologising. The man
mumbled something, head low, tough job, long day, don't
know what . . . Then he said: Thanks, guv, and went, not
glancing at Marjory's stony face. Not to worry, Marj; Grandad
took her hand as they walked back, watching for ice. Now her
tears would start; she sniffed and rubbed her nose with a
blackened glove. Grandad said: He'll be all right now, good
man really. He was *hitting* him, Grandad, in the face, on his
nose, it was *awful*. Yes yes I know, but he'll be all right now.
There, cheer up.

'But did you have to make so much noise about it, Marjory?'
Gran said, bringing food to table. 'Everyone was looking out
of their windows, old Mrs Barton came right to her door she
was so alarmed. What a commotion, dear me.'

'She was a bit upset, my dear, that's all,' Grandad said:
enough to silence Gran, who sliced instead into boiled beef.

'You and animals,' Uncle Ron said. 'I don't know. Why
don't you train to be a coalwoman? Or a kennel-maid?'

'Animals are nicer than some people,' she said, louder than
intended. Auntie Molly and Auntie Ada looked up, making
Chuh! noises.

' – Or,' went on Ron, 'you could go and muck out stables
or pig-sties?'

'Not at table, thank you,' Auntie Ada gasped a little.

'Or you could just be a good lady going round saving skinny
horses, rescuing mice from traps, mending broken wasp wings,
turning over upside-down beetles – '

'I want to be a vet.'

In the silence Marjory felt her throat rise in fear. It had

been said, wallop, without her planning. She looked at Grandad.

'A *what?*' Gran's knife was in mid-air.

'A *vet?*' Molly laughed quite loudly.

'For goodness' sake,' Ada said.

'A vet, ugh,' said Susie.

Grandad was surprised, then grinned: 'Well, always said she's good with animals, didn't I?'

'Certainly fond enough of 'em,' said Ron, 'can't deny that.'

Gran's smile at her husband and son was tolerant. 'I hope we all are in this family, but it takes more than that, surely? Exams, hard work, like a doctor. But I don't know that it's a job for ladies, is it?'

'Mr Stopps said I could do it.'

'You asked Mr Stopps?' Gran almost gaped.

'When I took Buller. He said he didn't see why I shouldn't, if I worked hard.'

'Ha – *if,*' Auntie Molly said.

Marjory drummed the table leg instead of kicking her. 'Well I would, *wouldn't* I?' she cried.

'Marjory!' warned Gran.

'Can just see Marj as a vet,' Uncle Ron was elbowing her, doing his music-hall comedian act. 'Remember the time I caught you teaching Jimmy manners?' It was a favourite funny story. 'There she was, in the kitchen, how old was she – about six? What a scream, giving the cat his tea, letting him take a bit of food and then grabbing hold of his jaw, like this – ' Uncle Ron demonstrated on her ' – holding his mouth shut. I said to her, here, Marj, I thought you liked animals, what're you doing to poor Jimmy? You know what she said? I'm trying to teach him some manners, Uncle Ron. Eat with your mouth shut, Jimmy, stop yaffling. Uncle Ron, he will keep *yaffling,* it's not very polite.' Uncle Ron leaned back in his chair and laughed; they all echoed him.

'I was only little then,' she said.

'Oh hark at her,' Auntie Molly said, 'all grown up.'

Auntie Ellie said: 'I think it's a very *brave* idea, Marjory, I really do.'

'You'd have to do operations and things,' said Susie, 'cutting them open. How could you? Ugh, it makes me feel sick.'

'I wouldn't mind, they'd get better.'

'I suppose,' Grandad said, 'there must be lady vets nowadays.'

'I wouldn't know,' Gran sighed. 'The things the child thinks of.'

'I thought of it ages ago,' Marjory said.

'We'll just have to see how you get on at school then, won't we?' Grandad was reasonable. 'The scholarship and everything. You'd have to do mathematics I imagine, and I think Latin would be needed, so I've heard.'

'We'll have to see what your father thinks, anyway,' Gran said. 'It's Henry who will have to decide in the end about the child's education, after all.'

But they hadn't actually said no.

Susie was speaking to her mother, just loudly enough: '. . . and Marjory got the *cane* . . .'

'Tell tale tit!' she cried.

'Marjory! Your language!' said Gran as Susie went 'Ooooh!'

'What had you done?' Gran inevitably asked.

'Ate a bit of toffee.' You wait, Susie.

'In class?'

'This is the one who's going to work so hard,' Auntie Molly pointed, Ada clicked.

'Marjory. Can't you behave properly *ever*?' Gran asked, all weariness.

Her father said nothing at the weekend about her being a vet. Perhaps Gran had told him, perhaps not. She sat near him when he was working on his plans; he drew meticulous lines and numbers, checking each detail, engrossed. She sorted his pencils quietly in groups: 3B, 2B, B, HB, 5H. Makes a change that does, he said, most kids want to mess them about. When I think of young Nora and Madge a few years ago, my goodness what scamps. But she could sit all day and not ask him the most important thing, she could not force out the words. But she told him about the Christmas Show: could he come? It's for three nights – Wednesday, Thursday, Friday. Gran and Grandad and everyone are coming on the last night. Don't know about that, Marjory, he said, have to see if I can get away, it isn't easy.

*

Susie all holy for three nights in her white headscarf and halo and blue gown. Herself something like a Christmas Puck, a green Page limping behind King Joe Wenceslas. That's the same colour as your eyes, he said, and turned red then walked away. Keziah the darkest angel: I suppose it's all right doing this, the angels were out of the Old Testament, weren't they? As if it matters, Mrs Hope told her, Jesus was real and it's a story, and he was only a baby anyway – what harm could a baby do? No, she said to Marjory, we can't come on the Friday, but we'll let Keziah off this once. She had wanted them to meet Grandad, and maybe, maybe, to say: Mrs Hope, this is my father. But he wrote a card: Sorry, my dear, I just have to work until late that day – pity, but there it is.

Auntie Flora in a hat a heap of feathers, a huge multi-coloured flowing dress which should cover but emphasised her pregnant bulges; Teddy in suit and stiff collar, a paper bag in his hand he said held rotten tomatoes. Auntie Molly and Uncle Fred Barnes, both silken, sleek, perfumed. Auntie Ada in extra flounces, a pale new boy friend putting her hand through his arm. Uncle Ron without his girl, acting escort to his over-flowing sister Flora: Uncle Bertie's at his pictures as usual. Auntie Ellie and Uncle Wilf, crisp, well-ironed, all pride for their Virgin Susie. Gran in her black lace bonnet, tiny beside Grandad in his grey wool suit, his white mane nodding as he stood talking to Mr Smiley about horses and scholarships. Blimey, Teddy said, look at 'em all, dressed to kill, what a sight. She heard him cackle in the middle of the hall when she came on as the green Page, and hissing and hushing from Flora.

Success: the audience was noisy, one or two even cheered. Mistakes were not serious. Once the prompter shouted into a lull, Susie cracked the Saviour's head on the edge of the manger, Joe nearly tripped over the curtain as he strode on as King, Keziah laughed aloud when a shepherd knelt and toppled at her angelic feet, but it seemed to fit. There was applause for paper snow impressively falling, for every solo, for Mr Beach's pounding the school piano. The audience was on its feet for four curtain calls. Then there was somebody in the aisle walking towards the stage, someone vast and floating and feathered, fronted by an enormous cellophane-crackling bouquet. Marjory ducked behind the Three Kings. Auntie Flora swooped into the lights, rose like a bright mountain up to the stage, and placed the flowers in the Virgin's arms, smothering the infant Jesus. Congratulations, Susie! Flora's words were heard by everyone: a polite pattering of hands in the middle of silence. Mr Smiley stared beneath brows, Marjory looked at the dusty boards, the cast looked at her and at Susie. Mr Smiley would say nothing now, but would wait until Assembly on Monday; she could hear it already, about the Nativity Play being, as he had said before, a serious and beautiful thing, not some frivolous concert party, and the more that players and parents and relations remembered that, the better. And all the school would stare. Too confident to hear the hush, Flora smiled back to her seat.

Cups of tea, coffee, jugs of lemonade, piles of sandwiches and cakes, waited at the back of the hall. I'm leaving my make-up on, Susie said, there isn't time to hang about here, come on, Marjory. She went out all lipsticked, swinging her skirt, the leading lady: Uncle Ron pretended to flirt with her. Grandad, this is my friend Keziah. Heard a lot about you, young lady, he said. She's going to be a lawyer, Marjory spoke loudly near Gran. Joe Bale said, talking through a chocolate bun, come and meet my Mum and Dad. Mum, this is Marjory Bell, she was the Page. And very sweet too, dear, said the lady in maroon. Marj, this is my Dad. Oh, she said, how do you do, but looked at his face for less than half a second: awful, it was the man from the Park who'd been behind the bushes. She looked instead at the brooch on Joe's mother's coat: a bird of Paradise with a very long tail. He might tell her off now in front of everyone, a naughty little girl who likes to stare at people when she shouldn't, what could she say? But he seemed not to remember her, only saying loudly, Well done, what a show, quite a little effort, eh, well done, you kids, how about a piece of plum cake. Joe looked embarrassed at his joviality, and confided: Dad lost his job a few weeks back, a lot of men have, you know. Actually, he's been ever so brave.

The approach of Christmas rustled in corners, was lit in the shops. Everyone was coming to Gran's house. After that, Marjory's birthday: she'd be eleven, scholarship age.

Joe said: This is for you, for Christmas, see you next term, eh Marj? A box of fondants, gold paper: she looked and touched. Thank you, Joe. Oh, Joe, she thought, you are nice; but it was impossible to speak the words. She had only a card for him. But I made it myself, I couldn't get you anything, they have to know what I spend the money on. I don't mind, he said, it's a lovely card. She told him about being a vet: I didn't say before because nobody knew then. He accepted it and said that's all right, fancy being a vet, you have to be quite clever really.

Teddy kept saying on Christmas Eve: Blimey it's another boy, who wants another boy, one vile brother's enough for me. Auntie Flora was all flat in front again, Uncle Bertie kissing her neck with everyone looking. Nora and Madge and Auntie Hennie and Uncle Joe, Auntie Liza and Uncle Walt and Val and Archie, Auntie June and Uncle Gerry and baby Bertha, Uncle Arthur and Auntie Rachel and their three grown-up, quiet-mannered, beautiful children, Rita, James, Esmie, not often at Gran's now they were out in the world and earning a living, Auntie Ellie and Uncle Wilf and Susie, Auntie Ada and Auntie Molly and Uncle Ron, Gran and Grandad, and last Daddy. All in the drawing-room, or crammed into the kitchen watching Ron pull the innards out of a goose and a turkey, helping and instructing with decorations, whispering parcel secrets, heaping glittering things under the tree, stealing sausage rolls, running away from Teddy who had a turkey's foot, opening and shutting the toes by pulling the sinews, Gran ordering Henry and Gerry to put the extra leaves in the table, filling acres of mince pies, ladling out soup and braised kidneys for supper, smiling round at all her sons, silly old fool said Marjory, and Teddy fell back off the long bench cackling.

Cards everywhere, wrapping paper, the smell of warming pastry and boiling pudding and roasting, chocolate, fruit, cigarettes, people. Ribbons on the floor, rustlings, exclamations. You know what it is, Archie shoved a huge star-covered bulk across the floor: inside, the dolls' house, unbelievable, furnished, perfect. Don't clean the floors with turps, he told her, or the paint will come off. Goodness, said Auntie Ellie, what a very clever boy you are, did he really make it all himself, Liza? It's the best present, Marjory said, but quietly. Daddy gave her a soft leather case with a fountain pen and pencil: That'll help you pass your exams, he said. He had had her name exquisitely engraved. Thank you very much, Daddy. Goodness yes, said Gran, I shouldn't think she'll expect birthday presents as well as all this luxury.

After hours of Christmas dinner everyone sat and burped, or picked at nuts, or slept. Auntie Molly sat and pedalled at the pianola: excitement yesterday when Uncle Fred Barnes had arrived with his beribboned gift in a special delivery van. There now, Molly, you can play whatever you like: just feed in the cylinder and you push the pedals and out comes Brahms or Beethoven or Old Man River, it's easy. They all had a go, it was like a conjuring trick. Fred's so thoughtful, Molly said, pumping out a Hungarian Rhapsody. Then: Come on, you kids, sing, do some entertaining, we've been doing all the work. Everybody sang something, nobody insisted on I Am a Little Beggar Girl and Swannee, or Auntie June out-stared Molly. Nora and Madge announced a party piece, rolled back the Persian rug and bullied everyone into moving back chairs and tables. They took up hip-jutting positions, elbows and hands and feet at angles, Nora in a white dress with five rows of fringe on the skirt, Madge in sugar-pink tiny pleats, and sang:

'Timothy Maginty was very nearly tight
Walking through a meadow at ten o'clock one night
Underneath an oak tree there he saw a bull
Waiting for a lunatic to give his tail a pull
Timothy approached, the animal arose
Tim up'd with his fist and punched him on the nose
In another minute he had to do a dance
For up came an earthquake and struck him in the pants
Then the band played and up to the moon he bunked
– All through tickling a bull that poor young man's
   defunct!'

They swung into a wild tap-dance, repeated the last two lines, and fell laughing into chairs. Applause. Marjory leaned on the arm of Auntie Flora's chair: Will you make me a dress like Nora's one day, when I go to a dance, will you? How about saying please? Please. Will you? All right, I dare say I might think about it, what colour? Pink, salmon pink, really vivid. Where on earth did you learn that song? Ron was asking Madge and Nora. Dad taught us, they grinned, and Uncle Joe said: You should hear the other verses. Honestly, Joe, said Ada, it's not very Christmassy, I'm not sure you should encourage such flippancy in your girls, they're quite modern enough. Look at Madge's hair, ever so short, like a boy. Doesn't look like a boy to *me*, Uncle Ron winked his secret towards Marjory.

He came with her often now to the Park on Sundays with the dogs, and did so again this Boxing Day, to meet his own short-haired girl by the side gate. The girl said: Hello, Marjory, happy Christmas, and Marjory replied Hello, same to you. The girl had looked sad, waiting, or perhaps just cold, but she smiled now at Marjory and turned her smile to Ron. But as the smile ended her mouth fell again. They walked away holding hands; Uncle Ron turned to wave.

Marjory's birthday began the new term. Eleven, and the Scholarship hung nearer, dreadful, and yet its falling would be a relief. Work, came the anxious chorus: Mr Beach, Mr Smiley, Miss Loyal, Mrs MacTavish, Mrs Popham. Work, muttered Keziah, it's all they ever think of. I don't mind, Marjory said, I'm going to be a vet, I am. Oh blimey, said Keziah, you're going to be unbearable, happy birthday anyway.

Susie in the evening rushed smiling downstairs, stopping at Marjory's room and interrupting equations. 'Marj – Marj! Daddy's got another job! Yippeee ...' she clattered on down to give the news.

Uncle Wilf said at supper: 'Don't fool yourself, Ron, I was lucky. It isn't going to be easy for everyone.' But although he stooped his face was less creased, and Auntie Ellie chirped around him.

'We'll all miss you here though,' Grandad said, and Gran agreed, yes, certainly they would.

'Are we *moving*?' cried Susie.

'Yes, darling. Daddy's new job's in Hampstead,' Ellie told her, 'and he thinks he might have found us a nice flat.'

'Golly,' Susie was round-eyed at everyone, 'we're moving.'

'You mean, you'll have to leave Christ Church? You won't live upstairs any more?' Marjory gaped. No more Susie for her and Teddy to tease and torment, to provoke to tears, to tell tales on them, to squabble with: she'd miss her. And Auntie Ellie's softness, Uncle Wilf's kind interest, she would miss them badly.

'Susie will go to a nice school in Baker Street,' said Wilf, 'but of course she's due to leave in the summer anyway.'

'Golly,' said Susie and Marjory together, and looked at each other.

Uncle Ron was saying: 'You weren't just lucky, Wilf old chap. A good man can do anything if he puts his mind to it.'

A shadow of Uncle Wilf's mournfulness crept back: 'Well, that's how you'll always see it, no doubt.'

Marjory thought: Uncle Ron must be right, that must be right. Or how could people ever do what they wanted? She went away from their voices as supper ended and into the quiet conservatory, to lean on the bench where the water-pipes were warm beneath the silkworm cage. They had finished all the mulberry leaves, these strange light caterpillars, and lay as if lifeless, glutted. Others, ahead of them, were already at work, spinning their magic silk cocoons. Spinning and spinning for a week, all movement and existence given to spinning, nothing else, only the creating of these fine silken unbelievable hiding-places. Some were ready, the chrysalids invisible within. She must take those to school, to the big cage with sections specially made where the moths might emerge, creamy and clumsy; then they laid their eggs, to be kept warm for hatching, and then again came the soft pale caterpillars and the collecting of mulberry leaves so they could gorge themselves, and then again the silk. Miss Robinson showed them how to wind off and re-spin silk from discarded cocoons: perhaps with this worm-created, re-made thread they might yet have enough to weave something. But you need more than one and a half thousand silkworms to make a pound of silk, they said. If a silkworm stopped to think of that, surely it would lose courage. Or perhaps those quiet ones, who seemed to lie exhausted from their intense greed, had actually paused to consider what lay ahead. While they digested the mulberry leaves and created within them liquid silk, maybe they also built up some determination just as strong for their seven days' work.

Grandad came: I hear it's your bedtime, Marjory, thought I'd find you here. He bent beside her to look into the cage.

Never stop, do they? She said: Those have, there, they're waiting to begin. She added tentatively: Or thinking about it. He laughed: Thinking about it? He bent and looked again. I dare say they could be, why not? And as soon as the idea had been accepted, she dismissed it, deciding inwardly: No, they're not; they just go on and on, blindly, they have to. If they stopped to think about the week ahead, the week which was the rest of their caterpillar life, then they'd stop for ever. She felt it now as a fact. But perhaps too, they sensed, for all one knew, that their unique silk was beautiful; she hoped so.

*

'It's foggy, look,' Keziah whispered, 'what if it's still there in the morning? We'll get lost going to the scholarship.'

'Don't be dotty,' Marjory said. 'It's getting dark, that's all.'

But it was dense when the bell rang. Mr Smiley was stopping children who didn't live near. 'Wait a bit, it may lift; are your parents on the telephone? Ah, Susie, Marjory – do you think you can find your way?' They said yes, Keziah would stick with them, Joe Bale too and two boys who lived round the corner on Brixton Hill. He let them go. 'But stay close together.'

They went in a row, arm in arm; Joe Bale managed to hold Marjory's hand. The fog was yellow-green where a lamp showed through, a blurred glow. 'Hey, it really *is* thick,' Joe said, 'you can't see the walls.'

'You can't see the kerb, never mind the walls,' Keziah said. 'Pooh, doesn't it pong?'

'Oh goodness, suppose we get completely lost,' Susie began to quaver. 'Whatever shall we do?'

'Wait 'til it clears, then they'll find us, six weeks later, dead of starvation,' a boy said. 'What d'you think?'

'Here,' said Keziah, 'we've come to a corner. That was Catherstone, this must be Holmewood. If we cross here, and we follow the kerb – look, I'll walk along it – we'll find the way, won't we?'

With Keziah's left foot as guide they followed the kerb, stepping slowly, holding each other, having to peer to see even the nearest face. Every few minutes somebody said: 'Hey, isn't it thick? It's getting thicker.' The smell, choking. 'We might as well sing,' said Joe, and they sang, it seemed warmer.

'This kerb goes on for ever,' Keziah said at last.

'We ought to've come out of Holmewood Gardens by *now*,' said Marjory. 'Where are we, anyway?'

They stopped. 'Oh, we're lost, we're lost!' Susie was about to cry.

'Shut up,' Marjory and Keziah said. They couldn't be lost. Scholarship day tomorrow, getting across Streatham by two different buses, the big school, to sit down at nine-thirty prompt and take the examination.

'Hang on a mo,' Joe said, and pulled at the line so that he could peer at a house gate. Then he groaned, 'Oh blimey, you know what *I* think?' Everyone said What? He told them: '*I* think we've walked round and round Holmewood Gardens following the kerb. That's what I think. We must've walked past my house a few times, we're on the opposite side now.'

'Maybe if we shout loud enough your parents will come out,' Marjory said.

'They wouldn't be able to see us even if they heard,' said Joe. 'Anyway, I'm not even sure they're home.'

'Crikey,' said one of the boys, 'we've gotter get out to Brixton Hill yet, somehow or other.'

'Everybody yell,' said Marjory. 'Yell your teeth out.'

They yelled. The fog stayed round them, silent, dirty, cold, green. They yelled again.

'Oh damn it,' Marjory said.

'Oooh!' said Susie.

'Oh *Susie*, you are an absolute *fool*,' snapped Keziah. 'I'd bash you if I could see you.'

Susie gasped, ready for an outraged reply, but instead shrieked with terror: 'Oh! Ow! What's that? Help!' Something large and hairy snuffled close, pushing, grunting faintly. 'It's a wolf! Help!'

'It's a dog, stupid. Here, here boy – who is it then?' Marjory reached out, a nose came into her hand, a tongue licked. 'Hey, it's Empire. Hello, Empire, did you hear us then? Did you come to find me? Good boy.'

'Who the devil's Empire?' Joe asked.

'Auntie Flora's Alsatian, they've only had him a few months, he's still a puppy really. Isn't he clever? He must've heard me.'

'He's *enormous*,' a boy said.

'He's supposed to be. Here, Empire – where's home then? Eh? Home, boy. Where's home?'

' – and he took us along Auntie Flora's road, so those two boys knew then where to go to get home, only just round the corner, then back to Joe's house and then to Keziah's road, and then here – honestly, Grandad, he did, and he's only a puppy still, he's awfully clever. If it wasn't for Empire we'd still be going round and round Holmewood Gardens.'

'That was Keziah's brilliant idea,' Susie said. 'Follow the kerb, huh.'

'Well, if we hadn't, we might have been *any*where, and Empire wouldn't have found us, so there. He was absolutely *brill*iant, just coming out of nowhere and – '

'Yes yes, Marjory,' Auntie Molly took aspirin; it was one of her pale days. 'We've heard all about it, and Empire is *too* clever.'

'It's your magic touch with animals again, Marj,' said Uncle Ron, 'that's what it is.'

'I told you they were cleverer than people.'

'Actually, you said *nicer*,' Susie said.

'Well, sometimes it's the same thing.'

'Nonsense, Marjory,' Gran was pushing chairs. 'Have you washed your hands? Then sit down. I should have thought it's far more important that you have to go out in the morning in this weather and sit for that scholarship. And if the fog hasn't cleared, how are you going to find your way to school I'd like to know?'

'Not just to school,' Marjory sat and took her napkin from its ring. 'To the big school, right the way down Streatham Hill and then all the way to – '

There was a din, everyone cried out at the same time.

Gran: 'What? They expect you to get all that way on your *own*?'

Auntie Ellie: 'My goodness. I don't remember Susie having to go that far. And in the fog too – we can't allow it.'

Auntie Molly: 'She'll have to take two buses. If there are any. Heavens above, what are schools thinking of these days?'

Auntie Ada: '*I* wouldn't venture out in it, let alone send a child.'

Then Grandad said: 'It'll probably clear by morning.'

Uncle Ron said: 'Empire can take her.'

'Why didn't you *say*?' Molly accused. 'You must've known you can't go all over there.'

'I must go, I must go!' Marjory dropped her cutlery and Gran clicked at the noise. 'It's scholarship. I can find the way, *easily*. I know which buses, and Keziah's going too. Mr Beach told us how to get there *exactly* and anyway I've been there before for hockey – '

'I'm not sure about it all,' said Gran.

'But if it isn't *foggy*, Gran, and even if it *is*, I could still find it – ' Gran would stop her going, stop her doing the scholarship, stop her going to the High School, stop her being a vet . . . 'I *must* go. Grandad, I can, can't I?'

'If the fog has cleared, I shouldn't think there need be any problem,' he said, all quiet sanity.

'Ho,' Auntie Ada said, 'I'm far from sure that it's safe, even so. These days, you never know who you'll meet. A child alone on the buses, goodness knows . . .'

'Oh Auntie Ada, that's just tommy-rot – '

'Marjory!' Gran, Ada, Molly, even Ellie, all cried out together while Susie mouthed Oh. Gran added: 'We will *not* have that sort of language, Marjory, unless you wish to go and sit on the stairs and have no food.'

'But, Gran – I won't be alone. I'll be with Keziah, and lots of others are coming. I'll be all right. I go out alone a lot, to the Park and everything, and nobody ever says anything – '

'Please keep your voice down, Marjory,' said Gran.

'But Gran – '

'And don't argue. We'll talk about it later when you've gone to bed, and besides nothing can be decided until we see what the weather's like in the morning. Sometimes these pea-soupers don't clear for *days*.'

Please God let the fog clear, please God blow it away, please God tell them to let me go. There were shadows on the walls and ceiling from the low gas-jet: it was always impossible to decide whether it was better with the flame low, as Auntie Ellie would thoughtfully leave it, with shadows that grew and threatened, or off, with darkness hiding movements and creakings, and the curtains shifting secretly. Drifting towards sleep and waking as her whole body jerked, a sense of wooden floors and something dreadful waiting out there on the stairs, waiting to open the door; and lying not wanting to sleep again, not wanting to stay awake. Voices murmuring downstairs. She could imagine: What a difficult child, such a handful, poor Henry. Please God let them say yes, make the fog go away.

The light outside her window was greenish but when she flung herself at the curtains she could see the end of the garden through swinging rags of dirty yellow tulle. Thank you, God, you did it.

Gran told her across the porridge: Grandad's taking you to the bus stop, so at least you'll be seen safely on to the first bus. Auntie Ada shook her head, a little velvet bow fluttered over one ear: I'm still not happy about it, Mother. I should think *not*, Molly dipped her silver teaspoon; making a child go all that way just for an exam. Ellie said: Well, Father seems to think she'll be all right, and the fog has cleared quite a lot you know. Oh *you*, Ellie, you don't *think*, Molly hinted at unmentionable happenings on Streatham buses. *I* can't feel happy about it, Ada said again. Oh dear, said Ellie. Gran said: Well, I'm certainly not going to argue with your father about it; if he feels it's all right, that's the end of it.

Grandad came, carrying his coat. Ready, young Marj? She fell off her chair. Get your hat and coat, off to the bus, big day. He straightened her hat for her in the hall. And if the fog comes down again later you'd better stay put, we'll find some way of collecting you. Auntie Ada called: You be careful now, Marjory! Auntie Molly: Don't speak to strangers! Gran: I hope you put your warm bodice on. Uncle Ron came downstairs: Hey, Marj, good luck then. You show 'em.

Keziah said on the bus: 'What're you looking all dumpish about? Nervous?'

'I don't know. Sort of. Honestly, Kez, they make me spit. The way they go on and *on*, Auntie Molly and Auntie Ada and Gran. They keep *on* and *nag* all the time.' It was peculiar, she felt like crying.

'Ah, never mind,' Keziah said. 'Don't take any notice, soppy lot. We'll soon be there, it'll soon be over.'

Rows and rows of desks in a hall five times as big as at Christ Church school. It was quiet, the children filed obediently, not looking much at each other. The whole room was pale and tense, a tall man with glasses waited with a pile of white papers. Sit down, children, when you have found your name. Arrange your pens and blotting paper. You will find plenty of ink in the ink-well. Papers, upside-down on the desks. Turn them over when the man says Now. Scratching pens, sighs, for an hour. Fifteen minutes' break, no talking, drink your milk. Another paper in two parts. Then it was the end. At lunch-time they could compare.

'Wasn't bad, was it?' Keziah bounced.

'It was easy. The English and General Knowledge anyway.' Marjory pulled sandwiches and an apple from a large grease-proof-paper bag. 'What did you think of the arithmetic?'

'All right really.'

Marjory looked into a sandwich. 'I couldn't do it all.'

'Some of it *was* hard, I suppose.'

'I made two mistakes, I know I did. *Stupid* ones. I knew as soon as I gave in the paper, ugh.'

'Oh, that always happens,' Keziah was airy. 'You always think of something too late.'

'Did you then?'

'Not yet, but I bet I will.'

'Arithmetic came first, that was why,' Marjory said. 'I hadn't sort of settled down, wasn't in the mood.'

'Crikey, I wouldn't be in the mood for arithmetic any time of day,' Keziah laughed.

'I bet *you* passed,' Marjory said.

'Well if *I* did, *you* did,' Keziah told her. 'You always beat me in class, nearly always anyway. Don't be soppy.'

'Well?' Gran and Grandad asked. 'How did you get on?'

'Pass, did you?' Uncle Ron looked over his evening paper. 'Flying colours?'

'It was all right really.'

'All right *thank* you,' said Gran.

'Thank you.'

'Easy, was it?' Ron asked.

'Some was. The arithmetic was hard though.'

'Arithmetic!' Auntie Molly was doing her eyebrows at the mirror by the door. 'You'll need arithmetic if you're going to be a *vet*, my girl.'

'I know *that*.' With luck Auntie Molly would jab those tweezers in her eye.

'Oops, temper,' simpered Ada. 'I'm sure nobody'd want to take little Fido to a bad-tempered vet.'

'I expect you're a bit tired, aren't you, dear?' Auntie Ellie said. 'You do look a little pale.'

'Sallow,' Gran agreed.

'I'm fine, really, thank you.'

'So what about this arithmetic?' Uncle Ron said. 'It's not so important. Only have to count up to four – most animals have got four legs, haven't they?'

'It was the very first paper, that was the trouble. If it had come second, or last – '

'Really, Marjory,' said Gran, 'I hope you're not going to be one to make excuses. *Some*thing had to come first, be sensible. And if you've failed, you've failed, and that's all there is to it. I'm sure it's not the end of the world. Susie didn't pass the scholarship and I've no doubt she'll do quite well for herself, something nice and respectable and ladylike. Why didn't you finish your sandwiches?'

The garden sieve was hanging on the back of her bedroom door. That was the wrong place. It should be on the wall, on the nail that Grandad put in, near the climbing rose by the shed. It was taken away from the climbing rose, it was hanging on the hook on her door. The door was swinging just a little, back, forward, hardly moving, perhaps it was only the shadows that moved, not the door. No noise, no creak, no sigh of wind, no draught at the curtains. The silence was over and under the bed, against her skin, among the blankets, across the room, by the sieve. The sieve was swinging now with the door, silent. The garden sieve which should be on the garden wall, it swung without noise, swing, swing, and then lifted itself from the hook on her door; it rose in the air, silently upwards and towards her, coming towards her, the sieve was falling, falling, falling, soundless, slow but fast, down over her face, right over, shadows and light and silence and air disappearing.

'Wake up, wake up, Marjory, don't hit me, dear, it's all right.' Auntie Ellie was holding her shoulders. Stop it, Auntie Ellie, stop the sieve, I can't breathe, take it away. 'What's she saying, sieve?' It was on my door it's on my face I can't breathe take it away. 'Nothing's there, look, nothing, you're all right.' 'Sit her up, show her.' 'There, see? Nothing on the door, nothing on the bed.' It was there, it was falling on me. 'Keep still dear – now look, look, Marj. Nothing. It was a dream, a horrid dream.' It was there, it was there. 'It's down the garden where it belongs, it really is. It was a dream. Nobody's hurting you.' She heard them moving away, saying gracious what a scream she gave, had quite a fright, she's all right now. 'My goodness,' Susie was out on the landing, 'I never heard anything like it. Poor old Marj, she's frightened of so *many* things.'

SEVEN

MARJORY (*to her son, then about nine or ten, who has been bemoaning some ill turn of fate at school*): Come on, you can't always have what you want, that's one of the hard facts of life. You did your best: *well* then – you couldn't have done any more, could you? That's how it is. If you don't get what you want you just have to make the best of it, don't you?

*

'Goodbye,' Auntie Ellie said, face flushed under her best white hat, 'goodbye.' She hugged Marjory and kissed her cheek. 'We'll come and see you and you must come and see us. Mustn't she, Susie?'

'Goodbye, Auntie Ellie, goodbye, Uncle Wilf.'

'Bye, Marj.' Uncle Wilf bent to kiss sadly.

'Bye, Marj,' said Susie. 'Hope you get the scholarship.'

'Bye,' Marjory said. 'Thanks.'

'Give your cousin a nice kiss then,' Auntie Molly instructed.

'Ugh,' Teddy said behind her.

'Lots of luck with the job, Wilf,' Uncle Ron tied the final suitcase on to the borrowed car. 'All the best.'

'You remember what I said, Ron.' Uncle Wilf's shoulders had still not quite straightened again. 'You just remember.'

'Nah . . .' Uncle Ron clumped his back. 'Not a bit of it. Things'll be all right, you'll see. We're English, you know, this is England.'

Wilf nodded slowly: 'That's the idea, Ron, that's the way,' but his tone did not agree. 'Come along, Ellie, let's be off.'

Goodbye, goodbye, good luck, they all called and waved, Auntie Ellie wiped her eyes, so did Ada; Gran and Molly stood with sad mouths. They won't have her to push around and wait on them, that's why, said Teddy. Goodbye, goodbye.

'Anyone'd think they were going to the other side of the world, not Hampstead,' said Uncle Ron, urging everyone back indoors, saying it was cold. 'The way you females go on. Look at Marj, gone all white.'

'It's not *them*,' she said. 'I feel sick.'

'Too much treacle tart I dare say,' Auntie Ada said.

'Hey, can I have some?' Teddy pounced.

'*May* I,' Flora pulled on her gloves, 'and no you may not. Unless you ask nicely at teatime and then only if Gran says so. You look after Harry and be good. Thanks for taking Reggie, Mother.' A woollen blue bundle looked wisely from Gran's arms as Flora went down the steps, jade crêpe wool draped from shoulder to hip, a close hat with one long pheasant feather over newly cropped hair. She turned and waved: 'You behave!' she called at Teddy.

'Hm.' Gran looked at Marjory. 'Fresh air probably. You children go and play in the garden. Go to the Park with the dogs if you like.'

'*She's* all right,' Molly said. 'Well enough to play hockey this morning, wasn't she?'

'I didn't feel sick then.'

'Go along out, do you good. Put on your scarf.'

'Yeah, come on, Marj.' Teddy pulled at her arm in the garden. 'Let's go to the Park and see that mynah bird that says rude things. Come on.'

'Don't feel like it, Ted. Honest, I feel sick and I've got tummy ache.'

'Oh pooh then, you're hopeless. Stay and droop about like a wet fish. I'll go on my own and I'll teach it to say Marj is a spoil-sport.'

'I'm not hungry,' she explained at teatime, turning down cherry-cake and treacle tart.

'Don't tell me you're sick at heart now Susie's upped and gorn,' Uncle Ron grinned, hands crossed dramatically upon his chest.

'Sick to death of her, more likely,' said Teddy.

'That's quite enough,' Gran told him, 'or you'll sit on the stairs and have no tea.'

'Horrid little boy,' murmured Auntie Ada, an echo of Susie.

'You,' Gran told Marjory, 'look as if you could do with a good dose of Salts.'

Gran was standing at the end of the bed, though her outline waved, fogged, distorted. Her voice was thin and far, strained through buzzing sounds. 'Why aren't you up, Marjory? I thought you were out with the dogs. I suppose you overslept. The times I've told you about reading late. Come along, everyone's at breakfast. Good thing your father isn't here this weekend, I don't know what he'd say I'm sure, lying about in bed. Come along.'

She pushed her voice out through a throat that hurt. 'I can't, Gran. I don't feel well.' She raised her head and at once dropped it.

'Nonsense.' Gran had reached the misty door, had turned. 'We don't have that namby-pamby attitude in this family I hope. Now come along. I want to see you get up.' She waited.

Marjory dragged a leaden body, half sat. The room was moving, there was a whining in the centre of her head. 'Honest, Gran, I feel awful, I've got this tummy-ache and my throat . . .' But Gran stood.

Marjory put her legs over the side of the bed, made herself straighten. Pains tore through her, she gasped, clutching at her stomach, rolled or fell back on to the bed. She turned her head, feeling her mouth pull into a strange shape, saying: 'I feel awful, Gran.' Gran's hand came into focus on the bedstead, tight and cold and irritated.

'Oh, get in then. Get *in*.'

She woke: the hands on the brass rail were gloved. Auntie Flora stood there, Gran in the doorway. She could see better now, less fog. Voices downstairs, Sunday lunchtime nearly, smells of food, horrible, her throat closed.

'Mother,' Auntie Flora said, 'this girl should see a doctor, just look at her.'

'Don't be silly, Flora. She's perfectly all right. Nothing that a good dose of Salts won't clear up.'

'Have you got a pain, Marj? There, see, Mother. She's not putting it on, look at her face. Good Lord, she's *grey*, she looks terrible.'

Gran's folded arms were stubborn. 'I don't believe in pandering to these things, Flora, you should know that. I'll fetch the Salts.'

'Mother. *I* think she should see a doctor.'

Something in Flora stopped Gran. 'Goodness what a fuss, Flora, whatever next? Well, don't imagine I'm going to call the doctor out on a Sunday. If she wants to see him she'll have to get up and go there, and that's that. *If* you insist.'

'Come on, Marj. Sit up. I'll give you a hand. What were you going to wear? Better be something warm.' Auntie Flora heaved her out of bed, propped her in the chair like a baby. 'You do look rotten. Want to go to the bathroom first, or have you been?' Marjory whispered: Been. Some time early in the morning she'd crawled there. She took the garments Flora held out, threaded her limbs into them. Her middle hurt, hot and sharp, her throat was choking her. She stood, her skin froze over, tight round her eyes, Flora faded out. 'You all right, Marj? Come on, hang on to me, that's it.'

'Does it hurt here? Here?' The doctor pressed cool quick fingers into her abdomen. 'Tell me where the pain is, there's a good girl.'

She flinched, nodded, and croaked: 'Yes, ow. And my throat too,' but perhaps he didn't hear. She could smell roasting beef from the doctor's kitchen, revolting, and a wireless was playing 'Tea for Two'.

'Hm,' he said, also sniffing the air, and turned to Auntie Flora. 'Child has appendicitis,' he was brisk. 'Best get her into hospital right away.'

'Hospital!'

'I'll make the telephone calls immediately. Take her home, the ambulance will come to the house. Get her things ready, nightclothes, toothbrush, that sort of thing. They won't be long, so let's not lose any time.'

'Appendicitis! An operation, you mean?' Auntie Flora herself looked stricken.

'Almost certainly. Best get it over with, it's very inflamed I should say.' He went away to his telephone and his Sunday roast.

'Good Lord,' Auntie Flora said. 'Appendix, fancy that. Come on, Marj, let's get your nightie packed.'

Gran and Flora rode with her in the ambulance, leaving the family at lunch. Nora had said, through a blur: Lucky thing, Marj, doctors are always handsome.

'I still can't believe it,' Gran said from her corner.

'Fancy getting appendix,' Auntie Flora said, 'honestly, Marj, and on a Sunday too.' She laughed, content that she had helped discover it.

'Lambeth Hospital,' Gran smiled at the ambulance man, 'is a good place I believe.'

'Certainly is, ma'am.'

The ambulance bumped and rattled, there were pains everywhere.

'Appendicitis,' Gran said. 'It's never happened in our family before.' Marjory didn't hear anyone reply.

Green curtains round her, a man and a woman both in white, only their eyes and hair showing. He was pushing at her, asking muffledly, does it hurt? Where? There? Appendix my eye, he said to the nurse, who snuffled a bit in her mask. Swab, he said. Open your mouth, little girl, Marjory is it? That's it, wider. Hm, yes, well that doesn't surprise me too much, does it? As if she could reply, with his fingers in her throat and something making her retch, dabbing about. Sorry about that, he said, not very nice. Never mind, over now. Stay with her, nurse, while I see the relatives. Is it the mother? Aunt and grandmother, I see. He vanished, white through green. The nurse's hand on her forehead, cool through the burning; Feel all right do you, dear? The white linen was blurring, her throat was suffocating her. Never mind dear, we'll soon get you better. Poor little thing. And who's got great big green eyes? There now, never mind.

Through the green curtains the voices, then the man was speaking loudly, angrily. Good heavens, my dear lady, how long has she been like this? Appendix nonsense, who on earth is your doctor, the child has diphtheria, yes diphtheria is precisely what I said, I trust you are not doubting my word. Isolation. Treatment. Danger. Diphtheria. Auntie Flora's high cries, Gran's disbelief, querying, dismissing. The man getting louder, faster, all of them talking, arguing. Pity she was not brought in before, frankly disgraceful. Diphtheria, and you might as well believe it, madam.

It was a small room, a wire-haired lady in the other bed. Green paint, and brown, chipped cream.

Something blocked her nose, bubbled, flowed. Blood. There's blood, all down my face, spilling all over the pillow, they'll be furious, they'll tell me off, where's my hanky . . . Nurse! Nurse! The wire-haired lady across the room was sitting up, shouting and staring. Nurse! For God's sake come quick, this little girl, she's bleeding something awful. The nurse came walking swiftly, mustn't run. Nose-bleed, is it? Nothing to worry about I'm sure. Her face altered as she looked from the doorway to Marjory. Heavens, she said, and ran: Sister! Running back, cottonwool, bottles, water. You lie back there, that's it, no, you won't choke.

I can't breathe, I'll die, I'll bleed to death, it's not going to stop whatever she does. Look at their faces, they're scared stiff, all my blood will pour out of me. There was a man got hit by a tram Teddy told me, he just lay there and bled to death before anyone came because the wrong vein was cut, it doesn't take long for all your blood to run out of you, I'm going to die.

Keep calm, nurse, Sister said, but her voice shook and she hurried too. Madam, please lie down, everything is under control. But the blood still ran out warmly. Everything possible is being done for the little girl. Calm, nurse, nothing to worry about, more dressings, nurse, quickly now. Gor blimey, across the room, poor little blighter.

'Took 'em 'arf an hour to stop it,' the lady said, 'I timed 'em. Luvvaduck, I fought you was a gonner and that's the truth.'

She had to lie on her back: don't move, the Sister said. Smell of rubber sheet under her head. Cracks across the ceiling. Her throat nearly closed, just a small hole to breathe through, making crackly noises.

'You're bein' moved tomorrer. Tooting Isolation, I was listenin'. Secondary infections in yer nose, that's what young Doctor Thingummywhat said, and gawd knows where else. I 'eard 'im. I'd say you're quite serious, ducks, that's what I'd say. You do what they tells you, eh, millions of kids dies of it.'

We'll soon get you better down here in Tooting, you see. They put a needle into her navel, huge, and injected. She watched the skin blow up, maybe it would burst. When they pulled the screens round, when the Sister came, it might mean the needle. Some days yes, some days no. Sometimes they saved it until the doctor came. Every other day they rolled her on her side: enema day today, dear, and the loathsome bubbling up into her bowels. Have you had trouble with your movements, child? The doctor is asking you about your bowels being opened, Marjory, before you were ill, he means. Laxatives? Ever had any? Salts, hm? *How* often did you say? Tell me, little girl, who has been giving you these Salts? I see. Well, I shall have to have a word with your grandmother, shan't I? Looking into her throat, stuffing things in her nose. Good girl. Not eating, hm? Try a little milk, maybe. We'll get you better, said the nurse with hair like Miss Clara Finch's, even if it takes us weeks and I dare say it will. Here are some letters, do you think you can read them? Shall I read them to you? Nobody can come and see you, you're too infectious. You might like to write when you feel a bit better; we fumigate your letters, see, otherwise everyone'd get your horrid old diphtheria and that wouldn't do, would it?

It'd be good if Gran got it.

Lying flat, ears about to split open any minute, throat sealing itself, some days gasping, choking. No I'm not hungry, can I have some water? Hello, Marjory: how's the tummy today, bit better? Ears still painful, yes. You lie there still and be good, we want to see that temperature normal. Now, nightie up, time for a little injection. My, you're a skinny little thing. Into the navel, ow. Can't see you running round the park yet a while, huh?

Grandad sent a parcel: an apple, an orange, some biscuits. Dear Marj, these might help buck you up if you feel like nibbling on something tasty. You be good and get better quickly, things are quiet here without you. Buller and Boney miss you, I don't think I move fast enough for them. So do the horses that bring the milk and coal, they'd rather have their sugar from you – I think you must cheat and give them more.

Dear Marjory, Daddy wrote, I would be glad to come and see you and cheer you up but I understand that visitors are quite forbidden. I expect they have explained that to you. I hope you are now feeling much better and able to eat a little, that's the way to build up your strength. The doctors tell me it could be a long business so try to be patient and do as they say, won't you? Everyone at home is well and sends their love. Thank goodness it didn't spread in the family, Auntie Flora was naturally worried about the baby.

Dear Marj, Teddy wrote on exercise-book paper, I taught the mynah bird in the park to say Gran's A Stinker, you should hear it. I've been taking out the dogs sometimes with Empire, but Grandad or Uncle Ron go mostly. Everything's OK but a bit boring. Hurry up and get better. I thought you were putting it on a bit when you said you were feeling sick. Maybe I'll catch it too, could you send me some germs? Then I'll come in and we'll have some fun. We went to tea the other day at Auntie Hennie's and I ate four cream puffs. That friend of theirs was there, the one we call Uncle Griff. I think he's a bit queer in the head, he keeps on picking imaginary bits of fluff off himself and jumping up and down.

Dear Marj, Nora wrote, you ought to see my new silver lamé and lace dress, it's got this big sash with a bow, a bit like a bustle really, in velvet! It's absolutely terrif!! Madge and I are going to a special dance on Friday and we're going to walk off with the two handsomest men there, only don't tell Gran I said so. The other evening we went to see *No No Nanette*, what a lark. Hope you're feeling much better now, Marj, Gran says you'll be there for ages. Hope they're nice to you.

Dear Marjory, came Joe Bale's writing, open and kind like his face. I was awfully sorry to hear how ill you were, I hope you're all right now. Keziah said you had it very badly and I know it can be serious. What's it like in hospital? Fancy not being allowed to see anybody at all, it must be funny. They say all the doctors and nurses have to bath in disinfectant before they're allowed home, is that true? It's a shame you missed the running and football, we've been winning a lot. And that girl Amy said they were missing you in the hockey team, I thought you'd like to know. Aren't you lucky, not having to do any homework or anything. I can't wait for summer when I leave, then I'll do something interesting at last. The papers are all full of this chap Alan Cobham who flew 8,000 miles all the way to Africa, wouldn't it be spiffing to do something like that?

Dear old Marj, said Keziah, what a swiz you being ill just when it's such cold weather and you can't sit and freeze with me in the classroom!! I hope you'll be much better soon, and the weather too. Mum and Dad and Benjie send their love, everybody misses you on Fridays. Is it true you nearly died? That's what Teddy said, he actually looked worried for once. I told Joe Bale too, just to make sure his love keeps on burning bright! ! ! You got Mr Beach's prize for writing again, it's getting a bit much, you winning all the time. Maybe the rest of us will stand a chance if you're out of the way for a bit. Still, I got the arithmetic so you're not the only genius. You're not missing much in the outside world, everybody's talking about strikes and politics and the miners are protesting all the time.

Dear Marj, Uncle Ron typed his letters, I'm looking after your silkworms so you needn't worry about them. What greedy pigs they are, I reckon they eat more than you do from what I hear. They just gorge themselves like real gluttons and then flop about and do nothing, I thought they were dead until I saw in your booklet that they always behave like that. Manners! What I want to know is, why wasn't I born a silkworm? I hear you're a bit better – that's the spirit, Marj, you're a tough one, you show them. I've been taking the dogs out for you quite a lot, and don't imagine it's just for the sake of my health, ho ho ho.

Dear Marjory, Gran's writing was quite large, Grandad has done you another parcel which I'm sending. He says he'll send you some fruit and biscuits every week, now isn't that kind of him? I hope you're trying to eat now and you're doing what the nice doctors and nurses tell you, you can be sure they know best. Auntie Flora and Auntie Molly and Auntie Ada all send their love and get well wishes. Auntie Ellie wrote too, and she and Susie and Uncle Wilf also send their love. They are enjoying life in Hampstead. Lots of kind people ask about you. We ring up the hospital often to find out how you are and so does Daddy. Uncle Fred Barnes came on Sunday, he very kindly drove Auntie Molly to Brighton, and he said to let him know if there's anything at all he can do for you, he's such a kind and generous man. Grandad says to tell you the dogs are well, so are Jimmy and Billy.

Grandad added a note: There was a lovely sight of Northern Lights the other day, you could see it from the rise in the Park. They say it was the best for fifty years, shame you missed it.

A card came, with roses and butterflies. It said Get Well in letters of gold, with love from Auntie. Auntie Violet: how did she know? Daddy, Watford. Next week, a small doll: love from Auntie, get well soon. The nurse said: Isn't she sweet? Who's she from? Violet, that's a nice name. You know, don't you, you won't be able to take the dolly home, because of infection? Never mind, another little girl will be able to have her and it will make her happy too.

Susie wrote: Dear Marj, It's ever so nice here in Hampstead and school is nice too. Daddy's job is going well but he says there will be a lot of strikes in the country. Mummy has made friends with the lady next door, her name is Millie Stanhope and she makes clothes, even better than Auntie Flora can. She is going to make me a costume for when I go looking for jobs. The other day a lady tried to shoot Mussolini, isn't that awful? She hit him on the nose but he was very kind and let her off.

*

How about that, said the Clara Finch nurse, you actually ate it all up. Some milk? And I do believe there's just the tiniest touch of colour in that funny old thin face. You should see the size of your eyes! Marjorie asked: Nurse, how long have I been here? Seven weeks, almost exactly. How about trying a step or two, eh? Upsadaisy. Do you like being a nurse? Course I do, wouldn't do it otherwise now would I? What d'you like best about it? Seeing people get better, what d'you think? Come on, less chat, I want to see some meat on these legs, get them moving.

The doctor said: So, you're eating. And walking too. Laughed at you, did they? Don't you worry, they'll fall flat on their backsides too. Now what we've got to do is fatten you up a bit. You'll be a bit feeble for a while so don't expect too much. Know how long you've been here? Oh, you do, eh? Well, we've seen quite enough of you. Tell you what we'll do. One more week and we'll send you off to Dartford for a bit. What we want from you is four clear swabs in four weeks and then you can go home. That's a good girl.

Dartford was fields, some of the trees were getting leaves, roses, the earliest buds by the hospital lawns showing pink and yellow tips in a mild spell. Country. Horses across by the far hedges, big white clouds, sun. Aren't you lucky to be in such a lovely place?

Four swabs, four weeks. Well done, girl, you did it, all clear. Get along with you then, we don't want to see you again.

Uncle Ron came by car to collect her, running from it and up the steps, winking at the nurses. This isn't Marj, is it? It's a shrimp, at the most a prawn. Oh wait a mo though. This looks like her hair, these are her eyes, it must be her. Bless me, what a skinny guts.

'Is it your car, Uncle Ron?' The sun shone on leather seats; their smell had tobacco about it, and perfume. They breezed between hedges, all sparkling. I'm out, I'm out, I'm back in the world.

'I might buy it,' he said. 'Friend of mine wants to sell. What d'you think? Better than the old motor-bike, eh?'

'Oh *much* better.'

'Har,' he said, 'you should be grateful to the old rattler, disloyal wretch. The times I've whizzed you home from the market or somewhere because you were jigging about dying to go to the lav.'

'You could still whiz me home by car. You should buy it, Uncle Ron, it's super. Uncle Gerry's got a car, why shouldn't you? And you could take out your lady friend in it instead of having to walk the dogs.'

He grinned, he might usually laugh. 'That's it, Marj. If she'd like.'

'Are they all right – the dogs? And my silkworms, what about them?'

'All fine, all fine. You'll see, nothing's changed.'

She watched trees, gates, cows, hedges, lamp-posts, streets. Her inside trembled, to be going home after so many weeks. What would they all say? What would they expect her to say back? She longed for Buller and Boney, their ugly laughs, their delight to see her, unquestioning, accepting.

Uncle Ron spoke again as if there had been no pause. 'Just between you and me, Marj, the thing is, how long will a girl wait?'

'What for?'

'Me, Marj. For me.'

'Oh. You mean, *marry*ing her? Oh!'

'That's what I mean. Well, Marj?'

After a while she said: 'I don't know.'

'There you have it, Marj. Nor does she, see? Nor does she.'

As Uncle Ron pulled on the brake at Leander Road the front door opened. Grandad, with Gran just behind. Ron got out of the car, bending and straightening his long legs: 'Here we are, hang out the flags, the traveller returns!'

Grandad opened Marjory's door, pulled her upright on the running board. Gran came to meet Ron, putting her arm through his, smiling up at him: 'Not too tired, dear?'

'Hey there, and who's this?' Grandad laughing, his hair looking very white. 'How's big-eyes then?' He picked her up as if she were a toddler, kissed her, and put her down on the pavement. 'Bless me, what are those matchsticks? Legs, you call them?' She held on to his hand with both of hers, laughing too much.

Gran said: 'Now, Marjory, don't get over-excited. Let's take your things indoors and then we'll have tea, and an early night for you. Daddy will be here tomorrow, and the doctor's coming to see how you are. He doesn't think you'll be able to go back to school for another week.'

Daddy said: 'You eat plenty of your Gran's good food, Marjory, you'll soon have roses in your cheeks again and a bit more meat on you. And don't worry if you find you're a bit behind at school – a spot of hard work and you'll soon catch up.'

Teddy said: 'Here, I saved this chocolate for you, it's smashing. Come on, tell us about the blood and the injections and everything.'

Auntie Molly sighed: 'Well, Marjory, I can tell you're back, I hope you're going to tidy your things in the bathroom.'

Auntie Flora said: 'Look, Marj, I made you a blouse, how d'you like that?'

Auntie Ada said: 'She'd better wear it on Sundays only or it'll be ruined in no time.'

Auntie Ellie on Sunday said: 'My, you *are* thin, dear, have another piece of Yorkshire pudding.'

Susie said: 'I've got a job at Peter Robinson's. In the Accounts Department, it's ever so nice.'

Uncle Wilf said: 'What d'you know, Marj, I seem to have this big box of fudge on me, you may as well have it.' And went on speaking to Uncle Ron: 'But it's true, the miners' pay *is* a disgrace to the community.'

Uncle Ron, grooves at his mouth, said: 'Don't go quoting that Communist at me, Wilf. You wouldn't be one of that lot, would you? All that stuff about a miners' strike being the end of Capitalism, load of bosh.'

Grandad said: 'Hey hey that's enough of that for now, boys. Seen the roses, Marj? Lots of buds but I think the blight's got to some of them.'

Auntie Ada said: 'Oh splendid. Marjory can help me in the garden this week while she's home. I'm sure she doesn't want to play with the dogs *every* minute of the day.'

Marjory said: 'I like gardening.'

The mynah bird in Brockwell Park said: 'Gran's a stinker, gor blimey.'

On her third day back at school Mr Beach was waiting at the classroom door as the line of pupils filed from the playground. 'All right. Stop here.' He waved them into a queue against the corridor wall. 'I want you to wait quietly, and come into the classroom one at a time, when I call.' He hitched his shapeless trousers and at mystified whispers yelled: 'Quietly I said!' He went into the room, calling: 'Right. First one.'

He had called 'Next!' three times when Keziah said: '*I* know. It's the scholarship results. He's telling us one by one instead of in front of everybody.'

'Oh, Kez, how awful. I'd forgotten. I feel sick.'

'Course you don't. It's nerves, dope. *You* needn't worry.' She added some unwelcome logic: 'Anyway, you can't do anything about it now, can you?'

'You go first,' Marjory said at the door.

She watched through the narrow opening, Mr Beach murmuring briefly to Keziah. Keziah blushed, grinned, and walked to her desk. 'Next!'

Mr Beach smiled as she came to his side. 'Marjory Bell. Well, Marjory, I'm rather surprised. It was the arithmetic I'm afraid. Missed it by only five marks.'

Little hairs stood up cold on her neck and arms. She looked at him.

'In cases like this,' he was saying, 'where it's such a near

147

decision, you have another chance to sit. You could do so at the end of the autumn term, near Christmas. You did extremely well in the other subjects, you'd pass them again easily. Indeed, I can't think how you missed the arithmetic, not like you, hm? Never mind, bad luck. Go and sit down.'

Keziah said: 'I don't believe it, Marj, are you pulling my leg?'

A buff envelope had come in the mid-day post.

'Mustn't cry over spilt milk,' Gran said.

'I'm not crying.'

'If you fail you fail, and that's that.'

'And you wanted to be a *vet*!' Molly had to laugh.

Auntie Ada followed her. 'My my, imagine that. Really Marjory, you'll have to lower your sights just the teeniest bit.'

Uncle Ron said; 'What, only five marks? What a swiz. You'd think they'd give it to you.'

'I can take it again, Mr Beach said. When it's only a few marks they let you.'

'Goodness, Marjory,' Gran landed floating white linen on the big table. 'I don't think you want to go through all that again, do you?'

'I don't mind – '

'Facts must be faced. If you didn't make it, you didn't.'

'Mr Beach said – '

'I'm sure Mr Beach was very kind, as one would expect.'

'Can't I do it again? They let you, near Christmas. Can I ask Daddy?' A thought worse than any exam.

Grandad said: 'I don't see why not, really, if the child wants to have another try.'

'Oh, very well. We'll speak to Henry at the weekend.' Gran placed silver and table-mats. 'Come, Marjory, make yourself useful, bring the cruet and glasses.' And after a pause: 'I'm sure young ladies never needed examinations in my day.'

Marjory went away from them after tea, into the Park with Buller and Boney. She ignored their running and circling, ignored the bending of paths, but took a straight line to the walled rose-garden near the Hall. The dogs leashed, she pushed the gate and walked slowly up one flagged path, down the next, then across and across; she saw only the blooms and buds, breathing their breath. Occasionally, since nobody was there, she halted to look deep into a velvet face. When I have a house, when I have a garden one day, I will grow flowers and flowers and roses and roses, everywhere; I know they will grow for me.

'Your Gran has explained everything to me.'

Her father stood by the drawing-room fire, sharpening a pencil to a needle. He looked at Marjory; his glasses needed cleaning. It was the only thing about him not always immaculate. 'It's a pity about the scholarship exam. I hope you're not too disappointed.'

Gran, sitting in the sewing-chair, said nothing.

'I can take it again, Mr Beach said so, as I only missed the arithmetic by five – '

'So I understand. But I agree with your grandmother, my dear. Why put yourself through all that again, and especially when you've been so unwell. It's not so very important, hm?'

'I want to go to the High School, Daddy.' She didn't know if he knew, but rushed on. 'I want to do things like maths and Latin and everything, I want to be a vet.'

'Hm, yes, I heard about that.' He peered at the pencil. 'Well, don't we all have these grandiose ideas when we're very young, and we don't know what's involved? But your Gran has a very sensible plan for you, and I agree with it completely.'

She did not turn her head to look at Gran.

Her father said, 'It would mean you staying on at Christ Church until you're fourteen – that's the leaving age isn't it? – but you wouldn't mind that I'm sure. You like it there, don't you?'

'Yes it's nice, but – '

'Well then.'

'But I'd *rather* do the exam again and try and go to High School, I'd *rather* – '

'Marjory. Surely we've covered that.'

'Well if I can't be a vet, can I be a nurse? I want to do something sort of medical, and – '

'A nurse!' Gran jerked in her chair. 'Good heavens, Henry. A nurse! Whatever will she think of next? We all know about

149

nurses, no decent girl becomes a *nurse*.' Her mouth was a small thin scratch on her face.

'They were nice, the nurses in hospital – '

'Nice! My dear child,' Gran made a half-smile towards Henry, 'you wouldn't understand what I mean.'

'But they *were* nice, and they worked hard and – '

'Don't argue with your grandmother, Marjory.' Her father, satisfied with the precise point of his pencil lead, put it away in his top pocket. 'You must accept that she knows best and has your welfare at heart. Being a patient in hospital – ' he returned his mother's smile ' – hardly puts you in a position to judge.'

'But –'

'But nothing. We'll hear no more of it, that's final.' Now he took off his glasses and looked closely at the lenses. From his pocket came a clean white hanky. 'I'm surprised, I must say, that you haven't asked about your Gran's excellent idea.'

She said nothing, keeping her face stony, watching the ironed whiteness rubbing round and round the lenses.

Henry sighed at her rudeness. 'There is a very good college in Southwark, and your grandmother has taken a great deal of trouble to find out all about it.' He paused, but the only response was Gran's breathing. 'It is a college for girls, it teaches everything there is to know about domestic science, cookery and housecraft and all that sort of thing. If you do well, you finish up after two years with a fine diploma. It is a very good college with a first-class reputation, and altogether seems to me to be very suitable.'

'*Very*,' Gran said to him.

'There is an entrance examination,' her father went on through newly glinting spectacles, 'which you would take at thirteen and a half – in two years' time, that is, not long at all. No reason at all why you shouldn't pass, plenty of time to brush up on that arithmetic, hm? Wouldn't you say?'

She wouldn't say anything.

'*I* should say,' he continued, 'you are a very lucky girl, having a family that thinks about your future with such care and consideration.'

Gran nodded at the compliment. 'It is a highly thought-of college,' she looked only at Henry, 'and Marjory will be extremely well equipped for her life. The best kind of woman's work.'

'I hope,' Henry still looked at his daughter, 'you are grateful, Marjory.'

There were answers, but none would be acceptable.

'*Well*, Marjory? Surely it would be nice to have a proper diploma in domestic science? Don't you agree that would be quite an achievement? You would be qualified, an expert, when you are a grown person with a home of your own. You could probably even teach the subject if you wished. Come now, don't tell me you don't want to do it.'

She kept her face stiff : 'I don't care what I do.'

EIGHT

*I don't remember a lot about those two years,
Marjory said to a daughter's questions. Funny, isn't
it? I remember being called to Mr Smiley's office
after school one day, and Mr Beach was there too.
They said they'd spoken to my grandmother about
the scholarship – 'but it seems she has made up
her mind'. You could say that again. They said
they were very sorry. Huh, not half as sorry as I
was.*

*Keziah? Oh, she was at the High. I didn't see any-
thing like as much of her but I still went quite often
on Fridays. I used to love that, the candlelight and
the singing, and Kez's mother was awfully kind to
me. Course, I had plenty of other chums at school
but I used to think most girls a bit silly; really I
preferred boys and boys' games. Oh, Teddy – yes,
he was still around though I saw much less of him.
His new school was a long way off, Dulwich or
somewhere. I suppose he had more work to do
there, I don't know, but except for the big Sunday
lunch he was hardly ever at Gran's, and he'd get out
of that if he could. He was at that age when boys
stick together in gangs and girls are only for making
dirty jokes about. We were always great pals
though when he WAS there.*

*Oh yes you're right, 1926 was the General Strike.
Well, to be perfectly honest it didn't affect us
much. We could hardly go short of anything, the
way Gran kept a store-cupboard. Teddy said to
her: 'So THIS is what it's all been for, you must be
a prophetess, Gran!' She didn't know whether it
was a compliment or cheek. Still, the fact is it
didn't touch families like ours, or not directly. I
remember Uncle Ron volunteered to drive a bus –*

lots of people did apart from students and troops.
He drove a lorry to Hyde Park too, it had FOOD
STUFFS, URGENT painted all over the side. They'd
turned Hyde Park into a vast food centre, it was
like a small town. Uncle Ron and Uncle Wilf had
one helluva barney about it all. Uncle Wilf said
he was helping to ruin the workers' cause. The
men went out into the garden that Sunday, all of
them, and there they were, shouting and waving
their arms at each other, and all the women looking
out of the windows wringing their hands, terrified
they'd come to blows. Uncle Ron said that half
the volunteer drivers were union men anyway –
that's what made Wilf blow his top. He began to
rail about Capitalist Propaganda, I thought he'd
burst something. They soon got over it though:
he and Ron never agreed about politics but they
were fond of each other.

Lord no, the women hardly EVER talked politics.
It was basically frowned upon. A bit like sex –
men could talk about it but nice women didn't, and
they certainly weren't allowed to enjoy it. Mind
you, Nora used to provoke them if she could, going
on about when-women-get-the-vote-just-you-wait,
that sort of thing. And I remember once she got an
argument boiling about some women's anti-strike
march – Welsh miners' wives I think it was –
and Auntie Ada and Auntie Molly were positively
squeaking with rage, and Gran was jumping about
like a parched pea, she was so horrified.

Apart from all that hoo-ha I suppose everything
went on as usual. Daddy used to come at weekends, Gran saved up my sins for him, she nagged
me and I cheeked her – or I'd escape to hockey or
to the Park with the dogs. Oh, that brings something back, damn sad it was too. Uncle Ron lost
his girlfriend. Don't know exactly when it happened, only he was looking sort of hang-dog
and there were two Sundays he didn't come with

me to the Park. I must've noticed he wasn't his usual jokey self because I remember asking him if anything was wrong. 'Oh well, Marj,' he said, 'no point in coming if she won't be there, eh?' I think I actually dared to say I'd thought they were going to get married, and he said 'Ah yes, but a girl likes a date to be fixed, doesn't she? Can't blame her, can we?' After then he went all drawn-looking and older than he really was, and he got pains in his stomach.

Now THERE's something I'd forgotten – it was around that time that there was an eclipse of the sun, I'm sure of it. I remember us all being out in the school playground with bits of smoked glass, watching the shadow move across. It was fantastic. The whole world went green – and then it was night-time, with stars and everything. When I told them at home Auntie Ada said, in that prissy way: 'GREEN, Marjory? What nonsense. I don't know how you dream these things up.' And Uncle Ron said, really snappishly: 'For God's sake, Ada, why on earth SHOULDN'T it go green?' It was so unlike him that everyone gawped – I can still see Gran and Grandad, mouths open. Poor Ron. Oh well.

No, I can't remember anything else. Must've been a quick two years, that's all. Or I worked through them without stopping to think, maybe.

NINE

NORA, in a letter to MARJORY, during the early
1950s: Thought I'd see you at Auntie Molly's
funeral, sorry to miss the chance of a chat. Auntie
Ada says it was peritonitis, Uncle Gerry said a
tumour, Auntie June just raised an eyebrow, you
can imagine, and Auntie Flora said she'd been told
TB. Got my own ideas, can't bring myself to put
them on paper somehow. Poor Molly, the way she
messed herself about, what a life. But it's weird,
isn't it, looking back, how nobody saw what was
under their noses? Do you think they just didn't
WANT to, or didn't such things enter their minds?

*

Around the same time, SUSIE, at tea with Marjory:
I suppose you're right, Marj, they didn't tell us
much in those days. But it used to be even worse,
when my mother was a kid. Did I ever tell you
about when she started her Monthlies? She told
me, she was so terrified at the blood she went and
sat in a bath of cold water to make it stop. Like
nosebleed. Gran found her there, crying that she'd
bleed to death. Gran just gave her a packet of
wadding and said: Here, you'll need this every
month, stop being silly, it's part of the cross that
woman has to bear. Mind you, Marj, there are still
some things I could never talk to my boys about,
I must admit. Like Auntie Molly and her Fred, for
instance – I NEVER talk about that. What are
you laughing at?

*

As if the route had been planned specially for Marjory, the
133 bus went from Brixton Hill and stopped in Southwark
opposite the narrow street where the Girls' College stood.
Buildings squeezed against each other, soot-red brick, dusty
windows, trams, buses, cars, vans, pony-carts; busier than

Brixton and Streatham, more smell, more throng, more voices, brighter clothes and lipstick, fish people from Billingsgate, nurses from Guys', Sainsbury vans from the big depot, traders from warehouses, vendors shouting muffins, newspapers, cockles.

Newcomen Street: a tall, dark brick building with arching windows, pointed roofs, once somebody's smart mansion. Taking the examination, young lady? Name? This way, please. Here is your desk, just wait quietly. A big room of light colours, desks with space and air, flowers in a sun-yellow window. Nervous girls waiting, like her, looking at their fingers, at other girls, at the girls already established at the College walking past in the hall, aloof and adult, neat navy blazers and hats with blue and gold ribbon. In spite of everything, it was interesting: an atmosphere of things happening, of knowledge waiting to be uncovered, a challenge.

Papers came, were written, were gathered. English, History, Arithmetic. The second part of the examination, Needlework and Art, came three weeks later, a woman with buck teeth and a Scottish accent explained. Take a piece of material, these lengths of ribbon, make whatever you choose, at home. Take this sketch book: draw and paint the following. Still Life, Landscape, Fabric design, Animal.

'Well?' Uncle Ron said. 'I bet it was easy.'

'Yes,' she told him, 'it was, quite.' She spread silk and ribbon on the table. 'Whatever shall I do with this?'

'Make some frilly knickers,' he said.

Gran said, '*Ron!*' And to Marjory: 'Easy? They told *me* the examination was quite a stiff one.'

'I could do it.'

'Honestly,' Auntie Molly said, 'what a swank.'

Billy rat posed for the animal drawing when she could persuade him from her shoulder. Roses for the fabric design, winding in and out of each other, dark spiky thorns. A landscape from memories of Yarmouth holidays: the fifth try was still hideous, she gave up. The still life took hours, days. An open feather fan, Auntie Ada's, and an apple. Hey, Marj, it's a masterpiece, said Ron. Gracious me, said Gran, you'll give the child a swollen head, and what are you going to do with that needlework, I'd like to know? It took her a whole week, hemming and seaming, pleating the ribbon round and round from edges to centre, stitching so that no thread showed. Look, it's a nightdress-case. I *say*, Marj, Auntie Flora inspected it; May I have it, after the exam?

Gran in her black bonnet beside her on the 133 bus, English lavender and mothball. An adult must accompany the examinee to the second part, an Interview.

Four men, one lady at a long table: they were Directors, nobody said their names; they discovered only afterwards that the lady was Lady Muriel Blythe, and Gran told Marjory off for sitting badly.

So you are Marjory Bell? Good morning, Marjory. Have you brought your drawings? The sketch book was passed along the table, each Director looked at each page, the man in the middle asked for it back and turned again to the feather fan and apple. Hm, he said, would you mind if I cut this out and kept it? Gran spoke from by the wall: May I ask why? Simply because I like it, said the man, no other reason. Only if Marjory doesn't mind, of course, he smiled. *I* don't mind, she said. Thank you very much, he replied. The lady fingered the nightdress-case, murmured to the men, pointing. She too smiled at Marjory and hand it back carefully, first rearranging the tissue paper.

Well *that*'s over, said Gran, though I don't know why you talked so much about animals when they asked about your interests, I'm sure. Marjory didn't care; the man had kept her painting. She told Uncle Ron: You know that painting you liked, one of the Directors wanted to keep it. *There!* said Ron. Extraordinary, said Gran.

*

Standing at the back of Christ Church school hall in morning assembly, now she was a senior girl though she felt just as small. The last term. If she didn't get the College exam. she'd go to Mr Stopps or some other vet and ask to be an assistant, and not tell Gran until afterwards. The hall had high windows, a good smell of wood and polish and paint and friends. I like this, I don't want to leave. Marj. Hey, Marj. Elbows were nudging, a finger jabbed her back. Mr Smiley's talking to you.

'Marjory Bell?' Mr Smiley said from the platform across all the turning heads. 'Will you come up here, please?'

There was further to walk as a senior, further to be watched, to wonder what was wrong, being called up in front of the school. Mr Smiley looked bland as she came up the steps. Mr Beach was looking down, rocking on his heels, pulling at a loose button on his jacket. Mrs MacTavish grinned upwards, even Miss Loyal nodded and smiled. Mrs Popham's curls quivered like suppressed giggles.

The Headmaster's hand on her shoulder, she was turned to face the school. 'Marjory Bell,' he said above her left ear, 'is the only girl in this school to have won a Scholarship to the Girls' College in Southwark.' Something pierced her below the ribs, her face was hot. 'She has not only passed an extremely difficult examination, but has done so with quite outstanding marks. We are all very proud of her, and I'm sure everyone here agrees.' Awful, all the clapping and cheers, good old Marj, where did you look but at the floorboards, a wide crack, a knothole with dust round it. 'Marjory, we all congratulate you.' Astonishing, Mr Smiley shaking her hand, Mr Beach too. 'Your name will be put on the Honours Board at the end of this Hall.' In gold letters, Marjory G. Bell, aged 14, a Scholarship to Southwark, 1929.

'They told you three *weeks* ago?' Gran held a letter from the College, the Principal Miss Robins was inviting Marjory to come and meet her and the Staff, an informal gathering to introduce new girls to the school, help them feel at home before they start. 'Three weeks! Why ever didn't you *say*?'

Marjory shrugged, pulling off her hockey boots in the scullery.

'You got it then, eh Marj?' Uncle Ron said. 'It was that painting, you bet.'

'I passed in everything.'

'Hark at show-off,' said Auntie Ada.

'Who told you?' Gran asked.

'Mr Smiley.'

'Fancy not saying,' Molly said. 'Typical.'

'How many passed?' Ron asked.

'Just me.'

'Heavens,' said Grandad. 'Just you, eh? How about that!' He found two half-crowns. 'Here, I should think you'll find a use for these.'

Auntie Molly said: 'With her father's brains, she should be ashamed if she didn't pass, that's what I think.'

Her father said at the weekend: 'There, see, Marjory? I knew you'd brush up that arithmetic, given time.'

He took her out on trams and buses, showed her hidden streets of London's City, the astounding ceilings of St Paul's, the treasures of the Tower. They watched the heavy great river from the bridge, he told her about ships and barges. Then they found a place for tea and cream cakes bulging with sweetness. He looked at her, his lower lip jutted, he smiled as if a little uncertain: Well now, Marjory, don't tell me you're not pleased you stayed on at school now, eh? She didn't know what to do but smile back and shrug lightly. She was only aware, and that vaguely, that she could not put words round the things that mattered most profoundly, and even if she could, they could never be spoken aloud. Not to him, not to any of them: perhaps to nobody, ever.

Auntie Ada beside her on the 133 bus: Gran had a chill, Ada would go with Marjory to see Miss Robins and Staff. It was raining, Ada was damp wool and Eau-de-Cologne, peach powder round her nostrils. Marjory wrote her name in the window-steam. Don't *do* that, Marjory, it's common, can't you ever behave like a lady? Marjory scratched minutely on the pane where Ada couldn't see: Silly Cat.

The bus rumbled on, stopped, picked up and spilled dripping, steaming people; through Brixton, Kennington, into the Borough. Nearly there, to face the teachers and other new girls. I've had it now, this is it, I'm in the College, women's work, that's that.

Miss Robins was unexpected, whereas she might have been like Gran, or domineering and aproned. She was neither tall nor short: brown hair tied back, grey stripes at the sides, broad long-fingered hands. A voice from the north of England, not loud but heard everywhere in the wide room. Welcome girls, and meet your teachers. Her smile followed her voice into all corners: Marjory thought of Keziah's mother though there was no clear likeness. This is my Deputy, Miss Brooks, who will teach you needlework. It was the buck-toothed Scottish lady from exam day. And Miss Northwell; she will teach you housewifery – that's everything from making black-lead to painting your own drawing-room. This is Mrs Westland, laundry and other housekeeping from wines and crystal to the arts of the hostess. Another Scot, from the way she said Good day girls; fat round the middle, pregnant sure as anything. This is Miss Peace, cookery, and when you can make a soufflé like hers you'll be a fine cook; Miss Peace smiled and blushed, young and dark and eastern-looking. Miss Holliday will teach you English, Mathematics, History – also hockey and cricket. Cricket! The room murmured and giggled. Miss Holliday smiled, head on one side, holding one little finger at the top and waggling it back and forth as if she would break it off. More names, smiles, subjects: Hygiene, Infant Care, Geography, Literature, Drawing, Household Accounts . . . And I, Miss Robins said, will teach Biology and the Humanities. (What are *they*? Ada whispered) But let me tell you something of the College background. Miss Robins spoke of a fine woman who left money in her Will to found the college, her idea being to clothe and educate poor children. Things are different now, but traditionally we still give clothing annually to the poor of Southwark. Last year for instance we gave to twenty poor women: one dress, one night-dress, one petticoat, six yards of calico, one pair of boots. Each gift cost three pounds and seven shillings, and I'm sure you'll all agree such an idea is worth continuing and be glad to know you'll all be part of the scheme.

Enough of all that, she said now, we'll have a break and meet each other. Coffee and biscuits over here, please do introduce yourselves.

Marjory looked into her cup and could not move. Ada sipped and sniffed. Then a beige-haired girl came boldly and smiled: Hello, I'm Ivy Clarkson, my father's a doctor, who are you? After that, several others: I'm Joan Stanfield, I think I must live near you, I saw you on the bus. I'm Jenny. I'm Mavis. I'm Dorothy. I'm Eva. I'm Minnie, I live near the docks, hope you're not as posh as some of this lot.

Miss Robins was on the platform again: Before we have to go, just a few words about our attitudes here and what will be expected of you. Don't look nervous, nothing alarming: her smile reached everyone. In general we believe that women are strong creatures, built for work! What harder work than bearing and rearing children, and running a home? We don't subscribe to that old myth that femininity and weakness are the same thing, far from it. Auntie Ada touched frills, breathed. Women live longer, must have a lot of stamina for their important role. Girls coming here must be prepared to work, to set out to achieve something and achieve it. No point in beginning without a belief in finishing. Old attitudes about women, they're outworn: Victorian. Vapours, fainting – downright nonsense. What people call 'poorly' times: we don't believe in such old-fashioned indulgences here. Of course if you are ill that's another matter, but natural things must be taken naturally; we don't treat girls differently because of a normal monthly function of the body. Auntie Ada gasping, some blushes, a snigger. Marjory felt something lift in her brain, or a door opening, a road clear, heaviness falling away, whispers vanishing. Something new. Looking forward, Miss Robins was saying, to seeing you all again in September, goodbye. Oh! Auntie Ada cried several times on the way to the bus-stop, the things she *said*.

The rain had left gleaming streets and roofs. Marjory looked out of the window, holding the lightness in her, not examining it for fear of it disappearing, not speaking to Auntie Ada until she said at Leander Road: Well, Marjory, aren't you going to *thank* me for taking you? At tea Ada was bulge-eyed, whispering to Gran and Molly: That Miss Robins, she talked about *Poorly* Times, in front of *every*body! Drawn-in breath: they stared at Marjory, who was guilty. She said: I *liked* her, she was *sens*ible; and she looked away from their faces. She left the table soon, before they could spoil everything.

*

The Headmaster and Staff of
Christ Church School
request the pleasure of the company of
MARJORY BELL
at a Dance
for School-Leavers and
Old Girls and Old Boys
in the School Hall on the Evening
of the Last Day of Term.
6.00 – 10.00
Refreshments

'They've got just the chiffon I want,' Marjory told Auntie Flora. 'Salmon pink, *bright*. And feathers – could I have two rows of feathers?'

'You're getting a bit of a figure at last,' Flora flicked the tape-measure. 'Don't you think, Molly?'

'High-stomached,' Auntie Molly said. 'Ought to have her fitted with a corset.'

'A corset! Auntie Molly, nobody wears corsets any more.'

'*Oh* yes they do, my girl, none of this modern flighty stuff. Every lady has a corset, and don't you forget it.'

'I'm not a lady.'

'You can say that again,' Teddy said behind a book in the armchair.

'You shut up!' she shouted at him for being hidden, for not having to be a lady, for having another life.

Come on, Auntie Molly said on Saturday, we've got an appointment. What? Where? Wait and see, Molly told her, and actually called a taxi. Here we are: she was being marched into FINLEYS, thin gold lettering on black. Fine Corsets, discreetly underneath. Oh, Auntie Molly, I don't need – I don't *want* – Shhh, Molly said, a high stomach is a high stomach, and the sooner corrected the better.

The embarrassment, standing behind purple curtains with a grey-haired lady who measured and stared. There, she said to Molly who sat on a gilded chair and watched, isn't that smart? Marjory gaped at herself, pinched at the centre, bulging above and below: I can't breathe, she said. The corset lady tittered, Auntie Molly said: You'll get used to it. Start now for comfort later.

I can't walk properly, she said in the street. I can't even sit properly she said in the bus. Honestly, Auntie Molly, I can't *breathe*. Oh *do* be quiet, Marjory, Molly stamped irritably along Leander Road, I never heard such a fuss, never knew such an ungrateful girl. And in a week or two she said to Marjory: See, you soon got used to it, didn't you? Oh yes, Marjory said easily. The corset lay at the back of her underwear drawer, hidden by school stockings. She put it on each morning, in case Auntie Molly should look in, and ran upstairs to undress and dress again before school, tearing the corset off and rushing out free.

'Hey, Marj, you've grown up,' Uncle Ron said.

She stood for inspection, salmon pink chiffon swinging from her shoulders, two rows of feathers at the hem, satin shoes with fine straps, Auntie Flora had them dyed to match.

'Oh,' she said. 'Have I?' She did not feel that she had, although from the mirror it seemed so. She had a sudden sense of dread, and helplessness.

'Quite the girl about town.'

'I certainly hope not,' said Gran.

'You're wearing *it*, I hope,' Molly murmured.

'And don't scuff those nice shoes,' Flora told her. 'Dance like a lady.'

'*If* you can,' added Ada.

'You'll be the Belle of the Ball,' Grandad said.

'Goodness,' Gran smiled at him, 'let's not give the child exalted ideas.'

'Nervous?' Uncle Ron asked.

'No I am *not*,' she said, and he laughed.

'As if you'd admit it. I'll come and collect you at ten.'

Keziah said: 'Stone the crows, Marj, you look absolutely te*rrif*.'

'Who me? Don't be daft.' Keziah too looked older, smart, her black hair tied back, her creamy dress of pleats. 'You look quite grown-up, Kez.'

'Hey *look* – ' Keziah shook her arm, ' – it's old Joe Bale.'

He was coming into the hall with another boy, talking but looking round. Marjory hadn't seen him for months, though occasional faithful notes sometimes came through Keziah on Fridays.

'Oh *Kez*, just look at him.'

'What?'

'That hat. He's wearing a *trilby*. Honestly.'

He asked her to dance, thank heavens he left the trilby in the cloakroom. 'Whatever were you wearing that hat for?' she demanded, and laughed.

He might have said: For fun, and laughed too. But he was stiff, telling her: 'That is my new trilby, and they are extremely fashionable, in case you didn't know.' She trod on his foot and fell out of love.

'Don't be mean about him, Marj,' Keziah said while they ate sandwiches and trifle in the interval. 'His Dad got arrested, didn't you know?'

'What?' Marjory said through a full mouth.

'He was doing something . . . you know . . . *dirty* in the Park. Mum told me. Don't say anything though.'

Marjory stared: 'What d'you mean? Dirty?'

Keziah was slightly pink: 'You know, Marj. *Show*ing things.'

Marjory looked across at Joe, and was sorry. But that was all. He was grown, different, distant.

Then Mr Smiley was speaking, calling for attention from the platform, there was no more chance to question Keziah. He made his speech about the School and his pride in the pupils, he hoped all leavers would come back and visit, everyone wanted to know how they got on. It was a pleasure to see so many old girls and boys here. He pointed at the Honours Board, the new names: he wished them luck. Ooh, Keziah said, I didn't see – doesn't it look *posh*, clever old Marjory.

The music was starting again. Mr Smiley stopped beside them on his way through the hall. She wasn't a pupil any more; the tone he used, she could be a parent or a visitor. You've done extremely well, leaving with honour. We'll always be glad to see you.

'May I see you home?' Joe asked during the Barn Dance.

'I'm afraid my uncle's meeting me,' she said. When the tune stopped she ran into the cloakroom.

'Whatever is the matter?' Keziah found her after ten minutes, and gave her a dry hanky. 'Did somebody say something?'

There seemed a lot of crying to catch up on. 'Oh Kez, it's *leav*ing, I hate it, I don't want to leave, everything's changing, everybody's gone or it's different, I can't be a vet, they bought me a corset, Joe's got a trilby, Teddy'll go away to college, you – '

'Oh Marj. We're growing up, that's all.' Keziah was all cool logic. 'You can't stop it, you just have to go straight on. Look at me, *I* don't want to leave our house, but we're moving off to Dulwich and – '

164

'You're moving! So there won't even be any Sabbaths, or hardly any – '

'Come on, Marj. Things aren't so bad. They change, but you just have to keep on – '

'That's the *point*, you *have* to!' But the sobbing was running down, eased by Keziah's grin.

'Don't you give in, Marj. You're leaving here with *honour*, crumbs, you heard Mr Smiley – you can't do any better than that. Anyway, I thought you said the Girls' College looked nice after all.'

'It is. Miss Robins is. Oh well, Kez.' She blew her nose and sniffed and combed her hair. 'I'll survive I dare say. It's just leaving. I liked it here.'

'Have a nice time?' Uncle Ron held out his arm for her to take; previously she would have held his hand.

'Yes, thanks.'

'Leaving somewhere's always hard,' he said. 'Still, new starts are exciting. D'you know what you're going to do with your life now?'

She kicked the pavement, then remembered the satin shoes. 'I,' she said, 'am going to be somebody who can really cook. I'll be a good cook, a *fine* cook.'

'Sounds all right to me,' he laughed. Then: 'Long way from being a vet though, eh?' She shrugged. 'You don't mind too much now?'

She made her voice spiky and direct: 'No point in thinking about it, is there?'

Ron put his hand on the back of her neck and said: 'Ah, you're a fighter, Marj.'

She said: 'I always did like cooking anyway.' Miss Robins had told them, no point in beginning without a belief in finishing.

*

She did not pause to consider it or feel surprise, but was by degrees aware: she was enjoying the College. The entire pattern of her days, the shape of her weeks, broke and changed. Away from the house early, home later in the afternoon, more homework in the evening; only at weekends did she see much of the family. Then she told her father and anyone who asked about what she did at the College. Her father listened, but it wasn't a man's subject: his eyes might stray to his newspaper and Gran said, Don't bore your father, Marjory – if you're so clever at all these things come and stir this and stop chattering or it'll burn. Auntie Flora asked about the needlework, Auntie Hennie liked to hear about recipes, Nora said, Golly, must be a bit of a bore without any boys around, Teddy said How's the housemaid's knee?

Keziah and her family had gone from their warm house: the candles, the hymns faded away. But Kez was right, you had to go on, can't stop things changing. And the change was in herself too, because of the College. She said in a letter to Keziah: The teachers here are somehow friendlier – no, I mean informal. It's as if we all muck in together, even though they're teaching us they're more like one of us, and it makes everything much more fun and interesting.

She discovered interest where she had suspected none. Learning how to care for wine, to know which was best for different foods, which drink for which crystal. Ten ways to fold a white linen napkin, to place the silver for a banquet of seven courses or more, to make black-lead or scouring powder, and she could teach Gran a thing or two or even three about making soap. A nurse came from Guy's Hospital holding a fat doll: One of these days you'll need to know how to handle a baby, yours or somebody else's, so watch. Miss Peace and her oriental smile: The hallmark of the good cook is a smooth shining sauce. For her Marjory made such sauces. For Mrs Westland she ironed a perfect polish on a starched shirt-collar, arranged flowers for different tables, set a breakfast tray for an honoured guest. School subjects for Miss Holliday, the finger-waggler to be imitated without mercy: she was too busy teaching well to notice, and, novel experience, introducing them to Debating. Marjory discovered she could stand up in front of others and make a case and argue it; she wished Keziah were there to see.

Miss Robins' lessons everyone looked forward to. The subject was not the important thing; it had to do with the atmosphere she carried with her, of frankness and sense, and interest in each of the girls. In an early Biology lesson, teaching of pistils and stamens, bees and pollen, seeds growing in ovaries which burst, she ended: Well I think I saw a grin here and there, I'm sure it won't have escaped several of you, the relationship between the bees and flowers and other forms of reproduction, humans included. Some wriggled that their smirks had been seen, others openly smiled. Some, like Marjory, nonchalantly covered surprise and ignorance. Miss Robins said: Well, all I'll add is, if any of you want to know *any*thing, any time, you only have to ask. You won't get any hedging or embarrassment from me. Personally I believe everyone should know just about everything. She smiled, nodded and went. The feeling of an opening door again, something to trust.

Marjory and Joan Stanfield looked out for each other every day on the bus. Joan, tall and lean with long red-gold hair, lived at the Brixton end of Effra Road, one bus stop away. Marjory kept her a seat in the mornings if she could, and watched for the navy hat and swinging hair in the queue. Joan's smile was a wide crescent moon, her long arms were made to embrace everyone. I'm going to be a kids' nurse, she said, baby-care and all that. Too many unhappy children in the world, that's what I say. They travelled home together almost always, and one day Joan said before she leapt from the bus: Why don't you come home and have tea sometime? What about tomorrow? Marjory asked Gran. Very well, she said, as long as you are no later than seven o'clock.

Joan dragged her into the house and yelled: Mum, hey Mum, where are you? We're here! Someone came who might be her sister, a woman with Joan's smile and hair almost the same colour. This is Marjory, Joan said, she lives in Leander Road, fancy that, and she's going to be an excellent cook, so I've heard the rumours. And this is my mother, her name's Barbara. I call her by it when she needs keeping in order. Barbara shook Marjory's hand and said: Welcome, Marjory, don't mind my dotty daughter, come and sit down. It was a room of flowers and bright pictures, warm airiness. Joan and her mother joked and laughed through the meal: Marjory watched and grinned. You're a bit struck dumb, Joan told her. You should hear her at College, Mum, never stops. Did I tell you about Marj debating? Honest, sometimes we have to yell at her to shut up. Never believe it now, would you?

I suppose I was a bit quiet, Marjory said afterwards on the

way to the bus stop. You and your mum – I was just
bowled over really. Joan said: How d'you mean? Don't tell
me we shocked you or something. Marjory said: I mean, I
never saw anybody with their mother like that. You're like
sisters, like *friends*. And she's young, somehow. The way you
can even call her Barbara. Joan smiled: I know, she's a bit
specially really, my mum. What's your father like? Marjory
asked. He's pretty nice too, actually. But I don't call *him* by
his first name, not unless I want to tease him. He says he
doesn't believe in attacks on male authority – what a
scream! What about your parents then, Marj? Oh, Marjory
said, my dad's strict really. I couldn't *talk* to him like you do
with your mum. When I was little I was scared stiff of him;
still am a bit if I'm honest. I don't see him much, only at
weekends – I live with my gran and grandad you see. I
haven't got a mother. Joan was stricken: Oh, rotten luck.
Marjory fished for change in her pocket, the bus was in sight.
She said: My mother's dead, as a matter of fact. Oh Marj!
Joan had tears in her eyes, and then through them surprise,
for Marjory had none. Oh that *is* rotten luck. Was it ages ago?
I was a baby, very small anyway. She saw Joan's question
forming and said: I don't know how she died. Joan was immediately indignant: What! Didn't anybody ever *tell* you?
And Marjory felt ashamed of them at home. She shrugged and
jerked her head. Joan said: Golly, Marj. They tell me
absolutely *every*thing.

On Sunday Marjory waited until Nora was alone in the kitchen. 'Do *you* know about my mother?'

A rare thing, Nora blushed deeply. 'What do you mean,
Marjory?'

'What I say. Nobody has ever told me anything at all about
her, d'you realise that? All I know is, she's dead. And Gran
says You'll Go The Way of Your Mother, like that, so I suppose she did something *she* didn't like. I couldn't ever ask
Daddy, and if ever they were talking about her it'd go quiet
when I came into the room. Or they'd say That Woman, or
sort of mouth "Greta" silently, or say "G" and put on those
funny faces. I just knew I couldn't ask anyone.'

Nora said: 'Oh.' And then: 'Well, don't ask *me*, Marj,'
flippantly, but she was uncomfortable and looked at once re-

lieved that Susie ran in, breathless. Susie, eighteen and wearing lipstick, though a delicate shade.

'Nora!' Susie panted, leaning on the table; she might have been near tears. 'Oh *Nora* – that Uncle Bertie, *hon*estly. Whatever can I do?'

Nora laughed. 'What?'

'What *are* you going on about?' Marjory said.

'Oh – *you* know.' Susie was red, biting her lip. 'And with Auntie Flora in the room too. Honestly, I can't stand *near* him.'

'Always said he was a dirty old man.' Nora squinted into the mirror by the door, smoothing an eyebrow.

'Honestly, Nora, his hand was right . . . *there* . . .' She made horrified gestures '. . . he actually *touched* me.'

'Well I hope you gave him a damn good slap, Susie, that's all.'

Marjory looked at them, her irritation broke. 'Just what are you two talking about?' she demanded.

'For goodness' sake, Marj, *you* know.'

'No I don't! I just don't, so why doesn't anybody damn well tell me?'

They were both staring and saying Marj! She ran out, slamming everything.

*

At College the girls said nothing, watching Mrs Westland's girth grow larger weekly, until the day Minnie Fisher knocked into her with an ironing board and Mrs Westland's Highland voice said: 'Watch, lass! Watch my bump!'

Everybody stopped, looked, and she laughed. 'Well, you wouldn't be telling me you hadn't noticed?'

Minnie got right to the point: 'We *thought* you was expecting. When's it due?'

'January.'

'You'll have to leave!' a girl said, and everyone made regretful noises.

'Afraid so. I'll work until December, I dare say.'

Minnie said: 'Can I feel it kick?' Some girls whispered: Oh, *Minnie*!

Mrs Westland said: 'If you want to.' Minnie laid a hand on the mound, and grinned.

'Bless me. Wouldn't care for a kick in the backside from that one!' Then clapped a hand over her mouth: 'Sorry miss.'

Mrs Westland was laughing. 'That's all right, Minnie, I often agree.'

To think of it, a baby inside, kicking. How did it lie there? What did it look like? How could it *be*, or breathe? The strangeness, right inside you like that, waiting and growing.

Ivy, the doctor's daughter, spoke to Marjory while they folded sheets: 'She's common, that Minnie Fisher.'

'Is she? What do you mean?'

'You know. The things she says, and the *accent*, dreadful. Of course, she's East End. Fancy saying that to Mrs Westland – *backside!*'

'That was quite polite, for Minnie. Usually she'd say arse.'

'Marjory!'

Minnie came top for their first cookery test, Marjory second.

'Cor, fancy me beating that lot,' Minnie jabbed her with an elbow. 'Put their posh noses out, eh?' She showed a wide row of crooked white teeth; her eyes were as black as Keziah's. 'Some of 'em think they're Lord Gawd Almighty, y'know what I mean, just because they live on posh streets in big houses and that, don't they?'

'Well, Joan doesn't. I don't either. *I* don't think I'm Lord God Almighty, stone the crows.'

'Didn't mean you, did I?'

Without further preliminaries they were friends. Minnie told her she had two sisters, worked at the jam factory down Tooley Street in the daytime. What do you mean, daytime? asked Marjory. Don't most people work in the daytime? Nah, come on, Marj, they do another job at night, don't they? Minnie winked. Christ, not that *I* would, thanks very much. She lifted her skirt, showing knee and thigh. *You* know. Blimey, catch *me*.

Miss Robins said in her Humanities class: 'Today I'm going to tell you about one of the scourges of society.' Hopefully they waited, and she wrote on the blackboard: Venereal Disease. And said: 'It's something that people pretend doesn't exist, or they talk about in whispers. I may as well tell you that I consider that unintelligent and unenlightened. The more that is known, the more likely it is that such evils can be avoided.'

Marjory glanced at Joan who smiled and rolled her eyes luridly: she knew it all. Then at Minnie, whose stare at the blackboard seemed fixed. Miss Robins was speaking again; she was brief, graphic, horrifying. At the end she said: 'Now, you know what I've said before. If anyone's puzzled, they can ask me *anything*. Right?' Marjory watched her go out of the room.

At lunchtime she asked Minnie lightly: 'Did you get all that, what Miss Robins said?'

Minnie didn't smile: 'Yeah.' After a while she said: 'Come on home and have tea with us, eh Marj? I'd like you to meet me mum.'

She asked Gran, but didn't say East End or docker's daughter. A girl called Minnie Fisher, lives with her parents somewhere near London Bridge. I can get a bus easily. I hope she's respectable, Marjory. Well, Gran, she came top in cookery.

Minnie took her between tall buildings black with London soot, past rattling iron stairs. Smells of urine and beer, tom-cats, dustbins, cabbage, onions. Up here, mind where you tread, Marj. Steep steps, litter, dogs' mess. Bilge, ain't it a dump?

She opened a juddering door, peeled paint and net curtains, and shouted: 'Watcher, Ma!' They walked through a small dark hall, wallpaper with brown flowers, brown paint, lino on the floor shining and smelling of polish. Minnie pushed an-other door; they were in a room which was everything, kitchen, dining, living, full of things, dim, muddled but clean. A big smile from a fat woman who held a baby to a gleam-ing white breast. Marjory looked up, down, not knowing where, but Minnie's mother said: 'So you're Marj'ry. Good-looker, even if you are skinny as a shrimp, eh, Min? Come on in, love, make yerself at home. Sit down, just shove them nappies on the side. That's it, nice comfy chair that one. Jenny an' Jinny'll be in soon, we'll have a spot of tea. 'Ere, yer little blighter, don't bite me tit orf!' She yanked the baby from her breast, it belched over her shoulder. 'Takes after 'is Dad, I tell yer.' Marjory laughed, Mrs Fisher cackled approval, told Minnie to put on the kettle. Soon she tucked the baby into a basket, buttoned her jumper, and asked Marjory to hand her plates and pans while she expertly prepared sausages, eggs, chips and peas at the gas-stove.

Jenny and Jinny came in sighing from the jam factory. 'Me feet, bugger me. Me back. Talk about fair wore out.'

Jenny was tall and so blonde she was almost white-haired. 'Don't let 'er kid you it's real,' said her mother. 'It's p'roxide, still it suits 'er, don't it?'

Jinny (Virginia, don't make me laugh, said Minnie) was dark with wide blue eyes, innocent and pretty. Both girls had long elegant legs, bright lips and nails, slender waists.

'I'm seventeen,' Jenny said, 'and by the time I'm twenty-one I'm gunna be rich, flat in Mayfair, just you wait and see.'

'Nah,' said Jinny, who was sixteen, 'it's a nice rich bloke I'm after. Who wants a flat in Mayfair all on yer tod?'

'Me, I do. That's who. All on me own, silk sheets, no blokes to muck me about. Smashin'.'

After the sausages they had thick crusty bread with lavish butter and four kinds of jam, cheap from the factory for the workers. Cake too: iced and fruit. Solid white cups of strong tea. They all talked at once, mouths full, and drank their tea while still chewing. Tell us what you did at College today then, Min. She's the brains of the family, Marj, just in case you hadn't noticed. Oh well, just our luck. Come on, better get ourselves changed into glad rags. Jenny and Jinny went into another room.

Marjory helped Minnie clear the table, offered a hand with the washing-up. 'There's a good girl, Marj, thanks ever so,' Mrs Fisher said. 'You help dry, that's the way. This towel, or this. They've done their stint in the bathroom. Their turn for the dishes now, then they can go in the wash-tub. Oh, we've got it all organised 'ere, 'aven't we?'

Marjory dried dishes with the grey towel of nameless odours, seeing Miss Robins, hearing phrases about mystifying diseases, remembering Minnie downcast after the lesson, Jenny and Jinny, blokes mucking about, a towel in her hand that had done its stint in the bathroom. She liked Minnie, liked her house and family, their happiness and frankness, the warm jumble. But she thought: I can't eat here ever again.

Jenny and Jinny came through the room on higher heels,

enough perfume around them to give a headache, hair ornate, vivid greasy lips. We're orf then, see yer later. Do yer 'omework, Min, there's a good girl. All right for you, you're smart. Still we'll all go up in the world one way or another, eh?

'Me dad don't know,' Minnie said. 'He thinks they work at the flicks, usherettes.' She was gloomy in the dusk, picking her way back down the iron steps. 'Thing is, Marj, we all have to get *out*, see.'

'Well you will, won't you, Min? You'll get a good job. You can't go wrong.'

'Har, go wrong, that's a good one, Marj. Yeah, but what about Jenny an' Jinny? All that stuff about being rich, Christ Awmighty. What a hope. And yer see, Marj, I should *tell* them, shouldn't I?'

'Tell them what?'

'What Miss Robins said. You know, VD and all that. Honest, they're so dotty those two, I bet they don't even know there's such a thing.'

Marjory said: 'Oh.' And there again was the confusion, and not knowing. Ovaries and seeds, Uncle Bertie touching Susie in a rude place, Jenny and Jinny and blokes. Miss Robins said, Ask. Marjory said as she got on the bus: 'Well, Min, you know what Miss Robins says. If you're going to do something, get on and do it. You'd better tell them, that's all.'

'Yeah,' Minnie said, desolate.

At the end of lessons next day Marjory said to Joan: 'Go ahead, don't wait. I've got something to do.' Joan asked no questions, waved and went.

Marjory walked round the front of the college. North House: where Miss Robins lived. Across the path, a patch of grass, the door. She breathed in, ran up the steps and into the square dark hall. Miss Robins' door had a gentle gleam of brass handle and knocker.

'Come in! Oh, Marjory, hello. What can I do for you?'

She sat in an armchair by the window, darning a lisle stocking. A table, lace-edged cloth, a pot of tea and some biscuits. A low lamp on the windowsill picked up the orange of the curtains and put a soft sheen on her face, and on the milk in the jug.

'Miss Robins, please, I wanted to ask you something.'

173

'You had that look about you. Sit yourself down. You might as well have some tea with me, it's just made.' She pointed at the other chair, reached for another cup from a trolley, and poured tea. 'Have a biscuit. Now – ask away.'

'Miss Robins. You said to ask if we were puzzled or if there was something we didn't know. Well the thing is I don't know *any*thing, they never told me, everyone else seems to know. I don't know about those diseases or how they happen, and I only *half* know about babies, what my cousin told me about men and women but it was hard to understand, and I *can't* ask them at home.'

'Don't let your tea get cold,' Miss Robins said. 'Well, Marjory, let me say two things first. I'm very glad you've come, for one. And for another, if it's any comfort, there was a time when I knew even less than you do. And I agree, it's time you knew. So, better start right at the beginning, yes?'

'Yes, please.' And she could sit relaxed in her chair looking at Miss Robins; her straightforward face, nothing hidden, nothing hesitant.

'We'll start with what people look like. The differences between girls and boys, men and women. You know what you look like, don't you?' She was pulling a thick book from the shelf.

'Yes. And I partly know about boys I suppose, because of Teddy – he's my cousin. We grew up together really.'

'Come and look at this.' They were into discussion, looking at drawings and diagrams, at ease. It was interesting in the way of a good lesson, it was a chat, sometimes funny, often surprising. She thought of Joan and her mother, Keziah and her mother : this feeling would be nothing new to them, sitting full of comfort, drinking tea, hearing honest words, free, clean.

Near the end of term, at teatime, she asked Gran if she could take a shilling out of her savings book. 'Mrs Westland's leaving, and we're clubbing together to get her a present – something, don't know what yet.'

'Leaving? She's going to another college?'

'Oh no. She's leaving to have a baby. D'you think a shawl would be a nice idea?'

Gran, Auntie Molly, Auntie Ada : all three were gazing at

her. Grandad looked at his plate. Uncle Ron looked at Gran, but was the first to end the silence. He said: 'Yes, I should think it would be a very nice idea.'

They hung back in the kitchen, letting her go ahead to the drawing-room. She waited, writing up some housewifery notes. Any moment one of them would come and start asking questions.

She was surprised: it was Grandad. He coughed and said: 'Hello there, Marj.' He sat with his pipe, then stood. It took a while; she went on writing. But at last he managed: 'About that lady at College, Marjory, the one you're buying a present for. You said she was ... erhum ... having a baby? Well. Tell me now. How did *you* know about something like that?' By the fireplace, he was looking over her head as if something might be happening outside the window, in the dark.

'She told us. Anyway, we could *see* she was expecting. *She* didn't mind. She said to Minnie, when Minnie barged into her with the ironing board. She said, Watch my bump!'

Grandad stared straight at her, she looked up at him. She grinned, he grinned, they both laughed. Then she was standing up rocking with laughing, they hung on to each other laughing, trying to keep it quiet so the others wouldn't hear. We must look crazy, she thought, and it made her laugh more, him about three times my size, both of us staggering about here crying with mirth, nobody supposed to know. Eventually he said, mopping his eyes: 'Oh my. Oh well. I'd better go and report.' He went back along the hall, controlling his snuffles.

They all sauntered into the room while she sat at the small table, still doing homework. Grandad winked when she looked up, the others said nothing to her until bedtime. Gran and Grandad went up early: 'I'm rather tired,' said Gran loudly, and didn't add that Marjory must finish soon. Ada drifted casually away, Uncle Ron soon after. Then it dawned: just Auntie Molly left, looking at a magazine. The volunteer, waiting.

Marjory stacked her books and whistled. She pushed them into their case. Molly flipped her magazine and shifted her chair and said: 'Well, Marjory,' and stopped. Marjory said nothing. 'You're um ... well, you're nearly fifteen now, of course.'

'Next month.'

'We – I've been thinking. It's time you were told some of the facts.'

'What facts?'

'The sort of facts you need to know, a *girl* needs to know, so she doesn't do anything . . . wrong. Facts of *life*, I mean.' Astoundingly she went on: 'It's easy enough to understand from, well, birds and bees and things like that – biology I mean. And then . . . well, *people*.' Molly, twisting her fingers, did not look at Marjory.

Marjory could stand no more. 'Oh for goodness' sake, Auntie Molly, I know all *that*. *All* of it. Men and women mating, and sperm and ovaries and *every*thing.'

It was wonderful to see Molly's face, and she almost lost her voice. 'How?'

'Miss Robins told me. She was giving us a talk on VD – that's venereal disease.' Molly was dark red. 'And she said that if anyone wanted to know anything then they should ask. So I did, and she told me all of it. What men and women look like, and what they do to make a baby, and ovulation and how babies develop inside the womb, and how there are so many sperm you could get *millions* on to a pin-head, and – '

'All right, all *right*.' Molly, if possible, was redder. She stood up and went to the door. 'It's time for bed, Marjory, so you'd better get a move on.' Then suddenly she was in a temper. 'And there's no need to sound so *cocky*, my girl. I'd like to know who you jolly well think you *are*.' But without waiting to hear, she went.

Marjory thought: Pooh to you, Auntie Molly; and laughed. Aloud she said: 'I'm *me*, that's who I jolly well am.'

TEN

*A day in 1934. The Morgue, Leander Road. June is
visiting Gran (now in her seventies and seated) and
the spinster daughters, Ada and Molly. The latest
scandal concerns Marjory.*

ADA: But the man's *married*, it's shameful.

JUNE: Unhappily married. But it seems he's in
love with Marj.

ADA: We might've known you'd say something
like that.

JUNE: I always did say, one of these days someone'll come along with some love to give her and
bang!

MOLLY: Really, June, sometimes you're impossible to understand.

GRAN: She had a good home, good family,
everything she wanted. The ingratitude!

JUNE: Everything?

MOLLY: She was always hard, even as a child.

JUNE: Maybe he'll bring out what's been hidden,
if he's clever.

GRAN: Your attitude is hardly moral.

JUNE: I'm not talking about morals.

MOLLY: You certainly aren't.

JUNE: Are you? (*A short sticky silence*) I'm talking
about what was inevitable.

GRAN: Inevitable! Nonsense. She was always
taught what was proper.

JUNE: Anything else?

GRAN: That surely was enough.

JUNE: That's what I mean.

ADA: You say such peculiar things, June, you
always did.

GRAN: It's broken Henry's heart.

JUNE: So he threw her out.

GRAN: Naturally!
JUNE: Inevitably.

*

Marjory, a few times during her adult life: 'All right, say I'm hard. Nothing new in that. All right, I hide my feelings – I know. If they don't like it, too bad. I can't let things like that bother me.'

*

Always, as she ran up this slope with Buller and Boney barging and gasping, she thought of the girl. Who had held Uncle Ron's hand, leaning against him, smiling right at his face; and had then disappeared.

It was a shock then, suddenly to see her now: as Marjory rounded the big tree, and called the dogs. The short glossy hair turning away, smooth legs hurrying, running down to the path. She hadn't wanted to be seen; or, if she had, could not speak. Marjory could call after her, but didn't know her name.

Marjory hurled through the kitchens calling Uncle Ron, not pausing as Gran cried behind her about her shoes, mud, what *are* you doing . . . ? Ron had his hand on the front door.

'Big bad bogey-man after you, Marj?'

'Where are you going?'

'Nosey Parker. Off to Vauxhall, see a man about the state of the financial world. Coming?'

'Hurry up, quick. Uncle Ron – I mean – go to the Park.'

'Hark at bossy. What the devil for?'

'Hurry *up*.' She stamped, jumped.

'What?' He stood, stupid, wasting time.

'Go *on*, the Norwood Road end, she was going – '

'Marj!' His face coloured, he was out of the door. 'Thanks, Marj – '

'Where,' Gran said at lunch, 'can Ron have got to?'

'He was going to Vauxhall.'

'Taking longer than he thought I dare say,' Grandad suggested. 'Business you know. Not to worry.'

'I just hope he gets something to eat. Going without food, it won't do. You know how he gets that awful indigestion, and he works so hard and forgets to eat.'

Marjory seized her fork. 'He's *thirty*, he can take care of himself.'

Gran spoke through an exceptionally small mouth. 'Thank you, Marjory, for your opinion.'

Auntie Molly said: 'A year at that College and she's definately getting above herself.'

'A year and a half nearly, as a matter of *fact*.'

'See what I mean?' Molly sighed, Ada joined her.

'Is it really, Marj?' Grandad said. 'Goodness me.'

'Final exams in the summer.'

'Then out into the big bad world eh? A job?'

'Do her good,' Auntie Molly said to her plate.

'That's right,' Marjory answered Grandad. 'A job.' She hadn't thought of it really, until he asked. A job.

Miss Robins told her: There's a big dance at the Grand, a Charity thing, and I'm suggesting some of you girls come along with me. I'd particularly like to introduce you to a nice family, good contacts for your future, Marjory. No point in getting top marks if you don't put them to good use. A job.

'I think,' Marjory told them at home, 'I'll wear my red dress that Auntie Flora made. Joan's grandmother once said to her, if you go to a dance without an escort, wear a red dress and stand near the punch bowl.'

'You can't go to a dance on your *own*,' Ada said.

'I won't *be* on my own, will I? Joan is going and so is Minnie, and Miss Robins will be with us anyway.'

'Your tone is very insolent these days, Marjory,' said Gran. 'And let's hear no more about hanging around by a punch bowl of all things. Really, I often wonder how you can allow such ideas in your head.'

Molly said: 'I could tell you.'

Ada said: 'She certainly doesn't get them from Henry.'

Dear Marjory, said a letter from her father, I'm bringing a friend home the weekend after next to visit the family. Her name is Miss Dolly Hawthorne and I am looking forward very much to introducing you to each other. You're sixteen now,

Marj, I'm sure I don't have to ask you to be good, but I hope you will make her welcome.

Dolly Hawthorne: sounded small and china-eyed, spiky-haired. Miss Clara Finch, Miss Dolly Hawthorne.

Uncle Ron pushed open her door one evening and whispered: 'Hey, Marj!' and laughed that she jumped. She thought: He looks better, not so papery. 'Wanted to say thanks, Marj, haven't had a proper chance to chat to you. What d'you know – ' he sat on the edge of the bed ' – I've got her back again. Who's a lucky fellow? Can't believe it.' She grinned at him grinning. 'Listen, Marj, secret. Don't tell. Going to marry her. Don't know when yet – ' She made a face at him and he said, 'Soon! Honestly, it's up to her, whenever she says. Only listen, Marj, I'm not telling any of 'em, not a dickie bird. One of these days you'll come home and I won't be around and they'll all say, Where's Ron then? and you won't say a thing, only you'll know I've done a bunk and gone and got spliced. Right?'

'Yippeeee!' she danced on the rug, he clapped a hand over her mouth and pushed the door shut with one foot. They sat, giggling. 'What's her name?' she asked at last.

'Rosalie. Didn't I tell you? Nice, isn't it?'

'Lovely. Oh, Uncle Ron, *goody*.'

He lit a cigarette, then winked and held out the packet. '*I* know what you girls get up to.' When he'd lit them both he said: 'Listen, Marj. You get a chance, you go. A good job, a chap you want to marry, whatever it is. Make it on your own, don't you listen to what anyone says.'

'Don't worry.'

'Bloody fool I was. Bloody lucky she waited.'

They sat a while, then she asked: 'D'you remember Daddy's friend, Clara Finch? He's bringing someone else home in a couple of weeks. Dolly, she's called. Dolly Hawthorne. If she's nice, maybe he'll marry her. Uncle Ron, can't you talk to him, make him get on with it?'

His comic mouth went down. 'Me? Tell Henry what to do? Some hopes. Anyway, Marj, it's *her* that's got to be strong; the girl, Dolly. That's what it takes.'

Small and china-eyed and spiky-haired. Let her love Daddy enough.

Minnie stepped back from the mirrors, the gold and cream, the velvet, the shining paint. Blimey, she said, it's a bit bloody posh. Come on, Joan said, you look just as posh, you look lovely, Min. It's Jinny's dress, seen a bit of life I bet. Look at Marj, golly, Marj, you look Spanish or something, you are lucky having that black hair, who's that bloke, the blond one, got his eye on you?

Miss Robins at the interval saying: Lady Deborah, could I introduce one of our best students. Marjory Bell. Marjory, meet Lady Deborah Thorpe-Marley. Tall and sequinned, a face of angles and big teeth, smiling. Meet my awful children, she hooted. Nancy, she prefers horses to dances. Laura, she's been dancing all night, like you. And this is my son, Conrad. It was the fair-haired man who had stared. Bashfully he said: I saw you dancing, your dress is too wizard, I hope you don't mind my saying. Oh *Con*, you made her blush; Laura Thorpe-Marley, small and fair, holding Marjory's arm, an instant friend. Blimey, Minnie whispered, it was *him* watching you, son of a Lord, talk about landing on your feet, Marj. It's a foxtrot, Conrad said, would you like to dance? Thank you, she replied, and inside her skin she was tremulous. How soppy, she thought.

'*Lady Thorpe-Marley?* Asked you to *tea?*' Auntie Molly's mouth was allowed to gape wider than her teaspoon.

'Oh, she's inventing it, *isn't* she?' cried Ada.

'Hay say,' Uncle Ron said, 'How fraytfully refayned.'

'They're nice actually. Not snobby at all.'

'They? Who are *they?*' Gran wanted to know.

'Lady Deborah, and her two daughters and a son. Nancy and Laura and Conrad. They were all there except Lord Thorpe-Marley, he hates dances, Laura told me. I danced with Conrad a few times.'

'A few times eh?' Ron ogled. 'Har *har*.'

'You'd better not get any ideas in *that* direction.' Auntie Molly's lips fitted her teaspoon again.

'As if I would! Don't be silly!'

'Marjory!' Gran cried, of course. 'If you can't be polite, you can leave the table.'

'Excuse me,' she said, and hoped her contempt showed blazingly clear as she left the room.

Miss Robins said: I'm so pleased, I thought you'd like each other, how did tea go? Marjory told her: It was nice. They're really friendly, and I met him, Lord Thorpe-Marley and he's not at all lordish if you know what I mean. He's fat and cuddly like Mr Belling at the grocer's. Oh *Marj*, said Minnie. It's true, Marjory said. I thought it'd be all . . . well, snooty, you know – Grosvenor Square and everything. But it was comfy, things everywhere, homely. And Laura's good fun, she showed me her clothes and let me try some on, we're nearly the same size, and Lady Deborah's super. She treated me just like family really. Miss Robins remarked: I should think so too. I think, Marjory said to Miss Robins, I just have the feeling she might be going to offer me some sort of job. It was the way she was saying about how they go to Scotland for the summer and stay there until after the shooting season's over, and she asked if I'd ever been. Minnie said: Stone the bleeding crows.

Saturday, Dolly Hawthorne Saturday. Gran was saying in the kitchen: 'Henry has invited her for the whole week*end*, says she will be leaving after Sunday tea.' She and Molly made subtle faces at each other.

'He must like her,' Marjory said, and as they turned towards her she smirked. 'Mustn't he?'

When she came, Dolly Hawthorne strode, all long lines. The arms, legs, body, lean and tall. Wide brows, a clear and lovely face, blue-eyed but not at all dollish. Her hair had no spikes; it waved softly, fair and fine. She said: 'Hello, Marjory, how are you then?' and shook hands with everyone, a look of private humour on her eyebrows. Henry watched her as if she might vanish.

She set the pace with few words. In the way she relaxed into a chair, crossing miles of leg; and looked directly, on the edge of a grin, when they questioned her.

Nevertheless, Gran tried. 'Of course, Miss Hawthorne, you're much younger than Henry, aren't you?'

'Oh, *much*.' Dolly flicked a piece of cotton from her prim-rose skirt, sent a teasing look at Henry. 'All of eighteen years, terrible, isn't it?' She smiled at them all; Henry might have frowned, but his mouth quivered and he smiled back. Perhaps he felt Marjory's stare, for he sent the tail of the smile to her. She looked at Gran, whose mouth was small but uncertain. Dolly said: 'And do call me Dolly, for goodness' sake.' Marjory slid down in her chair and danced inwardly. You've got them, Dolly Hawthorne.

'You are *slim*,' Molly said. 'Do you . . . diet?' It sounded immoral.

'Skinny, my mother calls it. Me? I eat everything. Don't I, Henry? Taking me out to dinner will make a pauper of him, he always says.' Dolly pulled down a fair curl and then pushed it back, laughing.

Always says. Glances shot among Gran, Ada, Molly. Grandad laughed: 'You'll have to try one of my fish suppers, Dolly, that's the answer.' Dolly smiled, that would be perfectly delicious; Gran studied the rug.

Dolly did not wait until she was asked, but suggested: Could she see over the house, it seemed so charming. Breathing, Gran led the way; Molly and Ada came behind, Marjory sauntered near, listening. Up to Auntie Ellie's old flat: Gran called it the guest suite. The room with the billiard table: Here is the recreation room. The big kitchen was a breakfast room; the Morgue, the work kitchen, and into this Gran stepped firmly. Running a house, she said to Dolly, hard work, organisation; this is where all the household wash is done. She began to point and demonstrate, saying: You're very young, you won't know about this sort of thing. Dolly leaned on a copper, all limbs and narrow waist, and smiled: 'Mother told me never to do my own washing if I can possibly help it.' She sidled out on the silence.

'Well,' she said as she and Marjory met in the passage, 'that certainly shut them up, didn't it?' And as they giggled through the conservatory: 'Silly cats.'

'I used to hide here when I was small.' Marjory showed her the secret grass, scrubby at the end of winter. 'And Teddy. They can't see you from the house.'

'When you were small? You're not so huge now,' Dolly said. 'And who's Teddy?'

'My cousin. Auntie Flora's his mum. I've got hundreds of cousins.'

'Oh Lord, have you?'

'How did you meet Daddy?'

Dolly looked at her from the far side of the pruned rose-bush: maybe she shouldn't have asked. But then she grinned. 'Bumped into him. Literally. Awful, *honestly*. Hanging about outside the shop, waiting for me every day. *Dread*ful behaviour, I told him. *Really*. I'm engaged, I said, go *away*. Did he take any notice? Not a speck. There he was again, mooning about. You don't mind if I walk with you to the bus stop? I'm going your way. May I carry your parcels? Why don't we have tea? What a cheek!' Dolly really did disapprove, but laughed too.

'Are you still engaged?'

'Ho ho. Wouldn't you like to know?'

'*Are* you?'

'Now, would I come and stay here for the weekend if I was, hm?'

Marjory breathed in deeply, leaning at the back door and looking along the garden. 'I wish it was summer.'

'What for? Beastly hot weather, can't stand it. All those awful people wanting to go *brown*, ugh.'

'The roses would be out, I could give you some. They're lovely. The red ones smell, oh, wonderful.'

Dolly smiled at her. 'I'll look forward to that.'

From the drawing-room door on Sunday morning Marjory could see their heads, close, over the back of the Victorian sofa. Dolly's light voice: But Henry, it's only *fair* to her . . . And he, with an unfamiliar gentleness, saying: I know, I know, but how can I?

Marjory came behind them and round the end of the sofa: 'Hello.'

They were holding all four hands together: he sprang into dignity but Dolly kept one hand. Both blushed slightly as if they had been talking about her: their smiles were bright enough. But she thought only: Daddy, holding hands.

'Gran says, Auntie Hennie and Uncle Joe and Nora and Madge are coming up the road, Auntie Flora's already here, can you give Grandad some help with the chairs and sharpening the carving knife, if you're not doing anything important?'

Dolly looked at him and snorted, then gave him back his hand. 'Go on. Be good.'

Teddy was here for once. Blimey, Marj, he said, look at

Uncle Henry, dead struck. Changed man you see there, Marj. Into a female's clutches, that's what it is, that's what it takes. I know a thing or two about the female, let me tell you. He leered and hinted. She's put the old stinker's nose out of joint though, eh?

Nora, meeting Dolly, laughed a lot, put an arm through Henry's. 'Why don't you like her?' Marjory asked later, finding Nora alone in the hall.

'Don't like her? Whatever do you mean, Marj? Of course I like her. She seems quite charming. She might not like *me* I would have said.' Nora smiled into the hall-stand mirror. 'Henry and I have always been close of course.'

'I *like* her,' Marjory said. 'I think she's really *nice*.'

'All right, Marj, I'm not arguing.'

'And *so* does Daddy.'

'For heaven's sake,' Nora cried. 'Who cares?'

After lunch, after the singing, she saw them all three walking round the garden. Dolly's hand on Henry's arm, Nora on his other side talking, her hands moving outwards now and then. It was cold, it might rain, but they walked round the paths, round again. Her father looked down, his whole body serious, and sometimes nodded. Then they were near the house again, and he put a hand on Nora's shoulder: they all looked at each other, Dolly was smiling, then leaned to kiss Nora's cheek. Rubbing hands they went into the house.

'What were you all talking about in the garden?' Marjory asked Nora. 'Looked very weighty.'

'You,' Nora said, and laughed.

'Oh yeah. Come on, tell.'

'Who's nosey then? What did curiosity do to the cat? Mind your own, Marjory Bell.' But she hugged her when she said goodbye: 'See you soon, Marj.'

'Thank you,' her father said to Nora just before the door closed.

Dolly said: 'I ought to be on my way too, Henry, if I'm to get a train before dark.'

Gran turned. 'You're leaving now?'

'Yes.' Dolly's smile was very wide. 'Thank you so much for all your hospitality. It's been lovely.'

'You could have walked along with the others,' said Gran. 'They're catching a bus to Brixton Station, didn't you know?'

Dolly's smile stayed. 'Oh, but Henry said he'd like to walk with me.'

'That's right, mother.' Henry brought Dolly's coat and bag.

'Dear Henry,' Gran sighed to Dolly. 'Such a gentleman.'

'Goodbye, Marjory.' Dolly kissed her. 'See you again soon I hope.'

Henry said : 'You certainly will.'

The door closed behind them. Gran and Molly and Ada walked towards the Morgue.

Marjory waited on the middle landing for him to come back. He might open the front door without noise, looking down at the doormat, pushing the door behind him without turning; if he did, they would have beaten him. Or he might step in : one, two, turning to close the door, head up. She hoped.

Gran came along the hall and turned on the gas, then returned to the kitchens. Auntie Molly came, stopped to clear the corner of one eye at the mirror, went into the drawing-room. Soon, strained Brahms from the pianola, Molly at the pedals.

The front door opened quickly. He came in. One, two. And he was smiling. She was on the stairs, running, wanting to call out : Oh Daddy, she was super, she was really nice! but saying nothing, for there must be better words, less childlike, more poised. He saw her, and then made her stop on the stairs, amazed. He put a finger to his mouth and beckoned, holding the front door open. She stood, he beckoned again. Then she was with him, being drawn outside, staring questions at him, mouthing What? but he shook his head, said Sshh, still smiling, and they were standing by the drawing-room window. Lights were on, Venetian blinds down but not closed, curtains still wide. 'Look,' her father whispered into her hair, 'look.' Auntie Molly at the pianola, alone and performing. Her feet pumped vigorously to produce the Brahms, but her hands, her arms, her body were pianist, conductor, the whole orchestra. And on the pianola top, grinning towards the prima donna, Auntie Molly's upper teeth.

He was laughing, Marjory was laughing, they were like kids together; the surprise of it made her stop and stare at him for a second, then laugh again with him as Molly's arms flung out, acknowledging audience. The great star, the conductor, chin back, top gum gleaming. They slid indoors, sniggering, conspirators. The memory, the secret, the whole delight of it made her grin or snuffle until suppertime. Honestly, Auntie Ada complained, what *is* so funny tonight, Marjory? You're being very irritating. Nothing, nothing, she told her, seeing, not believing, relishing the sight of her father smiling down at his hands, humming some of the Brahms. And *you're* not yourself today either, Ada resented. Molly said: Who's that humming at table? Manners! Marjory choked on a crumb and had to run out. She ran back still red and gasping, afraid of missing a word. They were talking about Dolly.

Grandad: 'Father a musician, eh? Fancy that. Yes, she seems an educated girl.'

'Really? A musician?' Molly said. 'Goodness.' And after a pause: 'Girls are very *bold* nowadays, aren't they?'

'She was certainly very modern in attitude,' Ada said, chin in ruffles.

'Very *young*,' said Gran.

'Hm, pretty,' Grandad nodded.

'Don't you think, Henry – ' Gran began.

'I'm glad you all liked her,' Henry said.

Uncle Ron widened his eyes at Marjory. 'She certainly sounds splendid, old man,' he said. 'Sorry I missed her.' He had been out, was always out now.

'*I* thought she was super,' Marjory said.

'Gran said: 'Try not to use common words like that, Marjory.'

Pooh to Gran. She smiled at her father, straight at him, the continuation of their laugh. His lower lip quivered, not a really wide smile with Gran watching, but enough.

*

'I've had a letter from Lady Deborah,' Miss Robins said. 'She says that she and Lord Thorpe-Marley would like to offer you a post. When you've got your diploma, in the summer. Just as you thought, Marjory. They'd like you to go with the family to Scotland. She says "I hope she won't see it just as a job. The children like her very much, and I would like to think of it as joining us as a family but earning some money too." Well, it looks as if your different tea-parties have been quite a

187

success. She says you'll love Scotland, they have a lot of fun there, just ask Laura.'

And Conrad. Last time at Grosvenor Square, he said: Wish we saw more of you, Marjory, you're a lark.

Miss Robins was saying: 'The idea is that you help with the cookery. I think you'll be busy enough, it's nothing for them to have forty to lunch during the season. But I think they'll make sure you have a good time too. What do you say?'

'I don't know. Heavens. Well, I'll have to write to my father.'

'Of course. Lady Deborah would like to know soon if you're interested, but she realises you can't say a definite yes until you have your diploma. Not that she minds about that, but she feels you would prefer to be fully qualified. And I certainly don't have any doubts that you'll be that.'

'There, Marj,' Uncle Ron said. 'It's your big chance. You take it.' He promised to tell nobody else. 'Hey, you must be good though, Marj. Offering you a job even before your exams.'

'They're friends of Miss Robins, that's what it is.'

'Nevertheless.' Then he asked: 'You want to go?'

'I think so. I don't know.' It was exciting, but she turned towards then away. Daddy, Dolly. Suppose he married her, and they said come and live with us. Suppose she went away and Dolly disappeared. Suppose she didn't and Conrad . . . Suppose Daddy said no, Scotland's too far.

Uncle Ron said: 'You want to go, Marj, so you go. Listen, if Henry gets difficult I'll have a word. Right? Anyway, you'll be back in London again when they've finished killing off all the grouse in Scotland, won't you? Maybe you'll work for them in jolly old Mayfair, what a whiz. So you can still keep an eye on your dad and his girl.' He laughed. 'And I'll tell you what. I'll try and get myself hitched before you push off.'

Gran handed the letter to Marjory: Daddy had written by return. 'I see you have become very secretive,' Gran said. 'You mentioned nothing to myself or your grandfather about this venture. A job in Scotland!'

She took the letter. 'I didn't want to until it was definite one way or the other.' She flipped the open end of the envelope on her fingertips. 'Anyway, you know now.'

Thank you very much, he wrote, for giving me your interesting news. A big step, taking a job as far away as Scotland, and my first reaction was to wonder if it wasn't just a bit too far. But after some thought I have to say that if you wish to go I certainly won't stand in your way. Miss Hawthorne sends you her very best wishes, and congratulations. Certainly it was a compliment that Lady Deborah should make you this offer, and you are quite right not to accept before you have your diploma.

Then he had begun a new thought, but had crossed it out too heavily to be read. He finished: This could be a new start for you, Marjory. Of course there will be hard things yet, things difficult to understand, and problems to face. But you won't let these get you down I hope. See you at the weekend. Your affectionate Daddy.

*

Nora tapped and pushed open Marjory's door. 'You there, Marj? Hey, you look busy.' She gave a small laugh, almost nervous, as if she had interrupted something, though Marjory was only sitting on the bed mending stockings and underwear.

'Hello, Nora. It's not lunch-time yet, is it?'

'No, I'm early. I came early specially.' Nora plonked herself in the armchair but did not relax.

'Oh, what for?'

'What for what?'

'What did you come early specially for?'

'Oh . . . *well*.' Nora was standing again, leaning before the mirror. There was nothing wrong with her hair, she turned again. 'To talk to you, that's what for, believe it or not.'

'Are you cross about something?'

Nora laughed, out of breath. 'Oh, Marj, good heavens no.' She sat on the bed beside her. 'Course not.'

'What's the matter then?'

'Nothing's the *matter*, not exactly. Just – well, listen, Marj. I said I'd tell you. You remember you asked me, ages ago – '

A nerve inside Marjory strung itself out like a tight thread. She buried the point of her needle in the stocking heel. 'Yes,' she said.

'– about your mother, I mean.'

'Yes.'

'Well. It was after that, I said to Henry there were some things you ought to be told. He said not to worry, you were young yet, plenty of time. I told him I felt awkward, you asking me about Greta and me not being able to answer you without asking him first, so it seemed as if I was telling you fibs. Oh, he said, don't worry, I don't suppose she'll ask again.'

'I see.'

'Well, you're sixteen now. Old enough to get married, for heaven's sake. Anyway, *he* seems to think it's time you were told everything at last, and I should jolly well think so too. Maybe it was partly Dolly's doing, I wouldn't know, but anyway he and Dolly had a word with me – that was when you saw us in the garden. He said he didn't know how to tell you himself, he was too involved, and he thought I might be able to do it better. As we've always been friends – haven't we, Marj? Of course I said I would, hadn't I told him that before anyway?'

Dolly leaning towards Daddy: It's only fair, Henry; and Daddy saying I know, but how can I?

'So.' Nora sat back in the chair now. 'I suppose I'd better go right to the beginning.'

Marjory waited, tidying the already tidy heaps of mending.

'The thing is, Marj, it might seem to you that people were bad, or not very nice, but try to see that they weren't really, they were mostly unhappy.'

'Who d'you mean?'

'Well . . . I mean your mother. Greta. She was left on her own with you just a baby when Henry went off in the war to France. She was lonely and pretty miserable. The honest truth is, Gran never liked her. You know Gran, the way she is about any girl coming near her beloved sons, and especially when . . . oh, the point *is*, Marj, Greta was already expecting you when she and your Dad got married, and from Gran's point of view that was Greta's fault, not dear Henry's. Henry was madly in love with Greta in fact but Gran wouldn't want to see that, would she? So the family didn't care about poor Greta stuck out there in Watford on her own with a baby, if she was lonesome it was her own fault, made her bed and she'd got to lie on it, and all that stuff. She was terrifically attractive, full of life, she liked having fun. Of course, she used to get awfully fed up.'

'Did you meet her? Did you know her?' Don't ask *me*, Marj, Nora had said.

'Yes, course I did. I was a kid, but we got on well. She was good to me; so was Henry, always. And mother liked her, always reckoned Gran was hard on her and Henry listened to Gran too much.' Auntie Hennie saying Rubbish Liza when Auntie Liza said something about That Woman. 'We lived fairly near then, you see. Mother used to look after you sometimes, me too, so that Greta would have a chance to get out with her chums. And Vi used to have you quite often as well.'

'Who? Vi?'

'Your mother's sister, Violet. An auntie of yours, in other words. She lives in Watford, she was the only family Greta had there.'

With love from Auntie. 'Auntie Ellie said she was a lady who used to know me before I came to live at Gran's.'

'Well, that's true.'

'But she was a *real* aunt. Why not *say* so?'

Nora looked out of the window. 'Oh, I don't know, Marj. Gran, I s'pose. Anyway, what happened was this. Greta met somebody else. I mean, another man. Henry was far away in France, and she was lonely, you see. She just fell in love with him, wham, and nothing else mattered. She dumped you on a neighbour and went.'

'How do you mean? Ran away with him?' You'll go the way of your mother.

'Just like that. Only Mother went after her and talked her into coming back, said she couldn't run out on her baby and Henry without so much as a word of explanation to anyone, and besides she was married and she'd made vows, and so on. Greta came back. Nobody else knew about it, Mum didn't say anything to a soul. Greta said she'd give it another try. But she was just *mad* about the fellow, Mike, he was called. I don't think she could live without him. She used to write to him and give me the letters to post; she'd pretend she was writing to Henry, but she hardly ever did. I didn't tell. To me it was all a bit of a game. Then one day she'd gone again, and nobody knew where you were. She'd left a note for Mum saying you were with friends – you could've been anywhere.

Vi said she'd been leaving you with all sorts of people and sneaking off to see her Mike. You were being passed from hand to hand, as far as anyone could make out, especially if Greta was away for a few days.'

'So what happened then?' Marjory rubbed chilled fingers together.

'Vi wrote to Henry to get him to come back from France and help find you. And naturally what she wanted was for him to make it up with Greta. There was a big search, though it was all kept hush-hush of course. As Dad was a policeman it was a big help, you can imagine. Anyway, Henry came back, you should've seen him, all thin and white. Where's Greta? was the first thing he asked my mother. Well, *she* didn't know, did she? You think about your daughter, she told him, that's what matters first. Well, they didn't find you for ages, weeks probably. It was my Dad who tracked you down. You were in a little room in this awful block of flats, a tenement. It was freezing cold weather and you were in just a cotton dress in this empty room, filthy, sitting on bare boards and half-starved. Some awful old hag was supposed to be looking after you, a great fat woman who stank to high heaven. God knows how long you'd been there, Marj, it was terrible.'

'Did you see her, the fat woman?'

'I wasn't there, Mother told me about it. Big fat slut with an apron, absolutely squalid.'

Cold air through the floorboards, the bear with an apron coming plod plod up the stairs, breathing at the door. It came across the room. They came across the room, glimmering, the tall man a policeman the woman with rough hands the other man, they would give her to the bear on the stairs.

'Was Daddy there?'

'Yes. And my mother and father. They took you out and took you home to Gran's house. You were screaming all the time and struggling, Mother said.'

'There was a motorbike.'

'How would you know that?'

'I think I remember. Something. Some people.'

'It was when they took you out of the tenement. What happened was, Greta and her Mike suddenly turned up. Maybe she was coming to fetch you, or to see if you were all right, I don't know. I suppose nobody asked her. Anyway,

Henry went sort of mad, rushed up face to face with her chap and actually hit him, right there in the street.'

'I was sitting on the pavement.'

'Greta was crying, Dad was trying to hang on to Henry, Mother was telling them to stop, and then all of a sudden Mike got on the motorbike and Greta jumped in the sidecar, and they were off.' Long silk legs leaving, going, Daddy crying, the noise going away, away, lost, sad. 'And that was the last Henry saw of her as far as I know. Mother said to him, face facts, Henry, you've just got to think of your child now, that's all. So they brought you to Gran's. The idea was that Auntie Ellie would bring you up along with Susie, but of course as Auntie June always said, that was bound to be a load of bunkum with Gran in charge of the house. In this house everyone gets a say and Gran has the last word. Still, she means for the best.'

Marjory moved her heaps of mending about on the bed, and did not speak. Shivering slightly, she crossed her arms and put her hands under her armpits; but Nora didn't seem cold.

'Don't think badly of Greta,' Nora said. 'She was young and mother said she was never one to cope very well. And I think she was confused. I don't believe she was really in love with Henry, not really and truly; probably if she hadn't got pregnant she wouldn't have married him. Then she met Mike and went head over heels. He was good to her and warm-hearted, nuts about her and showed it. She couldn't think of anything else.'

'Now I know why Gran hates me.'

'Oh Marj – she doesn't *hate* you. She did hate Greta, I think that's true. To her mind Greta was wicked but Henry could do no wrong – that's just Gran and her boys. And of course Auntie Molly and Auntie Ada back her up all the way. Auntie Flora too, mostly. They all thought Greta was bad, nobody ever thought about how she *felt*. Except Mum, and Henry himself. I think he really did try to understand it. Anyway, he always loved her, never got over her, not until now. He kept in touch with Vi so he'd know where Greta was. He's been terribly unhappy, poor Henry.'

'So where did she go? And what happened?'

'She went to Bournemouth, Mike had a job there. They

settled down, Henry gave her a divorce. *That* was hushed up, I can tell you – scandal! And she married Mike.'

Divorced. 'And then what?'

'D'you know – I went down there and saw her once. I was about seventeen I suppose. Found her in an office and said: I bet you don't know me. She looked at me and said: Blow me down if it isn't Nora. She nipped out for a coffee and a chat. She'd got two sons, imagine that.'

Marjory mouthed: 'I'd be about seven then.'

'That's right.'

'So when did she – '

'They'll be growing up too, won't they? Funny that, to think you've got a couple of brothers. Half-brothers, that is.'

'But how did she – '

'I suppose they're all still there, in Bournemouth.'

Marjory's throat had contracted, her mouth gave no sounds. She could not blink, staring at Nora: her eyelids had stuck open, dry as paper. I am a little beggar girl my mother she is dead. You'll go the way of your mother. Send you to a home for bad girls and orphans.

She heard Nora speaking. 'Marj! Oh *Mar*jory. You didn't still . . . You didn't *completely* believe she – she was *dead*, did you?' And as Marjory still was unable to move: 'But Marj, nobody ever *told* you she was dead, they never *said*.'

She had a voice, at last, although it emerged stretched tight. 'What do you mean? They did. They must have. They damn well *did*. I always thought – they *knew* I thought she was dead, they *did* tell me. Otherwise I wouldn't have thought it, would I? *Would* I?'

'Oh crikey, Marj. Look, maybe they just *let* you think it. I expect they thought it was easier if you thought she was dead – easier than having to explain it all to you when you were little – *you* know.' But Nora's voice collapsed without the support of conviction, as she looked at Marjory's face, which could have been rock, or ice. 'Oh, Marj, I'm sorry. I did sort of know you believed that once, but then I thought somehow you *must* know – oh, I'm *sorry*.'

There were tears in Nora's eyes, Marjory noted. She shifted further back, to the centre of the bed, and pulled up her knees, wrapping her arms closely round them. She was freezing; it must have got very cold outside suddenly. Nora sniffed, bringing out a hanky and blowing her nose; it was like a final trumpet. Probably she was relieved it was all said at last.

They knew all the damn time, Gran and Auntie Molly and Auntie Ada and Auntie Flora and *every*body, those cats those bitches, laughing at me singing their stupid songs, me thinking she was dead, home for orphans, I hate them. Bloody hypocrites, what about fatty Fred Barnes with his phoney name, of course he's married and anyone can see he's been in and out of Auntie Molly's bed for years, *I* know and they must all know if they're not blind, but that's all right I suppose because he isn't divorced or he's got money and a Rolls-Royce and she hasn't had a baby and he gives her jewellery and silk stockings and a stupid old pianola and pound notes like some bloated old sugar-daddy and they all mince around him and *simper*, bloody hypocrites, dis*gusting*, she's nothing but some *tart*, and there they are all *holy* about my mother, and what did she do that was so bad, she fell in love with somebody, and no wonder, my father a stuffed shirt cold as stone always doing what his mama says the old bitch I hate her.

Nora was at the door, standing uncertainly; Marjory remained unblinking and silent. 'Marj? Are you coming down?'

'No.'

'I hope . . . I hope you're not awfully upset, darling. Listen – would you like to meet her? We could arrange it, I'm almost positive. Henry's always known where she is, through Vi. Would you like to?'

'No.'

'Look, think about it. I expect everything's a shock and mixed up now. You might change your mind.'

'No. *No*.'

Nora still hovered; then she murmured she would see Marjory later, fluttered a hand, and was gone. Marjory heard her walking quickly downwards.

Of course my mother ran off, who wouldn't? How she must have felt, bleak and alone, knowing Gran and the others hated her. Marjory let herself fall or roll sideways on the eiderdown and stayed as she landed, curled with her knees up, arms crossed fiercely over her chest. Cold, utterly cold, dense deep waste of cold. And darkness sinking through her bitter limbs, down, dragging, filling her veins, out of the light, nothing to believe. I'll never trust any of them again, cheats, they cheated me.

The gas jet was on very low: Gran had done that, or more likely Auntie Flora. Dark, silent house. It could be tomorrow morning, it might be only nine or ten. No sounds, except from her stomach: breakfast was the last thing she had eaten. Nothing, go away, no no, she had told them, glacial and stubborn from the huddled eiderdown. Lunch, tea, supper smells had come and gone. So had Gran, Auntie Flora, Daddy twice. Don't want to speak to you. Go away. Don't want anything. Go away. Her eyelids were thick and sticky, she was still dressed except for her shoes; creased and chilled, squeezed by a blackness, a depression she could not understand, did not want; but she sensed, desolately, that this day might never completely leave her. Her stomach was loud in the silence.

Down, softly stair by stair. Past the drawing-room: men's voices, it wasn't tomorrow. Dining-room, empty. Past the cloakroom; there was a light on in the kitchen, door wide, nobody there. Stealthily she opened the larder door, took biscuits, a slice of ham, an apple. And from the half-open door to the Morgue somebody sighed; her hand stopped. Damn, they were in there. 'Well,' it was Flora's sigh, breaking what must have been a thoughtful lull, '*I* don't know what to suggest, I'm sure.' Marjory backed from the larder, watching the door. 'All she does is . . . well, mope. Whatever I said, she just told me to go away.'

Gran's voice: 'She'll get over it. Gracious, she had to be told sometime.'

Molly: 'I should've thought she'd be *glad* her mother's alive.'

Nora: 'It isn't that.'

Ada: 'I agree with Molly. Why, this should be exciting news, I should've thought she'd be grateful.'

Nora: 'It's not knowing, everyone else knowing and letting her think Greta was dead. And it's a shock.'

Flora: 'I tried to jolly her out of it but that didn't work either. She just went all blank.'

Gran: 'What about poor Henry? She wouldn't speak to him at all, he's so upset.'

Molly: 'As if he hasn't had enough to put up with. Let's be frank, we don't even know if she's *really* Henry's child.'

Nora: 'Auntie Molly!'

Ada: 'Well? *Do* we? With that woman it could have been *any* man. Just because Henry – '

She ran, hitting into a door, dropping a biscuit, up the stairs, up the next, breath painful. She sat in front of the mirror; breathe deeply, I won't be sick. She jumped up, turned the gas high, sat again and stared. Do I look like Daddy? Grandad had black hair once, Gran's eyes are greenish. Maybe she had green eyes too, Greta. I didn't ask Nora: What did she look like? Am I like her? Long silk legs. Could have been any man. Daddy. Dolly. Scotland: part of the family. Do I look like Daddy?

And now there was fear, or despair, in the blackness, too vast, too profound for her not to weep at last. Quiet, under the blankets, so they should not hear; but endless, and alone.

She wrote to him next day; he hadn't come to say goodbye in the morning. Dear Daddy, I'm sorry I didn't speak to you, I was just upset. I can't explain exactly.

She was in the hall each day when the postman came. At last, his writing, the coffee-coloured envelope. Gran behind her said: 'I'll take the post, Marjory.'

She gave the heap, keeping the one. 'This is for me.' She looked right into Gran's gaze: You won't ever make me cry again. Yesterday on the landing she had heard Auntie Molly say: You've only got to look at her these days and she's crying. And Auntie Ada: The fuss! Then Uncle Ron came: Don't be depressed, Marj, you're a fighter, aren't you? I won't cry, it's over.

Gran's hand was still stretched. 'Give me *all* of them please, Marjory.'

'This is for me.' She held it up so that Gran could see. 'From Daddy. It's mine.' She walked past to the stairs; Gran's hand wavered, dropped. When I've gone, when I'm in Scotland, you won't be able to touch my letters, nosey old cat.

My Dear Marjory, Thanks for your letter, sorry I haven't acknowledged it earlier. You weren't the only jumbled one over the weekend my dear and your description of your feelings very aptly covers me also. It was rather difficult for you, Marj, and I was more than pleased, or relieved, when it was over. Sometime you'd got to be told and now that part is done you mustn't let it worry you. If at any time you have any worries you must bring them to me and we can share them and make things lighter – or better still wipe them out altogether – that's a bargain.

Lots of colds about, hope you've escaped. I thought I had but developed a bit of a snorter this week. No news of interest to give you so will pack up hoping to find you feeling better when I see you. Please give my love to everyone and accept the same from your affectionate Daddy.

She put the letter in her box and locked it. Then sat, looking in the mirror.

On Saturday morning Teddy said: 'Blimey, Marj, what a cheek, they never told *me*. Fancy her being alive and kicking all this time.'

'I don't want to talk about it.'

'Don't you want to see her though? I mean, aren't you just the teeniest bit interested?'

'No I don't and no I'm not and why don't you shut up?'

'Crikey, what a blooming pepper-pot,' he muttered, and sat kicking the leg of her bed. Then he cackled and looked up: 'All right. This'll make you laugh. I was at Auntie Hennie's the other weekend. Remember that friend of hers, Uncle Griff? The one I said was a bit dotty, always thinking he had bits of fluff or hair or something all over him, and being all fidgety? Well, it turns out he's been shoved in the looney-bin. Honest! He went so barmy he was running around picking bits off everybody and saying "filthy! filthy people!" even in buses and restaurants. Naturally they got a bit peeved and told him to push off, and then he'd get annoyed back and in the end he went really mad. I mean, *mad*. Auntie Hennie said they were at his house and he started to fling things about and yell and say he'd got the message to save the world but nobody wanted to listen to him, they were all stupid and afraid. Next thing was he was being dragged off fighting and struggling to the asylum. Auntie Hennie said he'd been shell-shocked in the war, that was why. Uncle Joe said. "It's just nerves, he'll be all right." Just as if it was nothing more than a headache or something. Cor, what a scream though – wish I'd seen it, don't you?'

She had gooseflesh on her face. 'No I don't. I don't think that's in the least funny.'

'Gawd love us.' Teddy went away. 'Talk about a misery-guts, there's no cheering some people up.'

She sat in horror: the man Uncle Griff, distant in memory as likeable, plump, unexceptional. Flinging things and yelling, being dragged off. To be mad, to have no control; there was nothing to be feared more than that.

*

She ran in the front door to collide with Auntie Ada's frills. 'Where's Uncle Ron?'

'Good heavens, child, how should I know? And must you rush about like that? Won't you ever learn to be ladylike?'

'Hope not!' She leapt upstairs; Auntie Ada gasped and clicked.

'Caught in the act, guilty, guilty!' Uncle Ron was closing her bedroom door as she reached the landing.

'What are you up to?' And not waiting, she told him: 'I've passed, Uncle Ron. Got my diploma!'

'Hey – well done, Marj. What a clever old stick you are. Where's the bit of paper then, where's the proof?'

'Next week, end of term.'

'Knew you'd do it. Now take a look in there.' His thumb-nail tapped her door, his music-hall eyebrows wiggled. 'Go on, go on.'

He had bought her a trunk, russet-coloured, bound in strong pale wood. A label said: Go it, Marj! Love from Uncle Ron. 'That should hold all the woolly knickers you need for the frozen wastes,' he said.

'Oh! Uncle Ron!' She turned and kissed him, and they grinned at each other.

'Here.' He sat on the bed. 'Have a Woodbine.'

They smoked and turned the trunk inside out, and he asked about the exams. Thought I'd had it in cookery, she told him. There I was supposed to be making a blackcurrant bombe, and somebody had pinched my saltpetre – that's for the freezing, you see. So I had to tip the whole thing in another bowl and whip it up and decorate it, made it into a sort of moussey-fool thing. You should've seen Miss Peace's face! And in the end I got extra marks for initiative – what a scream. Ron said: You're pleased now, aren't you, Marj? Pleased you did it? She said: I think I'm pleased I did it *well*.

At tea Gran said : 'Surely your results should be out by now, Marjory?'

'Diplomas are given out at the end of term.'

Uncle Ron sent her a wink; Grandad asked : 'How d'you think you did, Marjory?'

'Oh,' she said, 'all right I think.'

Goodbye. Goodbye, Joan, Minnie. Good luck with the jobs, let me know how you get on. All right for you, Marj, set up with Lady Mucko and her handsome lad. We'll write, won't we? Keep in touch.

You've done excellently, Marjory, Miss Robins said. I can't see you ever lacking a job. I enjoyed your housekeeping, and Miss Peace remarked upon your lemon soufflé – I think her word was 'poetic'! As for the blackcurrant pudding – well, you've shown you can think on your feet, and that's an asset in a cook. You'll come back and see us, won't you? Oh yes, Miss Robins, I really will. Thank you – well, thank you for *every*thing. Miss Robins called after her : Just one thing, Marjory! Don't forget the pinch of salt in the pastry.

The diploma curled smoothly in her hand as she went sedately into Leander Road, with a lady's steps into the house. Auntie Ada was coming down the stairs. 'Good evening,' Marjory said decorously. 'Can you tell me, please, where is Uncle Ron?' She must unroll this parchment under his nose.

Auntie Ada clutched her ruffled wrists, then flung a hand over her face and with a moaning cry was in tears. 'Oh, oh . . . you *would* say that! Oh . . . Ron . . .' She ran gulping down the hall towards the kitchens.

Marjory pushed the door closed and stood on the mat. Uncle Ron. He'd done it, today. Him and Rosalie. Oh good old Uncle Ron. You'll come home one day and they'll say Where's Uncle Ron? And you won't say a thing but you'll know. Oh yippeeee, Uncle Ron. She threw and caught her diploma, tossed her hat on the hall-stand, danced some mad steps. Then she strolled, whistling, to the kitchen.

She was late, they should have finished tea. But there were no signs of a meal; they were all sitting at the big table. Grandad looked up as she came in but did not smile : 'Hello, young Marjory. Come along in. You'll have to know sooner or later. I'm afraid we've got some disturbing news.' Oh no Grandad, it's not at all disturbing, Ron and his Rosalie, it's good, it's wonderful.

Gran did not speak; she looked at her hands in her lap, not at Marjory. Molly was almost white, perhaps she had been crying, perhaps she was angry. Ada sniffed into her square of lace.

Grandad said: 'It's your Uncle Ron, Marj.' She saw his lip tremble and some chill reached her. 'He's been taken to hospital, he's very ill I'm afraid. They don't know what the trouble is yet, something inside, bleeding they say. Nobody can speak to him, he's asleep, unconscious, Marj, you see.'

'But – but Grandad – ' perhaps she spoke. Then she heard him saying: 'Hey, hey, sit down. Here you are.' Grandad's big hands on her arm, sitting her on a chair. Uncle Ron, Rosalie. 'Don't get upset, he'll be all right. It was a shock, we're all a bit shaken up, that's what it is. He was here, standing right by the back door, having a joke as usual. Said to your Gran he was off out, and she said, When d'you think you'll be home? He was pulling her leg, you know how he does, saying he might be gone a couple of days for all he knew. Then he went all white and said he felt bad, and the next thing was he was on the floor. Just like that, sudden as anything.'

'But, Grandad, he looked all right. Why should he be ill? What are they doing? Why can't we see him?' Rosalie. 'When will he wake up?'

'We're telephoning every hour, Marj, can't do more. Mrs Bates next door says we can go in when we like and use her phone. Maybe there'll be good news soon. They said they'd ring through when he comes round, don't you worry, we'll know at once.'

'Where was he going?'

'Whatever's that got to do with anything?' Molly cried.

'Didn't say, Marj,' Grandad answered. 'Out to see someone, that's all he said. You know your Uncle Ron, always acting the fool, pretending there's a big mystery. I expect he was going to se a friend – he'd got a few days off he said.'

Gran looked up. 'We might as well be sensible and eat.' Gran had been crying. Gran. 'Come along, Marjory, you can help me lay the table.'

'I've had tea,' she said. 'I'm going to the Park.' She threw her diploma on the dresser and was out of the door; Gran didn't call her back to change her shoes.

Rosalie was not by the big tree, not in the Park. Telephone her: but she didn't know her other name. Out of the gate, through the streets, a bus. At the hospital entrance she kept running, following signs along paths. Your name? I'm afraid we can't give you any information, my dear. No change in his condition. Please, if a lady called Rosalie something comes or telephones or anything, will you tell her about it? She's engaged to him and she won't know what's happened, he was going to meet her and he didn't get there so will you please tell her? Will you? There there, my dear. Rosalie did you say? Don't cry, I won't forget.

She was leaving and the man called: Listen, this Rosalie. She'll find out all right, don't you fret. Wouldn't she telephone him, p'raps at his office, when he didn't turn up? Then somebody would tell her, eh? See, things aren't always as bad as they seem, I expect he'll soon be on the mend. You run on home, miss, it'll be all right.

Two days of telephoning from next door, waiting. Grandad coming in, looking down. Nothing yet, my dears, no change, but they say he's comfortable. Doing all they can.

A third day, Grandad's head straighter, he called out as he opened the door: A bit better, they say! Good old Ron, on the turn.

A fourth day. Gran went with Grandad to the telephone, they came back out of breath. We can go and see him tomorrow, yes, tomorrow. He's been awake a whole hour, being quite cheeky, they said. Got a long way to go but they sound pleased. Just his parents to start with, they said. Telephone first, they said, make sure he's feeling strong.

Thank you, God, oh make him all right. What exactly are they *doing*, Grandad, the doctors? Molly snapped: *Must* you ask such pointless questions? Grandad said: They haven't told us yet, Marj, but he'll be in good hands, never fear about that.

She lay still in the fibrous warmth of the secret grass, breathing rose-scents, hearing the dogs' breath quicker than her own. Her fingers pushed through the green blades; there was another life below there, things moved, things too small to see. Miss Robins had taught about this microscopic life of the soil, cells tinier than imagination could hold, molecules, atoms. One could not think of it; it was too incomprehensible, peculiarly disturbing. She got up quickly and began to move from one rose-bush to the next, methodically, snapping off the dead heads. Stop mooning about, Auntie Ada had said, go and make yourself useful in the garden. Let him be all right, let him be better. I'll take him his favourite roses, the red and white climbers. Snap, snap, the dead heads. Some of the blooms dropped their petals on touch; some were firm, full, all perfume and plush; some hardly beginning to open buds.

And Grandad was next to her on the path, saying: Marjory, my dear,' quietly. He was back from the telephone, all dressed up in his good coat and stiff collar, ready to go to the hospital. 'Marj.' And she noticed how his skin and beard merged, the same colour. His next words could hardly be heard: 'I'm afraid your Uncle Ron didn't make it.'

*

Must you sit on the stairs, Marjory? I'm not in your way, I'm looking at the flowers, don't fuss. Auntie Ada hissed, Oh! Where's your respect? And on a day like *this*. Marjory read the cards as they arrived: on wreaths, sprays, bouquets, crosses. Your loving brother, Henry. Loving memories, Hennie and Joe, Nora, Madge, Liza, Walt, Ellie, Wilf, Susie, Flora. All of them, and unknown names too, friends nobody had met. And it came, a spray of small dark rosebuds: Rosalie, with all my love for ever. Who? said Gran. Who's Rosalie? Look, Marjory pointed, Dolly sent those lovely white flowers. Miss Hawthorne, if you please, Marjory.

Black, everyone came. The carriages, the horses with plumes: do things the right way, the old way, Grandad said; horses have dignity. Speaking of dignity, Molly said, who put that messy bunch of flowers there? Red and white roses from the climbers. *I* did, they're from me, Grandad said I could pick them, they were Uncle Ron's favourites and they're not messy. With love and thanks from Marjory. Oh, Molly said, I should've known, *really* Marj, where's your sense of – And Auntie June said: Don't be so damn small-minded, Molly, Ron would have loved them. Gran swung: Swearing! Behind her, deep breathing from Molly, Ada, Flora. June turned away.

Henry, Dolly on his arm; Daddy with eyes large, thinking, Dolly a beanpole in black, not smiling. Susie, adult in a veil. Nora, gold hair hidden. Archie, a man, uncomfortable. Everyone kissed and wept with Gran. Gran, the stiff net of her black bonnet making a web across her eyes.

Deep straight sides of earth, worms waiting. Teddy stood black-coated beside her and whispered: It was a growth as big as an orange, Mum said, and it burst.

The black box lowered, lay deep in the soil. Uncle Ron in there. She looked up, across the black hats, around. Don't fidget, Marjory, please. On the left, further away than the dark edge of the crowd, hair shining without a hat, a coat green not black, Rosalie. But she was away, turning from the tombstones before the crowd broke, slim legs quick down the gravel. I wonder how old Rosalie is. I'm sixteen and old, as old as I'll ever be. Don't stand staring, Marjory, everyone's waiting.

Go it, Marj, love from Uncle Ron. That should hold all the woolly knickers you need.

Auntie Molly and Gran at her door: What are you *doing*, Marjory? Everyone's asking where you are. Why aren't you downstairs helping? She looked at them: remote, irrelevant. I'm packing. I go on Thursday. Molly wheeled away to the stairs: My *god*fathers. Gran trembled: Haven't you any feelings at all?

ELEVEN

Around 1950, a visit is planned to Henry's home in London. In the West Country, Marjory and two daughters (about 12 and 13) are packing.

1st DAUGHTER: Fancy us not meeting our own grandfather till now. Fancy anyone not speaking, all those years.

MARJORY: He's written every Christmas.

2nd DAUGHTER: Now that's what I call goodwill.

1st DAUGHTER: Must've been some quarrel. Is is true that your father insulted you? That's what Dad said.

MARJORY: You could call it that. He said I was a prostitute and your father a cad – (*she grins a little*)

2nd DAUGHTER: – because Dad was already married?

MARJORY: – and I called *him* a bigoted old hypocrite.

1st DAUGHTER: What for?

MARJORY: Oh, that's a long story, about Auntie Molly. Tell you some other time.

1st DAUGHTER (*rather solemn*): You and Dad were rebels of your time, weren't you?

MARJORY (*who laughs*): I never thought of myself as a rebel particularly. A survivor, rather.

*

It was not the leavetaking she had imagined, although certainly Daddy and Teddy stood waving on King's Cross platform until they dwindled and disappeared, and so presumably had she. This train which contained her in its warm dust-smelling box, which held Uncle Ron's trunk some yards away in the guard's van, did not draw her slowly out of London, pulling taut the threads until they broke. It did not take her through back yards and smoky slates, English towns and countryside, creeping near and nearer to the northern hills, to Scotland. Rather it was a catapult, flinging her straight from London's centre to the station yard at Aberdeen, where Laura and Conrad and Nancy came in a huge car with Fergus who looked after the horses and Sandra who typed letters for Lady Deborah, arms legs beads wild hair, laughing, and fresh silk sky everywhere, mountains of navy blue striped with white water, hillsides soft and open: she was in a new world and there had been nothing in between departure and arrival. Did you have a good journey, Marj? I think so, I don't remember. Honestly, Marj, you are a scream. Isn't she a scream? This is our car, isn't it too delicious?

They drove down valleys and over hilltops, through stone villages against a pale bright evening, breathing the moors: Just wait until the heather's out, Marj, it's gorgeous here, just wait. The air's so fresh it actually smells, she said. Oh gosh, Conrad squeezed her hand, you say some killing things, Marjory. Fergus jabbed with a woollen elbow: Dinna take notice o' that laddie, he's an awfu' masher. Conrad said: Better than ponging of horse muck, frightful fellow. Nancy said: Lovely pong, take no notice, Fergus, good honest pong.

They sailed along the valley into Ballater, and Marjory felt no surprise as they came along a wide gravel drive to the house: perhaps because she had expected nothing in particular, because it was everything she had expected. A grey stone house that had grown there in solid lines, almost a castle. Well, Laura shook her arm, what d'you think, hey? That's our land from right over there to right over there. It's lovely, Marjory said. And it's big too. I should think it'll do. They laughed and tumbled from the car. She thought. I'm here, I've done it.

Goodbye, Gran had said, and kissed her. Be good, remember to work well for these kind people. Goodbye, Auntie Molly, Auntie Ada, Grandad, Buller, Boney, Jimmy, Billy rat. Goodbye, Auntie Ellie wept, Uncle Wilf, Susie. Good luck, Marjory, write to us. Goodbye, Auntie Flora; have fun, Marj. Goodbye, Miss Hawthorne. Call me Dolly, how many times do I have to say? Goodbye, Teddy, goodbye. Cheerio, Marj, blimey anyone'd think you were never coming back. I know, Ted, it feels like that; the thing is, I'll never live *there* again. Write to me, Ted. I will, Marj, you write too, watch out for the laddies in the kilties. Goodbye, Daddy, I'll write. Goodbye, Marjory, good luck, be a good girl, enjoy yourself, let me know you've arrived safely. God bless.

She leaned from her bedroom window: there were stars but it was not yet dark. The pines were black, though their scent was green, at the end of the lawns: but they were not a restraint or a barrier, for beyond was unlimited heath and mountain; another sweetness rose from below the sill, jasmine probably. It's only a small room, Lady Deborah said, but the view is nice. Sky, sky, more sky than anywhere. I'm here, I've done it.

Dear Daddy, I'm sorry I haven't written but I hope you got my card to say I'd arrived. I don't know where the time has gone, except I've been working so hard I just sleep like the dead at the end of the day. Well, starting at the beginning, I was met at the station by Laura and Nancy (they're the daughters) and Conrad their brother, and Fergus and Sandra who work here. We drove to the house – the estate, I should say. It's enormous, acres and acres, all country – it's as if they own about a hundred Brockwell Parks! The house has masses of rooms, and looks rather like a small castle, battlements and all, and it's even got its own little chapel in the grounds. I've got a lovely room, about four times as big as mine at home, though in comparison with most it's small. You should see the kitchens, they go on for miles! And the main drawing-room is gigantic with lovely furnishings, all very comfortable. Lady Deborah showed me round – so did Laura and Conrad until she (Lady D.) told them to go away because they kept playing the fool. Laura comes out (you know, debutantes and all that) next year, and she says after that she'll have to behave like a young lady, with her hair up, so she might as well make the most of life now! Lady Deborah introduced me to the cook whose name is Mrs Mudie and she actually says Scottish things like 'och' and 'the noo' – honestly! (I'm not making fun really, though if I did she'd be the first to laugh, she's awfully nice.) Mrs M said there wouldn't be all that much cooking until the shooting parties arrive next week so I said I'd help with anything. They took me at my word and I've been up by six-thirty every day, doing all sorts of things with the others (I won't tell you all the names of the staff, I'd fill the page at least) – like scrubbing the tables and floors. Picture several acres of white wood and flagstones and me toiling away!! Also cleaning silver and blacking ranges etc. etc., so my training has come in useful to say the least. Nancy keeps telling me she'll teach me to ride if only I'll stop working but so far my back's been aching too much for that! Anyway I feel I ought to work rather than mess about doing nothing.

Everyone's very nice. I don't see a lot of Lord and Lady T M really, but Laura and Conrad are always about. They come into the kitchens and generally muck in and we have a lot of laughs. Nancy's mostly in the stables or on a horse! In the evenings they take me out with them if they're seeing their chums in the village, and on Saturday there's a ceilidh which is a kind of Gaelic dance or party, and we're all going. I must write and tell Nora I'm learning the fling and reel now instead of the Charleston and so on.

I hope you're feeling well and also Dolly (she said I could call her that). I'll write soon to Gran and Grandad. I wrote to everyone I didn't actually see to say goodbye, had a really nice letter from Auntie June by return so if she's at Gran's on Sunday will you say thank you to her for me, please? Give Grandad and everyone my love, not forgetting Buller and Boney. They've got some lovely dogs here, mostly retrievers – working dogs and nothing less, as his lordship says – but I still miss B & B. Who's taking them for their walks these days? Lots of love from Marjory.

The cars came shining between the stone eagles at the gates and gleamed up the drive. Out stepped perfect tweeds, boots, baggage, furs, guns in glossy leather cases, shooting-sticks; clear voices rang, gloved hands beckoned and pointed. Conrad, waving an arm at the mountains, said: And Their Majesties have arrived at Balmoral, now it all begins.

Days of limp bodies, feathers floating brown and white through the scullery. Fuzz and fluff up the nose, in the hair; a clinging, heavy smell. Shooting-brakes piled with the dead, open the doors and the heads hang on senseless necks. Why do they shoot so *many*? Nobody can eat so many. Dinna be daft lassie, said Fergus, the rich folk of Aberdeen and Edinburgh and London will eat them well enough. But it's so cruel! Och, ye're soft, dinna break yeer hairt over a few wee birdies. She asked Conrad, tall and tweeded: What do you kill them for? Come off it, old thing, he said, it's for fun, sport, isn't it, and anyway they taste frightfully good. Och, Marjory, said Mrs Mudie, if ye say Puir Wee Things one more time I may lose control o' ma guid temper. The plucking, the feathers, the tables of bodies. After this I'll never pluck another bird all my life if I can help it. Aye weel, Mrs Mudie remarked, if ye're tae be a lady o' leisure that's another matter I'm sure.

Keziah wrote. Thanks ever so for your letter. I was awfully glad you came over to say goodbye, and Mum was really pleased too, though she said afterwards there was something *final* about you. What a shame you won't be here for Benjie's Bar Mitzvah, but I'll write to you about it and send a photo if poss. I should have my matric. results soon, so prepare yourself for brilliant news!! It sounds as if you're having fun, Marj, even if you're slaving away too. Reading between the lines I'd say you've got the Laird's son at your feet *and* Fergus-of-the horses following near . . . ho ho tell me more! Anyway, it seems you've stopped minding about not being a vet – is that true? Or is it just Marj's system, i.e. if it's beastly, don't think about it? Don't mind me asking, it's just I hope you're happy.

Something final; probably Mrs Hope was right. Walking along the village road with Laura and Conrad, the smell of heather blowing across her skin, and of tobacco, soap, perfume. You can't stop it, you have to go straight on; Keziah's words. Marjory didn't want to stop it now. Kez would write again, and Teddy, but not for ever. And this, Scotland, Conrad so good-looking holding her hand and Laura skipping ahead with the boy from the neighbouring estate: it was passing, something else waited. She knew: I can do anything I want in the world, really. I don't have to be a cook, I don't *have* to be anything I don't choose. Sixteen and a half, I could learn hundreds of things yet, who's to stop me? And I will, so there.

What a *bore* it was on Sunday, Teddy wrote. The old stinker was feeling croupy and was as grumpy as a rhino. The only interesting thing that happened was Auntie June having a few words with your Dad. I only heard some of it, but she was telling him he'd been dreaming about for years with his eyes and ears shut, and *he* was saying things like Goodness me, June! I had no idea! And *then* he said – I always thought she was a wayward child, never doing as she was told. Well – then I knew they were talking about you, didn't I? Worse luck, I didn't catch any more. Auntie June always did stick up for you but it sounded as if she was making up for lost time and reading him the riot act. Mostly though they haven't got much to say here – nothing to grumble about with you gone, and *I* haven't done anything wrong, at least nothing they know about . . .

Dear Kez, Marjory wrote, I can't believe so many weeks have passed here. Thanks a lot for your letter. I don't know about Fergus (who is nice, in spite of his stable aroma!) but you might be right about Con, who actually grabbed me and kissed me last night after we'd walked back from the village. I'm sure I don't know (much) what Gran would say ! ! Actually it was a bit wet but Quite Interesting. Trouble is it was by the stables and guess who saw us – yes, Fergus. He said to me in the morning: 'I saw ye leading the young laddie on.' What a cheek! I said I certainly was not and to mind his own business. *He* said, 'It is my business if ye come leaning on ma horses' doors.' Honestly, you have to laugh. I don't know what you mean really about what you call my system, Kez, but actually I do like it here. They're nice and besides I'm a *good* cook (and modest as ever, see)! Well, I don't think about being a vet any more – what's the point? But I do know there are a lot of things I could do, and I don't see why I shouldn't have a bash at them – I've got all my life before me, as they say! Let me know about your marks, I bet you do awfully well. Let me know exactly when Benjie's day is, I'd like to send something.

Conrad said: Mother says I mustn't get romantic ideas about you, Marjory. She laughed at his mournfulness. Oh really, and why not? Oh you know, family obligations. He was walking slower, letting Laura and Nancy and their boys go ahead. She felt his palm dampen against hers and he pulled her towards the road edge, a dark low tree; his body thumped against hers. Crikey, she thought as he kissed her, he'll break my neck. She said: I thought you weren't supposed to get romantic. He spoke into her hair: You know what I want, Marj, don't you, you know how I feel and even if you'd never say it you feel the same about me so don't tell me you don't want to as well. She pulled his several hands off her and said: Well I don't, so there, damn cheek. Anger or excitement or both, the struggle was hard. She laughed in the middle of some fear and a thrill in the way he panted and trembled; he pulled, she pushed, at last she kicked. Then it was he who pushed and she was on her back in a bed of nettles, half in the ditch. He was striding away from her, the young laird offended, dark along the road. Oh Conrad, she shouted after him, you absolute *pig*, what a rotten damn nerve! And somehow Fergus knew. See, lassie, ye should ken I'm a better man for ye than yon laddie who must marry a rich lassie. She plucked him from her and said, Oh, push off. Och, ye're a tough wee thing and hard-hairted and I'm sorry for us all.

Men! she wrote to Nora. And after all that pawing and grabbing I saw Conrad kissing a girl outside the dance hall – honestly! And then when he asked me to dance I trod all over his feet, *hard*.

Her father's letter was thicker than usual. He was glad to hear she had got used to the hard work; I knew you would, Marj, if you stuck it, that's the secret. And speaking of work, remember I was talking about going into business on my own? Like you say, no point in messing about doing nothing when you've got a good idea, so I started making enquiries. Your Auntie Molly very kindly mentioned it to (Uncle) Fred Barnes, and in no time he'd suggested a meeting. The next thing I knew was that he was being incredibly kind and generous, as always, and putting up a sizable lump of capital to help me. Well, I've seen a property near Hammersmith Bridge which might be just the thing, so with luck I might be able to go ahead, quite soon I hope.

She read that twice. Fatty Fred Barnes: *him*. Then she read the next part and nothing else deserved a thought.

I must tell you now what is uppermost in my mind. Her father's writing took an even neater slant. Perhaps it is something you have already guessed at, my dear. The plain fact is, I am hoping to be married, to Miss Dolly Hawthorne. But, and this really is a but, she has said she will accept me only on condition that you completely approve. Of course I at once agreed to write to you. I believe you liked her on the occasions you met and so of course I hope you will be happy at this news and wish us well.

Dolly, Daddy. Uncle Ron: Anyway, Marj, it's her that's got to be strong; this girl, Dolly.

She ran to the village with her letter. Dear Daddy, Dear Dolly too, I can't tell you how pleased and happy I am, it's the news I most wanted to hear. When will the wedding be? What would you like for a present? Where will you live? Congratulations, congratulations. What shall I wear?

Dolly's letter crossed with hers. Please be your usual forthright self, Marjory, if you have any doubts; you have had a few ups and downs in your life and I don't want to be another 'down'. I couldn't be happy with Henry if I thought that, and would rather say No! and go away. So, for heaven's sake say what you think and not what you think we'd like to hear, won't you?

Marjory posted her a spray of heather and a card saying: Don't say no! Heaps of love.

She was awake very early nowadays, Daddy and Dolly in her mind. From her window she saw the small grey granite chapel, lit from the side by the young sun. She hadn't been inside: now, under the clean shell of sky and no sounds but birds, she would go. Not to pray exactly, perhaps just to sit, or only to look and think. Wet grass, sharp air. She stole to the door and crept inside with its creaking. The smell was wrong: it ought to have been a small echo of Christ Church, cosier perhaps. But it was cool and remote in spite of its dolls'-house size, a hint of fungus or damp stone; no warmth of scented smoke and polish, of people. There's no spirit here, she thought, and startled herself, so that she swung outside rather than dwell on the idea. Oh, and who cares? She looked up at the sky, and sky and sky, and said: Who needs a church, anyhow?

Of course you must go down for the wedding, Lady Deborah said. What awfully exciting news for you, Marjory, too thrilling. We'll be leaving for London ourselves just a matter of days after that, so if you wished you could go straight to Grosvenor Square. That is, if you have decided you will be with us in London? That's splendid. I'll write to Biggins at once and tell him when to expect you and which is to be your room.

*

Watford.

I was born here, perhaps in one of these red-tiled houses with net curtains in an avenue of trees. Straight-edged half-empty flower beds, stiff standard roses too symmetrical, shut behind privet clipped like walls. Streets of shops and shining windows, whitened doorsteps, smudgeless brass letterboxes, washed sills.

Nothing of me is here.

Nothing of me in this bright moving wedding crowd, mauve, white, pink, beige, blue; nothing but its shining centre, its focus, Daddy, Dolly. They smiled, crisp, ironed, ribboned. Dolly's amused eyebrows; she looked at her husband's family and then at him, and laughed. Sternly he was not going to join her mockery, but with her he had to laugh, and actually winked at Marjory.

Oh *Marjory*, Auntie Ada floated through in a mist of lilac chiffon, you *would* wear green, and on a day like this, don't you know green is unlucky for weddings? Marjory said: Nothing is unlucky for this wedding, that's just superstitious rubbish. Oh my, Marjory, Ada sighed and faded, you don't change, more's the pity.

Daddy and Dolly glimmered above the white cloth, napkins, silver; white shirt, hat, smiles, roses, cake.

The others flowed towards her and away; she saw teeth smile, heard questions, politely replied or nodded, but was not of them. Nora was there suddenly, eyes and hair shining, a ring on her left hand. Guess what, I'm engaged. Must be something catching in the family, he proposed to me the first day we met, in Kew Gardens, imagine! Just haven't had a minute to write and tell you – Dolly and Henry only just beat me to it. It'll be your turn next I dare say, Marj, you *do* look nice.

Gran, a stony blankness looking mostly towards Dolly: Of course, Marjory, if you'd prefer to stay in Grosvenor Square instead of with us, I quite understand. That's fine then, Marjory said. Flora under a halo of feathers that might have come from the Scottish scullery: Teddy isn't here, drat him, he's

213

got himself a job in the west somewhere, honestly I never did know what that boy would do or think of next, and as for the telegram he sent they can't possibly read it out. You look ever so smart, said Susie. You're not saying much, said Auntie Hennie.

Silver on white linen, crystal sending broken light, Daddy and Dolly looking at each other, sometimes at her. I think, said Auntie June, she might bring out the human in him at last. Had a few words with your father, Marjory, should have spoken out years ago. I really do wonder if he thought of anything or anyone but Greta all that time. Marjory said: He was always kind to me, you know. I was afraid of him but that wasn't his fault. He was shy in a way, I see now, and I suppose he was unhappy. Marjory, said Auntie June on a kiss, you have grown up.

When there was talk of changing clothes, calling cars, she was at last next to them; Dolly made a gap between her and the rest. 'I have to admit,' she disapproved, 'I was appalled, Henry letting his daughter go into service.' The ribbons flipped on her wide hat.

'Into *service*? Oh come on, Dolly. They're my friends, I work for them.'

'It is *still* service. *Really*, Henry, I told him, a daughter of *yours*, whatever were you thinking of?'

'Oh Dolly, you are funny.'

'Nothing to laugh about,' though Dolly would always grin at someone else's amusement. 'Now you listen, Marjory. We've found a nice house near Hammersmith, it's quite big. There's plenty of room for you too, I'd like you to think of it as your home. What do you think of that, hm? Your father would be delighted – ' she picked at his arm as he came near ' – wouldn't you, Henry?' She grinned behind her fingers as if hatching mischief and not kindness. 'I'm not old enough to be your mother, heaven for*bid*, but – well, *you* know.'

Henry said: 'Find a job for you in the business, no trouble at all. You'll have to work, mind.' He smiled.

'Thank you,' she said. 'I'll see.'

And when Dolly had one foot on the car's running-board, she said: 'You will come, won't you?' She was very serious, no wiggle of the brows.

'Thanks, Dolly, really. I promise I'll think about it.'

Dolly was triumphant, pointing at her from the leather seat:
'You'll come.'

Confetti, waving, Gran patting her eyes, Grandad standing until the car had gone. Uncle Ron or Teddy would have tied streamers and tin cans to it. Well, that's over; Marjory felt Auntie Hennie's sandpaper hand on her arm. I suppose it's all back to Leander Road for tea then, hey? Not me, Marjory said, I can't, got to get to Mayfair. Until the end of the year, she thought, or until Laura's a deb, and then I'll see. She would go back one day to Leander Road, to visit; not yet. Shame shame, Grandad said, haven't had a decent chance to speak to you, Marjory. What a young lady you look, hardly recognised you, my oh my. His face was the same, would always be, the white hair and beard; maybe he would never die. Nora once said: Grandad's the most good person I've ever known all my life, he never sees the bad in anyone.

And Nora said as they were finding their coats: 'While you're here, Marj, you could go and see your Auntie Vi. You always used to wonder about her, didn't you? All those birthday cards and everything. Well, she lives not very far away.'

Marjory said: 'It doesn't matter now.'

Grandad took her arm as everyone moved away. 'How's it all going really, Marj? Are you enjoying the job? Tell me, how does it feel to be out in the big bad world after all, eh?'

She smiled at him and said: 'Fine.'

She thought: Free.

*

MARJORY and daughters during their first stay with Henry and Dolly.

1st DAUGHTER: He seems friendly enough with Daddy now, anyway.

MARJORY: I should hope so; all that was ages ago. Though I suppose if it hadn't been for Dolly he might never have come round. She's been good for him, he's changed. I can actually talk to him at long last.

2nd DAUGHTER: You're ever so like him. To look at, I mean.

215

MARJORY: *Am* I? (*She turns to a mirror*) Do you really think so?

2nd DAUGHTER: You're pleased, aren't you?

1st DAUGHTER: D'you mean you didn't realise, Mum? You're his image.

MARJORY: Well well. Pity Auntie Molly can't hear you.

1st DAUGHTER. Why's that?

MARJORY: (*Still looking in the mirror*) Something she said once about him maybe not being my father.

2nd DAUGHTER: She must've been nuts, or blind as a bat.

1st DAUGHTER: I reckon you've never been sure, ever since. Crumbs, all those years.

MARJORY: I thought I'd forgotten it. Funny, I suppose one never does. Like my nightmare of the bear on the stairs, it still comes back.

1st DAUGHTER: You know what, Mum. It means you must look something like your grandmother, how about that? You said your father was like her.

MARJORY: There's a thought.

2nd DAUGHTER: And *I* look like *you*, so maybe I'll finish up looking like her too.

MARJORY: Stone the crows, there's no end to it, is there?